ADIA KELBARA
AND THE
HIGH QUEEN'S CURSE

ISI HENDRIX

PROLOGUE

Captain Perpetua Edochie was known throughout Zaria for many things, but patience wasn't one of them. She was a sharp woman – with an even sharper sword – who had no qualms about yelling at anyone who accidentally set her off. And it didn't take much to set her off. Perpetua hated tardiness, laziness, vanity and tepid water. She hated cowards, braggarts, people who spoke too softly and people who were too loud. Anyone who'd known her for more than a few days wondered if there was anything or anyone Perpetua *did* like. Because it was plain as day that she didn't even like her own son – and Darian Edochie, the Warlord Child, was an emperor.

An emperor who was currently trying not to sigh as his mother flew into a rage.

"Do you know what people are saying about you?" Perpetua snapped. Her soldiers would have cowered at the anger coming off her, but Darian didn't so much as flinch. She had to give the boy credit. He was the only person alive who didn't seem to be afraid of her. Good. It would have reflected poorly on her if she'd given birth to a weakling.

"I asked if you know what they're saying about you?" Perpetua repeated. "About your latest decision."

"Who's they?" Darian asked, his face blank.

Perpetua let out a slow breath and tried to speak in a calm, reasonable tone, despite her son behaving in such an unreasonable manner. "The nobility, your council members, everyone in the capital who matters."

"Oh. *Them*," Darian said, his tone unconcerned. "I'm sure they say many things. What critique is it that concerns you the most, Mother?"

Perpetua would have pinched his ear if she didn't think it would knock off his crown.

"They say," Perpetua said through gritted teeth, "that ever since you got back two months ago it's as if you've been possessed by a demon."

She'd hoped Darian would feel some level of embarrassment that being under the influence of dark magic was the best explanation people could come up with for his recent decision-making. But his only reaction was a raised eyebrow.

"And what would you do if I *was* possessed by a demon?" Darian asked, walking over to a window and peering out over the land he ruled. "Would you travel the world to find a cure? To find someone who could exorcise me? How do you think you'd even know? Could you look into my eyes and know it wasn't me?"

Perpetua gasped. "What are you talking about? I'm your *mother*. Of course I would know. That's why I'm here now. Something is clearly wrong with you. You've had a meteoric rise to power and now you're trying to throw it all away with this plan of yours to outlaw Drops. You're going to have to help me make sense of this."

"It's a pretty straightforward decision, I would think," Darian said with a shrug.

"Straightforward?" Perpetua gaped at him. "My dear child, you were the one who came up with the idea to give Drops to the peasants. It might go down as your greatest achievement. They never stop wanting it. Drops make them happy, submissive and easy to control, which makes the nobles rich, happy and easier for *me* to control. Truly a win-win scenario. No one is getting hurt. So I can't understand why you would want to stop production."

Darian frowned. "Have *you* ever taken Drops, Mother?"

Perpetua blinked. "Only once," she admitted. "To see what all the fuss was about. I'll admit it made me feel foggy for a few hours, but it didn't harm me in any way, if that's what you're worried about. And you know it's a completely natural substance – nothing more than a medicinal tonic made from agrias vines."

She'd hoped her answer would calm whatever concerns

the boy had about Drops and was annoyed when his face remained as unreadable as ever.

"I never have, you know," Darian said, his voice sounding older than his thirteen years. "Taken Drops. And I never will. They do more than make you foggy. They make people weak and susceptible to outside influences and..." His voice trailed off.

Darian knew that his mother would think he'd lost his mind if he'd finished his sentence. That, in reality, Drops weren't the calming tonic to make you more receptive to the Bright Father's love that the missionaries claimed they were. They were a poison that drained victims of their energy and power. And then gave that power to a demon.

"You admit you wouldn't take Drops yourself," he said, collecting his thoughts, "but you want to ship it all over Zaria for the peasants to drink? To villages just like the one you grew up in?"

"Darian," Perpetua said with a sigh. "I rose to this position so that my people would have someone in power who could help protect them. If having to deal in Drops will keep me in that position, that's a sacrifice I'm willing to make. But my concern right now isn't the peasants of Zaria. It's us. Our family."

Darian rubbed his forehead, his exasperation clear. "We're never going to see eye to eye about this. I have a council meeting in a few minutes. I'm sorry, but my decision is final."

"Darian." Perpetua tried again to reason with him, but Darian held up his hand, signalling that their conversation was over.

"It was good to see you, Mother."

Perpetua raised an eyebrow. "Come now, Darian. We may not understand each other, but we never lie."

That was true. He and his mother had always been too honest with each other.

"All right," Darian said. "It's been bloody awful seeing you. But you're the only family I have in this world so...don't be a stranger."

Perpetua narrowed her eyes. "I know there's nothing I can do to change your mind. But be careful. No one is happy about this. Which means it's going to happen sooner than I'd thought."

"What's going to happen?"

"A rebellion," Perpetua said. "A coup. A mutiny. Whatever you want to call it. Be careful, my boy, because mark my words, they're coming for your crown."

"Is that a promise?" Darian muttered, pulling the crown off his head and tossing it on a table after his mother left his chambers. "So they think I'm possessed by a demon? It's a little late in the day for them to put that together."

No, he wasn't possessed by a demon.

Not any more.

There were only a few people in Zaria who knew the truth.

And his mother wasn't one of them. The truth was that Darian Edochie was no emperor, and never had been. He was a boy who had been possessed by Olark – the most dangerous and murderous demon the world had ever seen – for the better part of a year. And he had only agreed to keep pretending he was an emperor so he could help clean up the mess Olark had made while possessing his body. But cleaning up after a demon was turning out to be more difficult than Darian had imagined. Because even with the demon gone, the people who'd benefited from Olark's reign had stayed. And they had no interest in giving up their new-found power.

He glanced at his pocket watch. His mother's unannounced visit had delayed him, and he was about to be late for a council meeting where yet more people would yell at him about banning Drops and thus effectively ending the surplus of money the capital had been collecting from sending that poison to the poorer citizens of Zaria. But to Darian, every coin that came from Drops represented someone like him – someone who'd had their free will taken away. Maybe not as violently as a demonic possession. Drops were a subtle poison – so subtle you wouldn't even notice that you were susceptible to someone else's suggestions. Or that if you had any trace of shamanic power, Drops made it easier for Olark to see and steal it.

With a heavy sigh, Darian reached for his crown, but it slipped from his hands as a thunderous boom rattled the windows so hard a potted plant fell off the sill. It sounded as if a hundred horses pulling heavy wagons had crashed through the palace gates all at the same time.

"What was that?" Darian muttered, rushing to the window. Were they under attack? His mouth fell open as he took in the scene below.

"Mother!" he yelled. He ran out the door, dashing down the long staircase that led to his private entrance. But before he could take a step outside, someone jumped in front of him.

"Majesty! Please wait. We're not sure what happened. We don't know if it's safe."

"Move!" Darian yelled. "My mother was just there."

The ground where Perpetua had been standing was gone, replaced by a massive crack that extended as far as the eye could see. A cloud of smoke rose in the distance as everyone near the chasm ran away in panic. Darian didn't know which emergency needed his attention more – the sudden split in the earth, or the concerning amount of smoke that was now rising from beyond the treeline. Whatever had just happened looked to be a widespread disaster. But before he could do anything else, he needed to make sure his mother was unharmed.

"Darian!"

"Mother!" Darian sagged in relief as Perpetua pushed her way through the growing crowd to get to him. Somehow she'd managed not to fall into the chasm. Of course she had.

She would have jumped out of the way the second she sensed something was off. He looked up at the sky to say a quick thank you to Alusia and all the guardian gods who dwelled on the ancient star, but then he froze. For better or worse, everyone around him was too busy focusing on what was going on with the ground to notice what was happening in the sky.

"It can't be," Darian whispered.

"Your Majesty. Captain." A Gold Hat pushed his way forward, approaching Darian and Perpetua. "Permission to send riders to find out what happened and assess the damage? It appears to be a massive earthquake."

"How could it be an earthquake when the earth didn't quake?" Perpetua asked sharply. "Did it, Darian. Darian?"

Darian ignored them as he stared up at the clouds in a daze. But all that was left was a trail of grey that looked like a heavy rain cloud about to storm. And a storm *was* coming. Because nothing good ever followed what he'd just seen, written across a background of blue.

Hear my words throughout the world
And read them in the skies...

There was only one fallen celestial who was powerful enough to weave Words of Power in the sky. But Olark had been killed months ago.

"Darian!"

His mother's sharp call drew him out of his stupor. He

turned from the sky and met his mother's steely gaze with one of his own. He couldn't let fear overtake him. Not now. Not when it was clear the nightmare he'd thought he had been freed from was about to begin all over again.

"No. The earth didn't quake." Darian turned to the Gold Hat. "Send out the riders."

"Of course," the Gold Hat said. "But, um, did any of you by chance happen to see..." He ran a hand through his hair, accidentally knocking off his golden helmet.

"What's the matter with you?" Perpetua didn't have time for the men around her to fall apart. "Do as your emperor commands," she said, her voice fierce.

"Yes, of course, Captain," the Gold Hat stammered as he quickly picked his headgear off the ground and fumbled to put it back on. "It's just that... You'll call me a fool if I say it."

Darian's shoulders tensed. Had the Gold Hat seen the writing in the sky too?

"Speak quickly," he said. "What did you see?"

The Gold Hat straightened. "It's just that I was standing over there," he said, pointing to the treeline. "As soon as the ground split, I saw someone run into the forest. They were carrying a flaming torch."

Darian looked at his mother.

"It's not even close to evening. The only reason someone would be carrying a torch right now would be to start a fire. That might explain the smoke coming from the forest."

"Can you describe who you saw?" Perpetua asked.

"Well, that's the thing, Captain. I can describe him perfectly. The person I saw was Lucas Grim."

Darian had no idea who Lucas Grim was, but his mother clearly did.

"You're right," Perpetua said after a moment of consideration. "You are a fool. This one is in shock, Darian." She pointed at another Gold Hat. "You there. Send out the riders. Your companion here is relieved of his post."

Both Gold Hats rushed away as Darian raised an eyebrow at his mother.

"Lucas Grim?" he asked.

"A trainee who died two years ago," Perpetua muttered. "During a routine patrol. His horse got spooked and he fell off a cliff. The ground is splitting open, a forest fire is raging, and a Gold Hat thinks the dead are walking among us. What is going on?"

Darian wanted to know that too.

"Mother, go with them and report back to me. And remember, we're to provide aid to people. Keep the Gold Hats in line." The elite group of soldiers weren't known for helping the people of Zaria so much as extorting money from them. They were a menace – and next on his list of things to clean up as long as he was stuck wearing this crown.

"And where are you going?" His mother stepped in front of him, forcing him to stop. Darian glared at her in frustration.

"I have to take care of something."

"Take care of something?" Perpetua stared at him as if he'd grown horns out of his head. "Darian! We're in the middle of a natural disaster."

"Trust me, Mother," Darian said, his eyes so fierce that Perpetua faltered. "There's nothing natural about what just happened. Please do what I ask."

Perpetua looked as if she was about to argue, but something in Darian's eyes stopped her. She nodded and stormed over to her guards.

"You two, with me. The rest of you will go to the nearby districts and see if they were affected. Jonah, delegate who goes where."

Darian breathed a sigh of relief as everyone ran to do his mother's bidding.

"And you," Darian said, once his mother was out of earshot. "I need to get a message to someone. Have your fastest rider deliver it."

The Gold Hat stood to attention. "Of course, Your Majesty. Where will the message be going?"

"To the Academy of Shamans," Darian said. "I need to get a message to Adia Kelbara."

CHAPTER 1

An orange cat jumped straight into the air, his fur standing up in about fifty directions as he let out a horrible wail.

"Good grief," Adia muttered, peering up from her book and shaking her head at how hideous Bubbles looked. Living in the dangerous wasteland that was the Horrorbeyond might have made the pair of them a little too feral. They could both do with a haircut. And a bath. When Bubbles hissed again, she glanced around to see what was upsetting her cat so much.

"What's the matter with you?" Her lips twitched in amusement when she saw the cause of his distress. "Oh."

A vine was slinking its way through the sand in a snake-like fashion. Adia couldn't blame Bubbles for mistaking the agrias vine for a limbless reptile. It stood up like a cobra about to strike and shot towards her. But Adia only laughed as the vine wrapped itself around her torso, giving her a squeeze.

"I guess this is a goodbye hug," she said when the vine finally untangled itself. "You know we're leaving tomorrow, don't you?" Her mood immediately dropped as reality sank in.

After saving the life of Emperor Darian, Adia had agreed to go from kitchen cleaner to student at the Academy of Shamans, but she'd regretted that decision almost immediately. The only reason she'd been offered a spot at the prestigious school and cleared of suspicion of any wrongdoing was because Darian had declared her a hero of the realm. The Academy professors had been mortified to find out the girl who'd been honoured by Zaria's ruler worked downstairs scrubbing pots and pans and she'd been given a full scholarship right then and there.

But since part of her "act of heroism", as the headmaster had called it, involved rescuing a bunch of kidnapped students, the Academy had been shut down for months pending an investigation to make sure it was a safe place for parents to send their children. Which is why she was here in the Horrorbeyond instead of there.

"As if anyone learns anything at the Academy." Adia sighed as she huddled under a tree, trying to avoid the rain.

As if anyone would be safe at the Academy while she was there.

A familiar feeling of guilt crept into her stomach. She was the reason Darian and those kidnapped students had needed rescuing in the first place. They had been innocent pawns in the fallen god Olark's game to find the one person in Zaria who could give him everything he'd ever wanted.

The way to Imo Mmiri.

Created from waters so powerful that fire couldn't burn there, Imo Mmiri was the only place in the mortal realm that contained the power of a star. And Olark the Tormentor had wanted to use that power to turn himself into an indestructible god. But the mythical water kingdom was guarded by powerful shamans, and Viona, Adia's doppelgänger ancestor, used her immense power to cloak Imo Mmiri in a veil, forever hiding the land so that only someone from her bloodline of shamanic protectors would be able to see it. As the last direct descendant of that bloodline, Adia was that someone.

Olark's original plan had been to burn Zaria to the ground until the only thing left standing was the one place that flames couldn't touch. But when he'd learned of Adia's existence, he realized it would be faster to possess Adia and use her eyes to find Imo Mmiri. But by some twist of fate, when the two of them had finally come face to face, Adia had been the one left standing. And Olark had vanished.

The rain was getting heavier now. The palm tree above Adia bent at an angle so that not even a drop of water touched her head or the textbook she was skimming.

"Thanks," Adia murmured, burying her nose back in her book. Even without trying, she was in tune with every living plant around her. Herbs, shrubs, trees, flowers – anything that drew energy from the sun gravitated towards Adia, whether she wanted it to or not. She knew that shamans were supposed to have mastery over their specific ability, but more and more she felt like it was the other way around. That the plants didn't listen to her so much as they dragged her along for the ride. They were in control, not her.

She set the book to the side and let her mind drift as Bubbles snuggled against her hip, the sound of the rain and his purring making her drowsy. She hadn't slept well last night. Ever since Olark had briefly possessed her, she'd been plagued with nightmares. Sometimes she'd force herself to stay awake just because she was scared what she might see when she closed her eyes. But right now, it was impossible to keep her eyes open. She wrapped her arms around Bubbles and let herself drift off.

Almost immediately, reality gave way to a lush rainforest. Colourful birds flew overhead, singing in unison as Adia slowly walked through a dream world. She stuck out her hand and let her fingers run along the branches and leaves, smiling when some of them curled up against her fingers. The only clue that she was in a dream was that the butterflies Bubbles kept trying to catch would vanish, then reappear above his head.

But suddenly the birds went silent as shadows rose from the ground like giant claws all around her. The dark, smoky hands stretched forwards, quickly swallowing the forest and sky and casting Adia into the darkest of nights. But the darkness faded as quickly as it had come, giving way to a flash of light. No, not light – flames. The forest was ablaze. And she was standing in the middle of the eye of the fire.

With a cry, she clutched her head and fell to the ground as whispers hissed at her from every direction.

"You woke her up."

"Someone help me!" Adia screamed, her eyes watering from the smoke. She could feel the heat from the fire. She couldn't breathe.

"She's coming."

A huge clap of thunder sounded, and Adia woke with a sharp gasp. Her heart raced as she tried to catch her breath. It was just a dream. But the fire felt so hot and real she couldn't help looking down at her arms to make sure she hadn't been burned.

"You'd better scream," a voice called out. "You were *this* close to getting singed a few seconds ago, you know. How many times have I told you not to be out here when it rains? Lightning loves to strike the Horrorbeyond."

Taking off her glasses, Adia breathed a sigh of relief as Thyme glared down at her. Her friend was right to be annoyed, and Adia knew not to take Thyme's warning lightly. No one knew the Horrorbeyond better than the warrior girl. Thyme had spent a whole year living in this hellscape before Adia had rescued her – actually it had been more like five hundred years, seeing as how she'd been carrying the bloodstained stone, a celestial object that had taken her out of space and time. She was Adia's best friend now, but Adia never forgot for a second that Thyme was from a different period of Zaria's history, when creatures who no longer existed used to roam free.

"Sorry, sorry. I didn't mean to fall asleep," Adia said. "If it makes you feel any better, I was having the world's worst nightmare. I was about to be burned alive." She cringed as she pushed herself up, realizing she was emitting a purple glow. And not just from her hands.

Adia worked on calming her power as Thyme frowned at her. It took a few seconds but, finally, the glow disappeared. "That's the second time this week," she muttered.

"Third," Thyme said. "Last night when I got up to throw Bubbles out – he was screaming at ghosts or something and I couldn't take it any more – I passed by your room. You were glowing so much in your sleep that I could see the light from under your door."

Adia blinked. She'd had no idea her powers were coming out in her *sleep*.

"I must have been having another nightmare." Thyme knew all about the dreams that had plagued Adia these last few months. In her dreams she had no choice but to relive the moment when she and Olark had wrestled for control of her soul over and over. But she didn't want to think about that right now. And she didn't want to think about the strange phrase from this latest hellmare: *You woke her up.*

"This storm looks serious," she said, deflecting. "Let's get out of here."

"It's never been this bad," said Thyme, peering out at the turbulent waters of the Serpentine Pass as they walked back to their cottage. "Not even the year I was trapped here. I don't know why the weather's been so angry lately. How are we going to get out of here in one piece? Do you really think we can sail through this?"

"Maybe it's a sign that we're not supposed to. Get out of here, that is," Adia said. "Maybe we should just stay for ever."

She was only half kidding. The Horrorbeyond had been a safe haven for them for the last two months and she wasn't in a hurry to leave it.

"You know Gini would never allow that," Thyme said.

Adia winced as she thought about Gini. Right now, the circle of people in Zaria who knew the full extent of Adia's shamanic ability and her powerful ancestry was contained only to Thyme, Darian, and her cousin EJ.

But the Alusi knew of Adia's existence too. Three of the powerful guardian gods had come down from the stars to stop Olark as he ran around possessing people so he could search for her. Who knew what would have happened if the most powerful Alusi, Ginikanwa, hadn't decided enough was enough and descended from the stars to stop him.

"You need to learn how to control your ability better. Until you do, Gini wants you at the Academy," Thyme continued. "Besides, maybe it'll be fun to be back. I bet everyone is going to suck up to you now. They'll probably pretend to be your friend so you can get them into palace dinners with Darian and all the rich people. Just like—" Thyme cut herself off when she saw the stricken expression on Adia's face.

In the time that they'd lived in the Horrorbeyond, there had been next to no rules. They woke up when they wanted, they did chores when they wanted (which in Thyme's case was never), they ate when they were hungry, and they went to bed when they were tired. A freedom most almost-thirteen-year-olds could only dream of. There had been only one unspoken rule that, up until that moment, Thyme had never broken.

Don't. Mention. Nami.

"Sorry," Thyme said with a wince. "I didn't mean to bring him up."

Pulling herself together, Adia shrugged. "It's all right," she said. "I need to get used to acknowledging Nami's existence. He'll probably be back at school too."

"I still say you and Darian should have thrown him into the same prison cell he put you in," Thyme muttered.

Adia took a deep breath and looked up at the sky, letting the water run down her face. Wishing it would douse the anger inside her. She stuck out her tongue to catch a few drops.

"Come on. The storm's getting worse, and we need to pack," Thyme said, picking up her pace.

Adia closed her mouth and hurried after her. Thyme was right. They needed to finish packing. It was officially time to face facts. In a few days, they'd be back at the Academy.

Where everything Adia had spent the past two months avoiding would be waiting for her.

CHAPTER 2

When they reached the door to the house Thyme had built, someone was standing outside.

"Ferryman!" Adia said, smiling at the cloaked figure. Even though he stood tall and straight, she knew there was nothing behind the cloak – no face, no limbs, no person. A fact that had taken her some time to get used to. He was what Gini called a Soulless, and he was also the one who ferried them to and from the Horrorbeyond.

"Come on, we're getting drenched," Thyme said, hurrying to push the door open.

They stepped inside and Adia shook her hair, sprinkling water all over the room as Thyme patted down the soft fuzz on her once-bald head. As a warrior of Nri she'd had to shave her head to show her dedication, and she'd kept it shaved until she met Adia. When she realized that she'd been trapped in another land and time for centuries and that everyone she'd ever known was dead, Thyme had decided that she would never cut her hair again, and it was growing in fast. Though she would still have to cover her head with a scarf while she was out and about on account of her pointy ears. They were a dead giveaway that Thyme wasn't Zarian. Or even fully human, for that matter.

"It's good to see you," Adia said, "but why are you here so early? We're not leaving until tomorrow morning."

She didn't expect an answer. Gini seemed to communicate with Ferryman telepathically, but Adia's conversations with him were usually one-sided. This time, though, she heard something. Not a human language, at least not one that she recognized. More like vibrations and hums. But somehow she understood.

"Go now?" she said in disbelief. "We can't leave tonight! Look at this storm! We're leaving tomorrow."

More vibrations in her head. Louder this time, repeating that they had to leave *immediately*.

"I know you're not human, but there are certain things you need to understand. Like how unacceptable it is to tell someone they need to show up to school early," Adia said. "We're leaving tomorrow morning like we planned."

"Adia..." Thyme's eyes were wide, and her ears were pinned back. Bubbles did the same thing when he was nervous.

Adia pointed at Thyme and gave Ferryman a self-satisfied smirk. "See! If even *Thyme* doesn't want to do something, you know it's not safe."

"No, Adia, I don't care about leaving tonight," Thyme said, ruining Adia's argument. "Although Ferryman had better have some way to turn himself into a covered boat if we have to go sailing in this rain. But how do you know all this? You've never been able to talk with him before. Only Gini can do that. And Mbari and Ikenga and the other Alusi, I guess. So how are you talking to a creature who has no soul?"

"I—" Adia blinked. She'd been so annoyed about going to school early that she hadn't even processed what she was doing. There was no denying it any more. Ever since her battle with Olark, her shamanic powers had been growing and changing. She wasn't the same girl she'd been before. Though she still wasn't ready to admit that out loud.

"Maybe Ferryman's always been able to communicate with me but needed a while to decide if I was trustworthy?"

It was a weak excuse, and Thyme wasn't buying it.

"I don't like this," she said with a shake of her head. "You're getting too strong, and you have no idea what you're doing! Don't think I haven't noticed. Sometimes you're here and other times it's like you're in a different dimension. It's..."

Her voice trailed off.

"Dangerous," Adia finally said, looking at the floor. If anyone had a right to be concerned about Adia being a threat, it was Thyme. Adia still felt ashamed when she remembered how, as she was first coming into her powers, she had gone so far into a trance that she'd almost hurt her friend. She'd almost become the ogbanje her family and village thought she was. A demonic child who brought misery and misfortune wherever they went. Doomed to reincarnate over and over to release untold horrors into the world.

"I just think maybe you shouldn't use your powers so much until we get to the Academy," Thyme said quickly. "Why does Ferryman want us to leave now anyway?"

Adia turned back to him to ask but, to her shock, Ferryman flopped to the floor, becoming nothing more than a pile of fabric.

"Ferryman? Are you all right?"

She knelt and touched the crumpled fabric. There were no more vibrations. There was nothing. Ferryman was gone.

"Thyme!" she cried. "Something's wrong." She held up the cloth and tried not to cry.

"Do you think he's..." She couldn't finish the sentence. She didn't want to say it out loud.

"No," Thyme said quickly. "He's not technically alive so it's not like he can die. But I don't know what's going on. I say we do exactly what Ferryman told us to do and get out of here."

Thump. Thump. Thump.

Adia stood up slowly. Thyme put a finger to her lips and motioned with her head. Adia nodded and quietly got behind her as Thyme slowly picked up her bow and notched an arrow, ready to let it fly if she didn't like who was on the other side of the door.

The banging grew more insistent. Thyme narrowed her eyes and pulled the arrow taut as the door flew open.

"Oh, for the sake of the stars, Hiroma," Thyme said as she lowered her bow. Adia exhaled in relief at the familiar, if not disconcerting, sight of Hiroma the Headless, carrying her head in her hands. "You *would* be wandering around in this hurricane. What are you doing—"

"You have to go," Hiroma said, her voice strange and terrible. She may have looked like an eight-year-old, but Hiroma was ancient in her own right. Whenever Adia asked the girl to explain how it was that she had come to rule the Horrorbeyond – and more importantly, how she'd lost her head – Hiroma would skip off, saying in her usual sing-song voice that she'd tell her when she was ready to hear it. But now her voice was that of an ancient and powerful creature. Low and deep, and vibrating with such force that the chairs rattled.

Even Thyme took a nervous step back.

"Hiroma?" Adia said shakily. She couldn't keep the fear out of her voice. She'd dealt with too many people possessed by demons, herself included. If Hiroma getting possessed was the reason Ferryman had wanted them to make a run for it, they might as well just curl up in a ball and accept death.

Hiroma's eyes softened. "Sorry," she said, her voice back to its usual soprano. "I didn't mean to frighten you. But I have to get you two out of here. Now."

"What's going on?" Thyme asked, lowering her arrow, but only barely. If even Hiroma was spooked, then something was definitely wrong.

"I'm not sure," Hiroma said. "But something is reaching out, trying to find Adia. I was redoing my braids, and the ground where I was sitting split in half. My head almost fell in. Imagine! I've spent three days on this hairstyle, only for my head to fall into a *chasm*? But almost ruining my hair isn't the most pressing matter."

"It's not something that matters at all," Thyme snapped.

"Wait, I don't understand," Adia interjected before Hiroma and Thyme could start fighting. "You think something or someone bad is trying to find me just because there was an earthquake?"

"No. I want you to leave because there's only been two earthquakes in the history of the Horrorbeyond. The first was one year ago when the bald one showed up," Hiroma said, tossing Thyme a sour look. "And just like that wretched day, I can sense a new presence on the island. The ground only cracks when someone who shouldn't be here – in our land and time – shows up. And whoever just arrived belongs here even less than Thyme did. Can't you feel it, Adia? Can't you feel the wrongness and the chaos in the energy? Honestly, open your eyes!"

Adia was startled by the annoyance in Hiroma's tone.

"I..." She tried to focus on whatever it was Hiroma was

talking about, but she didn't feel anything. "I don't see anything," she said, giving a helpless shrug. Hiroma couldn't hide her look of disappointment and Adia blinked back tears, feeling like she'd just failed an important test. She was useless if her powers only decided to work when she was terrified and in mortal danger.

"It's not your fault," Hiroma muttered. "Ginikanwa taught you nothing about your abilities. She was probably too busy staring into a mirror admiring her own reflection, the peacock. You haven't even scratched the surface of what you can do yet. But never mind that. We need to get you out of here."

"Agreed," Thyme said. "I don't understand a single thing you just said but it's clearly time to go." It might have been the first time the two of them had had a conversation that didn't descend into yelling within thirty seconds. But Hiroma and Thyme seemed to have some sort of silent agreement that their usual bickering would be put on hold if Adia was in danger. "Adia, get Bubbles. Leave behind whatever you haven't finished packing."

"I packed everything already," she called over her shoulder as she ran into her room and snatched the cat, stuffing him into her bag. He screamed and swatted at her in protest, but she paid his claws no mind.

"Thyme, your bag," she said. Thyme hadn't moved from her warrior's position.

"Forget it," she said. "Getting you to safety is what matters."

"Oh, for the sake of the stars," Adia said, running into Thyme's room before anyone could argue. Thyme hadn't had any earthly belongings until they'd met, but Adia knew her friend secretly loved the colourful little cloth dolls she bought every time they stopped at a market. She grabbed Thyme's half-packed bag and quickly swept all the dolls into it then ran back out, putting both bags on her back so Thyme wouldn't be weighed down by them if she needed to fight. But Adia winced at how heavy it was. What exactly had Thyme packed in there?

Thyme gave her a small smile before shifting back into position again. "Let's go."

"But what about Ferryman? How are we supposed to leave here without him?" Adia still didn't know what had happened to him or why he'd vanished. She hoped he was all right, wherever he was.

"You'll have to sail yourselves," Hiroma said as she shoved them out the door. "I have my own boat. You can use that. It's the only way out of here except via Ferryman, so you shouldn't be followed. Hopefully, once you're on the water whatever is trying to reach Adia won't be able to sense her."

"What do you think it could be?" Thyme asked. "Some sort of monster or demon that's come up from the Underworld or fallen from the sky like Olark?"

"I have no idea," Hiroma said with an irritated shake of her head, which she held in her hands. "It's like something is stretching out a great big hand trying to grab her. Like—"

"Hiroma!" Adia gasped and pointed behind them, where orange flames shot up several metres above the treeline. "The Horrorbeyond is on fire!"

"What in all the hells is that?" Thyme shouted. "How could a fire have started when we're in the middle of a monsoon?"

"Stop talking and run!" Hiroma shouted.

Thyme and Hiroma didn't break a sweat as they raced to the shore, but Adia could barely breathe by the time they reached the water. Running – or anything athletic – had never been her strong suit. She was agile of mind, not body. But she mustered up as much strength as she could to help Thyme drag the small boat Hiroma had waiting for them into the water.

"Get in!" Hiroma shouted.

Adia shook her head stubbornly. "No. We can't leave you. Come with us."

"It can't hurt me," Hiroma said, staring down the fire. "Besides, I'm not what it wants. I'm guessing the second you get on the water it'll put itself out. I left food in the boat for you. Get in."

Adia sloshed back out of the water and bent down to give Hiroma a quick hug.

"Are you sure you'll be safe?" Adia asked as Hiroma shoved her towards the boat. "If this thing already knew we were here—"

"I can take care of myself," Hiroma said in a cheerful voice, sticking her head back onto her neck. "I'm almost as old as the dawn of time, you know!"

"Yes, you're the spitting image of primordial evil," Thyme sniffed, but she dug into her pack and pulled out a dagger, tossing it to Hiroma. "Here. I'm sure you know how to use this."

As baffled and terrified as she was about what was going on, Adia couldn't stop a small smile from creeping to her lips. As far as she knew, she was the only person Thyme had ever gifted one of her weapons to. It meant something that she was giving one to Hiroma.

"A Nrian blade," Hiroma said slowly. "There are only a few left in the world."

While Hiroma pretended not to be moved as she examined the dagger, Adia quickly knelt and touched the ground. Thankfully, she felt her body heat up and her hands glowed purple as the earth responded to her.

"Protect Hiroma," she whispered.

The trees around her rustled as their branches bowed in her direction. She knew they had heard her. Yes, Hiroma could take care of herself, but there was no harm in asking the plants to protect her as well.

"The boat will find its way back to me," Hiroma said as she pushed the girls towards the water. "Go now. The Serpentine will keep you safe."

Adia hugged her bag and Bubbles close as Thyme grabbed the paddles and started rowing.

"Look, Adia," Thyme said. "Hiroma was right."

They watched the Horrorbeyond grow smaller as they rowed away, but that wasn't the only thing growing smaller. Within minutes, the fires had completely extinguished. Adia was relieved for Hiroma's sake that the fire was gone, though still shaken that it might have happened because of her. She closed her eyes, willing herself not to cry. The Horrorbeyond had been her refuge for months but, in the end, darkness had still tracked her down. And who knew what they were sailing into now. She took a deep breath and gave Thyme a brave smile, repeating Hiroma's parting words. "Whatever is going on, we're all right for now. The Serpentine will keep us— Ugh!"

A huge wave crested over the boat, knocking Adia out of her seat and filling the boat with water and snakes. Thyme rolled her eyes as Adia leaned over the side and coughed up the seawater she had just swallowed. She knew she had about a dozen river snakes in her hair, but she tried to channel Gini, straightening her shoulders and presenting herself as a picture of calm and grace.

"The Serpentine will keep us safe," she coughed out.

Thyme shook her head and sighed as she continued rowing. "Yeah...we're definitely doomed."

* * *

Underneath the boat, something pulled itself up out of the water. Enough so it could breathe, but not so much that the two girls would notice they had a hitchhiker. It was going to be a difficult journey, clinging to the underside of the boat and dealing with the snakes of the Serpentine, but it had to be done. Everything was set in motion now.

Smiling to itself, the creature whispered, "You woke her up. She's coming."

CHAPTER 3

The girls walked down the path to the Academy gates in silence. It had been a tense boat ride through the Serpentine, and they both had been lost in their own thoughts on the walk over from the dock at the Macobar Jetty. Without Ferryman's speed to propel them through the Serpentine, the trip had taken four days instead of the usual three. Adia had been annoyed to leave the Horrorbeyond early, but with the delay, they'd barely made it back to school on time. As it was, they would hardly have time to unpack before tonight's orientation dinner.

Adia had been so anxious about their frantic departure from the Horrorbeyond and the fiery scene they'd left behind that she'd forgotten to be anxious about school. But there was no avoiding that now.

They'd arrived.

"Is it just me, or is this place even uglier than when we left?"

Adia winced at the volume of Thyme's observation. Was her friend wrong about the Academy of Shamans being one of the ugliest structures in the known universe? Of course not. But loudly voicing that sentiment wasn't something a person should do – at least not within hearing distance of the school. "The walls have ears" wasn't just a proverb when it came to the Academy. It was a legitimate warning.

"Could you please lower your voice before a window decides to slice our heads off?" Adia sighed when Thyme gave an unconcerned shrug. Her friend hadn't spent enough time at the Academy to truly fear its personality. But she would learn soon enough. "Besides," Adia continued, pushing up her glasses. "So what if it's hideous? Beneath the beams that slap students over the heads and the doors that hold themselves shut so teachers can't leave the toilet beats a heart of gold."

She gave Thyme an earnest smile. Unfortunately, the Academy decided that was the perfect moment to let out a groan of agony as part of the building collapsed to the ground with a thud. The weight of having students back in its hallowed halls must have been more than it could take. Adia could hear her classmates screaming all the way from out here. One boy almost fell out a window, and two of his friends had to grab his arms to pull him back up.

"A heart of gold." Thyme mimed pushing up imaginary glasses as she mocked Adia, who was currently coughing from all the dirt and debris the school had kicked up with its theatrical display. "Our school is literally trying to kill its students."

But Adia paid Thyme no mind as she took in the Academy.

The first time she'd seen the decrepit school, she had been nothing more than a runaway. Back then, apprenticing in the kitchens had been the only way out of her horrible life as an orphan in the Swamplands.

But now Adia had been *invited* to attend the Academy. She was here as a first-year student, not a dishwasher in the Academy kitchens.

She couldn't say she was thrilled about having to attend class with the rich, mean students of the Academy – like her nemesis Mallorie Amber – or the most useless teachers ever to grace the field of education. But Lebechi and Maka were there too, and she was excited to see her old friends.

With a purr, Bubbles jumped from his perch on her shoulder, dashing into a small hole and disappearing into the school.

"Happy to be back, are you?" Adia said. She turned to Thyme. "I bet he's going straight to the kitchens to steal fish."

As much as she hadn't wanted to come back, now that she was standing in front of the school again, it felt like home. Her ugly, weird, crotchety home.

"Let's go. Our room assignments should be listed in the main hall."

Adia ignored the stares and whispers as they entered. Any

hope of the other students forgetting what had happened two months ago was dashed. People gawked at her as if she was a carnival attraction as she walked over to the room assignment list. She kept her eyes trained on the paper, refusing to acknowledge her new classmates.

"I've got our room number," she said, turning to Thyme. But Thyme was focused on something else.

"Umm, Adia... They seem to have added some new decor to the place."

Adia turned to look at what Thyme was pointing at. Her mouth fell open.

A wall that used to have gold tapestries on it was now covered with a mural of poor Darian when he was still possessed by Olark. Except he wasn't alone in the mural.

"What is that monstrosity?" Adia said slowly.

She was standing underneath a life-sized painting of herself, smiling serenely down at Darian, who appeared to be wounded. He gazed up at her as though she was an angel who had come to bring him back from the dead as a group of people in long grey cloaks raised their hands to the heavens.

Thyme moved her head back and forth. "Wow, the artist is really talented. It's like your eyes are following me wherever I turn."

"Thyme!" Adia said in exasperation.

Thyme cleared her throat. "Right. Not important. Let me read the plaque." She leaned forward.

*In honour of the Academy Council for rescuing
Emperor Darian Edochie.*

"*Who* rescued Darian?" Adia said, her voice strangled.

"Wait, there's more," Thyme said. "I almost missed it. The print is really tiny."

Adia Kelbara was there too.

Adia stared at the mural in disgust. "Oh, was I? I'd almost forgotten. And what am I putting in his mouth? Is that a bottle of *Drops*?" She took a deep breath to stop herself from screaming. "You know what? I don't care. Come on," she said, spinning on her heels. "Let's go."

"Go where?" Thyme asked in confusion.

"Back to the Horrorbeyond," Adia said, dragging Thyme behind her. "Or to live on a boat in the Serpentine and become one with the snakes. I don't care. But we're getting out of here."

But when she tried to pull the doors open, they refused to budge.

"Oh, you hateful building," Adia cried. "Let me out!"

"Let's at least make it through orientation," Thyme said, dragging Adia away from the door. "I'm tired from rowing. We can sleep here tonight, and if you still want to take off tomorrow, I'll help you escape."

Adia glared at everyone who dared look at her as she stormed up to their room. She knew this wing of the school well. It was where the richest students were housed. She used to bring them their morning tea.

"It's this one," Thyme said. Adia groaned.

"Great. We're right next door to Mallorie Amber. Last time I was in this hall Mallorie was yelling at me. Though I suppose there were some good moments too. Like when Bubbles threw up in her face cream." The memory made Adia smile as the door to their room opened without them touching the knob.

"Wow," she and Thyme said at the same time.

Their room wasn't a room, so much as a giant suite.

"We have a fireplace," Thyme said, rushing forward and tossing her bag to the floor. "And look – the bookshelf is already stocked. I suppose that's for you. Stars know I'm not reading books outside of class. And someone left a fruit plate for us!"

Thyme grabbed an apple and flopped onto a large plush chair.

"So soft," she sighed happily. "I didn't think anywhere in the Academy could look this nice."

It was true. The school had clearly decided to go all out for Adia.

"This is so much bigger than Mallorie Amber's room," Adia said in shock as she ran her fingers over a small dining table.

She figured that when Mallorie got wind of the fact that she now had only the *second* largest room at school, she'd show up at the door with a flame-thrower and burn this one down rather than let Adia have it.

A horrible whistle sounded, and Adia and Thyme covered their ears.

"What was that?" Thyme groaned.

"It must be new," Adia said, lowering her hands when the piercing sound finally stopped. "But look at the time. Orientation is about to start. I guess that was our signal to get moving."

Adia tugged at her orientation kaftan. It had been hanging in her closet with a note pinned to it about white being the best colour to wear to channel energy. Being from the Swamplands, Adia hadn't worn white clothes a day in her life. It would have been an invitation for mud stains. And her powers worked just fine no matter what colour dress she was wearing. More nonsense from the Academy teachers, no doubt.

"Ready?" Thyme asked, looking just as uncomfortable in her own outfit, which had a hood to cover her ears. Gini must have seen to that before she left.

Adia nodded and they entered the dining hall. As usual, there were vines running up and down the walls, but someone had added more plants to the space. There were even trees growing out of large pots. Maybe Darian had ordered it done? He knew how comforting she found plants. The hall was packed and noisy, but a hush fell over the room as everyone turned to stare at them. Adia sighed. She hadn't been going for a grand entrance, but it had taken an extra ten minutes to drag Thyme out of their suite once she'd found her chest of weapons. Gini must have seen to that too. As if Thyme didn't already have enough pointy objects.

"It's her," someone whispered. "Adia Kelbara."

"Show us your power," another student yelled out. At that, everyone started screaming and trying to get Adia's attention.

"If she even has any." A familiar, shrill voice carried above the rest.

Adia's eyes narrowed as she slowly turned around. Mallorie sauntered up to her, a cool smile on her lips and a sharp diamond pendant dangling from her neck.

"My father says she probably drugged poor Darian and then somehow convinced him she saved his life. I wouldn't put it past her. So, Adia. Who'd you bribe to get into the Academy?"

"I'm afraid you'd have to tell me about bribing your way into places you don't belong," Adia said drily. "I wouldn't know anything about that. But you can think whatever you like. Just stay out of my way."

It felt amazing to be able to snap back at Mallorie without any fear of getting punished.

"Or what?" Mallorie said, stepping closer, but Adia clenched her fists and walked around her.

46

Except for when her powers had come out in her sleep, she hadn't lost control of herself in months. She wasn't going to let Mallorie Amber be the reason she messed up.

"Ignore her, Adia," Thyme said. "She's just jealous."

Adia kept her head down as she followed Thyme to a table, but she still felt everyone's eyes on her. Some of the kids looked excited as she walked past, but most seemed terrified. She wasn't sure if that was because of her or Thyme. After much pleading Thyme had kept her weapons hidden, but the expression on her face was scary enough even without a battleaxe strapped to her back. And it didn't help that agrias vines were creeping down from the ceiling and moving towards them.

"Adia," Thyme said, her voice sombre. She nodded to the back wall. Adia looked behind her and froze. A line of Gold Hats stood guard. One of the trainees was staring at her intently.

Nami.

So he was back at his post then. She knew the Gold Hats would have punished him for the commotion he'd caused. She wondered what the punishment had been.

"It's all right," Adia said, turning away from Nami's unhappy stare. "I knew I'd see him eventually. Just as long as I don't have to talk to him."

"Adia! Sit with us!" a boy called out, distracting her.

"Rusty, what are you doing?" The girl next to him nudged his side with her elbow. They looked shockingly similar, down to the same wavy brown hair and bright green eyes. Twins, maybe?

"Better to be on her good side, Mimi," he said. "I heard she's the most powerful magician who's ever lived."

"But we're at a school for shamans, not magicians," Mimi said in confusion.

"Same difference," he replied.

"No. Not same difference," Adia said, her voice dripping with irritation. There went her plans for trying to remain unnoticed, but there was only so much she could take. "Do you even know what a shaman is? Or a magician for that matter? Trust me, everything I do is real. Not an illusion or trick of the eye. Why are *you* at this school?"

Rusty stood up and pushed back his chair, his face red with embarrassment.

"Of course I know the difference," he huffed. "Shamans communicate with spirits and travel between realms and heal illnesses. I do it all the time."

Thyme snorted with laughter, which only made the boy angrier.

"You're not special," he sneered. "You're just the jerk who got school cancelled last semester right when I was about to meet the emperor. Darian's a friend of the family. He was going to invite me to a private meeting after dinner."

"Is that so?" Thyme laughed. "What's your family's name? We'll tell Darian you send your regards."

"Well, I don't know him personally," the boy sputtered. "But our parents do."

"Rusty, stop embarrassing yourself," Mimi said. She had the decency to look mortified by the entire exchange. "They *actually* know Emperor Darian. You don't."

"Our family does," Rusty insisted, slamming his hands down on the table. Adia was about to tell him off, but the Academy did it for her. The table started rocking back and forth until Rusty's glass of water spilled down the front of his trousers, making it look like he'd wet himself. He jumped back and swore, frantically grabbing napkins as Mimi failed at holding in her laughter.

"Come on, Adia," Thyme said, shaking her head in amusement as she led them to an empty table near the front. "I forgot how, um, temperamental this Academy of yours is. No offence."

"Are you saying that to me or the school?" Adia asked.

"The school," Thyme admitted sheepishly. It had only taken an hour for Thyme to learn to treat the Academy with respect, or else. "Not sure what to expect from a sentient building."

"Expect epic tantrums," Adia said as she watched students struggle to stay seated in chairs that were more inclined to dump them on the floor, and to eat food off tables that kept trying to upturn themselves.

"You should see what's happening in the kitchens," a mischievous voice said.

"Lebechi!" Adia said, jumping up to grab the tray from her friend and giving her a big hug. "Please tell me you're not trying to *serve* me?"

"Of course not," Lebechi scoffed. "I'm deliberately manning this section so I can talk to you and keep an eye out. We thought you'd come see us right away! Maka even made you a special cake!"

Adia grinned. She was glad to know Maka and Lebechi had missed her too.

"We'll be down as soon as we can. You remember Thyme?"

Lebechi and Thyme grinned at each other. Adia hoped they would get along. She wanted Thyme to have more people in Zaria she could call a friend besides her and Darian.

"Now listen up," Lebechi said quickly. "Word in the servants' quarters is that the new headmistress is a real piece of work. There's been a whole shake-up with the staff too. The new head fired half the professors when she got the job."

"Headmistress?" Adia said slowly. "It's a woman?" She closed her eyes. *No.* She wouldn't dare do this.

"Oh! That must be her now," Lebechi said. "Shhhh."

A hush fell over the room as the faculty walked across the stage.

"Oh...no," Thyme groaned. "No, no, no."

Adia turned her gaze to the ceiling and took a deep breath. "Please don't let it be her," she muttered, before turning back to the front of the room.

"Hello, hello!" a voice boomed.

A woman with an air so regal it made the entire dining hall go still glided across the stage. Her hair, which usually trailed along the floor, now flowed down to her waist in locs that were decorated with gold flowers, and she wore the long green robe that Adia remembered seeing on the old headmaster. Her long, elegant fingers were wrapped around a tall wooden staff. The staff wasn't glowing purple the way it usually did, when it was covered with flowers that constantly unfurled and bloomed and died before beginning the process all over again. And at least she'd remembered to dampen the trail of stardust that floated around her when she wasn't paying attention. But even in a mortal disguise, Adia would know that voice anywhere.

The Alusi Ginikanwa – the most powerful guardian god in the known universe – stood before the completely clueless student body of the Academy of Shamans.

CHAPTER 4

Gini deliberately ignored Adia's glare, managing to look everywhere but at her and Thyme.

"Students and scholars, pupils and professors, friends and...and...ferversherss," Gini said, mumbling gibberish when she clearly couldn't think of another alliteration.

"What?" Lebechi said, tilting her head in confusion as the students began to murmur among themselves.

"Bahaha!" Thyme cackled loudly, and Adia nudged her in her side, trying to get her to stop. Gini – ever confident – carried on despite her flub.

"Welcome to the Academy of Shamans! I'm your new headmistress, Professor Inika!"

Adia rolled her eyes at Gini's name change.

"I'm delighted and honoured to have been asked to lead the Academy into a brand-new era. This school has been quite useless for centuries, has it not? Though that's to be expected, of course, when not one of you has a drop of ability except for—"

"And I'm Professor Mbari."

Adia dropped her face into her hands as Mbari shoved Gini out of the way before her brutal honesty did too much damage. Two Alusi masquerading as professors? Adia half expected Ikenga, the Alusi of victory, to come barrelling forward next with his horns fully on display. She didn't know Mbari well – not like she knew Gini – but she wasn't surprised that the grumpier Alusi hadn't bothered to change his name.

"Mbari, wait your turn," Gini said with a frown. "I was just getting to introductions. Now, this welcome ceremony is going to be quite different from any you've had before."

"Are we still going to be sorted by ability?" someone shouted. "Fire, water and plants."

And death, Adia thought. But she didn't think that was common knowledge. She'd learned that first-hand from Gini.

"My family channels water spirits," the student continued.

Gini stared at the student in disbelief. "*Sorted?* Where do you think you are? And what nonsense are you talking about, channelling water spirits? Your family can do no such thing. The last mortal water channeller was murdered over six hundred years ago by—"

"There will be no sorting," Mbari said, again cutting Gini off. "Because we are not psychics or magicians. If you have an ability, it will make itself known in its own time. Not when you wish it to be known and not on demand. But only if the spirits think you're worthy and decide to open your eyes.

Instead, we will be giving you a proper demonstration of *our* powers."

"Oh no," Adia groaned, closing her eyes for a moment. She might not have any love for her fellow classmates, but she didn't want to watch Gini set their hair on fire either. Well, Mallorie getting singed a bit would be all right.

"Adia, pay attention," Thyme said, clearly excited to see whatever chaos the disguised Alusi were about to cause.

Mbari looked embarrassed as he stepped forward. He caught Adia staring and gave her a small smile, which she returned. Of the three Alusi she'd met, Gini was terrifyingly chaotic for someone so powerful, Ikenga was just terrifying, and Mbari was...well, Mbari was impossibly cranky, but after being around Gini, Adia could understand why the smallest Alusi lived in a constant state of annoyance. But at least if he was here too, he should be able to contain Gini's worst tendencies.

"If you're going to attend this Academy," Gini said, "then it's high time you saw what true shamanic ability looks like."

Lebechi gave up all pretence of being there to serve dinner and plopped down next to Adia, resting her chin in her hands and staring at the podium in excitement.

"Do you think she's the real deal?" Lebechi asked.

"Oh, she's the real deal all right," Thyme said. "In fact, we should all be worried about how *real* this is about to get."

Mbari picked up a candle and walked over to Gini. She put

a hand over the flame and paused, closing her eyes as if she were deep in concentration. Adia knew this was purely for dramatic effect. Whatever Gini was about to do, it was nothing she couldn't do as easily as blinking. The flame grew larger, and the students leaned forward in their seats. Adia winced as her ears popped, as if she'd surfaced too fast from underwater. She glanced around to see if anyone else had felt it, but everyone was staring at Gini. Adia tilted her head. It was just a small flame, but she swore she could hear it roaring and crackling as if it was a large bonfire. Then, with a whoosh, the flame went out. As did every candle in the hall.

Several students screamed as the room was cast into darkness. Just when Adia was sure there was going to be a panic, the flames returned and the dining hall was once again flooded with candlelight.

"Now," Gini said to the stupefied room. "How did I do that? Was it magic? Of course not. Was it a trick? I'm sure many of you will tell yourself it was. Most people find a way to explain away the unexplainable. But what's the shamanic answer? Miss Kelbara?"

Adia froze.

"Do you know the answer?"

Adia swallowed. "You travelled between realms. You're a master of the realm of fire and you had a spirit put the fire out and then bring it back."

"Correct," Gini said, her eyes never leaving Adia's. "And

that's why I'm here. To make sure that you learn how to move safely between realms, and that you always find your way home. Because the worst thing that can happen to a shaman is to get stuck between worlds. Well, maybe there's one thing worse."

"What could be worse than that?" Mallorie Amber said with a shudder.

Gini tilted her head, daring Adia to respond, but Adia turned away. They were both well aware that she already knew the answer, but she didn't want to say it out loud. Gini gave her a sympathetic nod before answering her own question.

"Possession. Few can escape possession by a malevolent spirit if it sets its sights on you," Gini said. "In the worst situations, the host may even lose their life. If a shaman can break free from possession on their own, without anyone there to help pull them out? Now that's a power to be respected. And feared."

Gini clapped her hands, ignoring Mbari's wince as the vibration of her power caused the podium to shake.

Mbari cleared his throat. "Ahem. Table's a bit wobbly," he said, trying to cover for an unconcerned Gini.

"But no more talk of such scary things," Gini said. "Why don't you all give it a try? See if you can touch the realm of fire. Close your eyes and see if you can feel a heat source. I'll open the veil a bit to make it easier."

Adia sighed, preparing herself for Mallorie Amber to launch into her usual theatrics about her great power. And sure enough, Mallorie stood up and opened her mouth. But instead of her usual shrieking, she let out a big yawn.

And then fell down.

Everyone else followed. Some fell out of their chairs, others flopped head first into their dinner. Thyme caught Lebechi from falling into a bowl of soup and stared at Adia with her mouth open.

Adia jumped up in shock as she took in the student body of the Academy, passed out over their salads.

"Gini!" Adia gasped in horror. "What did you do to them? Lebechi!" She shook her friend urgently, but Lebechi was out cold. Adia leaned down and put her cheek next to Lebechi's nose, sighing in relief when she confirmed that her friend was breathing.

"They're asleep," Thyme said in confusion, waving her hand in front of a snoring student. "Good grief, Gini, this is a bit much."

That's when Adia realized that Gini and Mbari looked as shocked as they were.

"This wasn't you," Adia said slowly.

"It wasn't me," Gini said, quickly floating off the stage, all pretence of mortality gone as she hovered over the table. She put her hand on Mallorie Amber's forehead. Mbari leaped down as well and began sniffing the food and drinks on the tables.

"It's not poison," he said with a frown. "The food is untainted."

Adia walked around the room, trying to find some hint as to what had just happened. She tripped over something – no, *someone*. Nami must have wandered away from the wall to get a closer look at Gini and passed out on the floor. It figured that he would do something like that. He'd found orientation fascinating before. He would have been beside himself to see a real display of power.

An overturned pitcher was dripping a steady stream of water onto his face from the table above. Adia sighed. Who knew if Nami would help her if the situation was reversed, but she was better than that. She couldn't let him accidentally drown. She straightened the pitcher and dragged him by his feet so he wasn't lying in a puddle.

She walked around, examining students and shifting anyone who had fallen in a precarious position. Out of the corner of her eye she could see Thyme doing the same. She was about to ask if anyone was showing any sign of waking up when the heavy doors at the front of the room squeaked open. The sudden noise in the eerily silent dining hall made her jump.

Maybe a Gold Hat had heard the silverware crashing to the floor and decided to come see what the commotion was about. Adia swallowed. How were they going to explain why the entire student body was passed out? Adia hoped Gini or

Mbari could come up with a lie on the spot because she was at a loss how to explain why, out of a room of hundreds of people, they were the only four still standing. But it wasn't a Gold Hat who walked in.

Adia tried not to shudder at the jerky, puppet-like movement of the deathly pale figure approaching them. They lurched as if they were controlled by an invisible hand. Their clothes were so worn they were practically rags, and water dripped onto the floor behind them. A clump of seaweed fell off their leg. Had they wandered in from the Macobar Jetty? Had there been a shipwreck? Maybe their movement was so contorted due to a hit to the head or being tossed around the water. She felt guilty for being so unnerved. They could be injured.

"Are— Are you all right?" Adia asked, stepping forward. "Do you need help?"

But before she could go any further, Gini and Mbari jumped in front of her.

"What is it?" she whispered.

"Pay attention, Adia. Tell me what you see when you look at that person. What do you feel?" Gini said in a low tone.

"Feel?" Adia blinked. The urgency in Gini's tone was the same as Hiroma's the day she'd left the Horrorbeyond. Everyone expected her to be able to see something with her powers, but she wasn't sure what.

She tried to tune out her panic, and focus. And there it

was. Something *was* off. It wasn't exactly like the Energy Thieves in the Horrorbeyond, but there was something completely wrong about this person that reminded Adia of them. Something was missing. Where a soul should be, she could only feel a gaping hole.

Another clump of seaweed fell from their ragged and deteriorating clothes. Adia narrowed her eyes and focused in on the sea plant.

Where did you come from?

Almost immediately she felt a familiar snake-like energy. The seaweed had come from the Serpentine, and this creature had come with it, all the way from the Horrorbeyond. This had to be the presence Hiroma had felt – the one that made her send Adia and Thyme running. They had followed them all the way to the Academy.

"What is this?" she whispered. She didn't want to say it out loud.

"Another type of shamanic ability," Gini said. "One that's just as reviled as possession. Reanimation."

"Are you saying that person is..." Thyme said, her voice trailing off. She shuddered as the body crashed into a table with its jerky movements.

"Dead," Adia said in horror.

Thyme shook her head. "No. No, no, *no*. I draw the line at corpses. I'm going to scream."

"You're not going to scream," Adia said. "Someone is

controlling them like a puppet. It's not their fault." She turned to Gini. "We have to help them. Can't we do anything? It showed up right after everyone fainted. That can't be a coincidence."

But all thoughts of helping the reanimated corpse flew out of Adia's head when it stopped its stumbling and stared right at her. Its mouth opened, trying to gasp for breath with lungs that no longer worked, and a strangled sound came out.

"Adia Kelbara," it wheezed, stretching its hand towards her. "I tried to wait until you were alone. But time is running out. I need…I need…"

Adia took a step back. Why did this creature know her name?

"Who did this to you?" Adia asked quickly. "What do you need?"

"I need…to bring the High Queen…" it said in a hoarse whisper, "your eyes!"

The corpse lunged for her.

Adia flung her hands up and every plant in the room hurled themselves towards her.

"My eyes?" she whispered in horror. There was only one reason anyone would want her eyes. Which meant Olark wasn't the only one who knew that she could see through the shamanic shield that hid Imo Mmiri.

She felt sick. It wasn't over. Now that Olark was gone, she'd thought the only things she had to worry about were her uncontrollable powers and nightmares and school. But someone else was after her – someone who wanted to find Imo Mmiri. A queen – but what queen?

Mbari quickly pushed Adia aside. He clasped his hands together then extended his arms wide. As he did, a long iron staff appeared. Gini's staff was wood and had flowers springing all over it. Mbari's looked more like an angry scythe.

"Ginikanwa," he said, keeping the puppet-corpse away from Adia. "Can you wake the students? Adia's right. It's not a coincidence that they all lost consciousness just when this abomination showed itself."

The corpse tried to shove its way past Mbari, whimpering in its desperation to reach Adia. It didn't seem to notice anyone else was in the room.

"I could try," Gini said. "But it's risky for me to tamper with their minds since I don't know what caused them to fall asleep in the first place."

"Well, we have to do something," Thyme shouted. "Chop its head off and I'll throw it in the fire."

"Hold on, everyone," Adia said. "Look at the plants."

The agrias vines had wrapped themselves around the corpse's legs, keeping it in place. More shot forwards from all corners of the hall, covering the body.

"Ugh," Thyme said with a shudder. "Are the vines *eating* it? Is agrias carnivorous?"

Adia couldn't begin to answer Thyme. She didn't know if

she would ever grasp the scope of what agrias was and how much it was capable of. But the agrias vines *did* seem to be devouring the corpse. Or, more so, helping it to decompose.

"I don't know," Adia replied as they watched the corpse disintegrate into dust. "But the vines are getting rid of it."

"Well, thank the stars for that," Gini said. "Adia, Thyme, get back to your table."

Adia and Thyme rushed back to where they had been sitting, shoulders tense as the corpse disappeared. Mbari slowly backed up but never stopped pointing his staff at the creature.

"Thyme, put your head down," Adia said, laying her head in her hands on the table next to Lebechi, whose brow was furrowed as she frowned in her sleep. Adia stared at her friend in dismay. What was happening to everyone who was trapped in this unnatural state of rest? What were they seeing? "Pretend we were asleep too. If this works, once the corpse is gone everyone should wake up. We can't let anyone know we weren't passed out too."

"Right," Thyme said, laying her head next to Adia's and staring at her with wide eyes. "But...why *weren't* we knocked out? The two Alusi I understand, but why are we the lucky students who got to meet a corpse?"

Adia shook her head.

"I don't know," she whispered. "Maybe because it came here for me? It knew who I was. Shhh. They're waking up."

The room erupted in noise as the students began to regain consciousness. Some were groggy and covering their mouths to yawn. Others went right back to the conversations they were having, not noticing they'd just taken an unexpected nap. And Mallorie was yelling at an exasperated-looking Mimi, accusing her of spilling her dinner because, as Mallorie was currently screaming, "How else did my robe end up covered in soup!"

But Adia wasn't paying them any mind. Another powerful being was after her – because anyone who could raise the dead and send them after her had to be powerful. She looked down and stared at the body. Or at least, where the body had once been. The plants were gone now, having done their job. All that was left where the corpse had once stood was a pile of dust.

CHAPTER 5

The walk back to the dorms managed to be both sluggish and chaotic as the half-asleep student body of the Academy started to piece together that something strange had just occurred. Several students tossed Adia suspicious glances. She did her best to avoid their mistrustful stares as she rushed down the hall after Thyme. Since their Alusi professors had taken off to try to get some answers – and Gini had bluntly told the girls they would only get in the way – there was nothing to be done except go to sleep. Except of course neither of them could sleep after what had just happened.

Whereas Adia was channelling her terror into unpacking, Thyme hadn't stopped speaking since they'd shut the door.

"People are going to put two and two together and figure out something weird just happened," Thyme said. "And we don't even know if it was contained to the dining hall or if it was everyone in the Academy. Maybe everyone in Zaria got lulled into a supernatural sleep! Maybe—"

"I know you can't survive without your weapons," Adia interrupted with a frown after she banged her elbow against one of Thyme's shields, "but can't you store some of these under your bed? They take up so much space. How'd you fit a shield in your bag anyway?" No wonder Thyme's bag had been so heavy.

"Oh, would you stop straightening up and say something," Thyme said with a huff. "Or are you really trying to pretend that a rotting corpse didn't show up wanting to spoon out your eyeballs?! Adia!"

Adia stopped fiddling with her clothes and rubbed her head as she walked over and sat down next to Thyme. "I'm trying to focus less on the corpse aspect and more on the message. What queen needs my eyes? The last queen of Zaria would have died…"

Her voice trailed off as Thyme stared glumly at the bed.

"Would have died when Nri fell," Thyme finished.

Thyme had lived in the last Queendom of Nri before she'd travelled through space and time and wound up here, unaware that Olark had burned her homeland to the ground along with everyone she'd known and loved.

"I'm sorry," Adia said quickly. What she knew as ancient history, Thyme knew as home. Adia understood how much it hurt her friend to think about all she'd lost. "We don't have to talk about it. I can research it in the library."

"No, it's fine," Thyme said. "Besides, someone who can give you a real account of the past is better than anything you'll find in a book. But I can't think of any queen who'd have an interest in taking someone's eyes. Plus we didn't have high queens or low queens or anything in between. They were just queens."

Adia shuddered. What had the corpse's plan been? Would it have killed her first before beginning its ocular surgery, or would it have just held her down, put a blade to her eyes, and started carving?

"I won't be able to sleep if we talk about this any more," Adia whispered. Bubbles crawled out from whatever hole he'd been lurking in and rubbed his body against her. He must have sensed how distraught she was.

Thyme gave her a sympathetic look. "Fair enough. We'll see what Gini has to say in the morning." She gave Adia a hug and hopped off her bed. "For now, let's get some sleep – seeing as how we're the only ones who didn't just have a long catnap. Goodnight."

"Goodnight," Adia said, pulling her blanket around her.

She lay there for a solid half-hour, staring at the ceiling. Thyme usually fell asleep the minute her head hit the pillow; she said it was part of her training. As a warrior she never knew when she'd get a chance to rest again, so she used breathing techniques to slow her heart and put herself into a deep sleep no matter how stressed she was. Maybe one day

Adia would ask Thyme to teach her those methods. But tonight, she was glad to be wide awake.

Once she was sure Thyme was asleep, Adia pushed off her blanket and climbed out of bed, grimacing when the floorboards creaked.

Don't act up, she thought. The Academy never messed with her, but she knew that if the school wanted, it could fling the bed against the wall and keep her trapped inside this room for ever. She grabbed a torch off the wall and tiptoed into the hall. Bubbles yawned but jumped off the bed to follow her.

It wasn't long before she stood on a trail outside, shivering in her nightgown as she stared at the dark forest that lay behind the Academy. She steeled her nerves as she walked off the trail and stepped into the woods.

"So many great memories here," she muttered to herself. Like running through the dark as Gold Hats led by Nami chased after her, the botched exorcism, and letting herself be possessed to destroy Olark. If she'd had her way, she never would have set foot in this forest again. But if she didn't make her peace with it now, she'd be terrified every time she passed by.

The corpse had said the *High Queen* needed Adia's eyes. Whoever was after her now, it was a woman, not Olark. Still, Adia needed to go back to the site of Olark's final exorcism. She needed to know if he was still here, reanimating the dead to hunt her down in his place.

When she arrived at the scene of her possession – the place where Olark-as-Darian had snarled at her that he too needed her eyes – Adia began to second-guess her decision. Her curiosity had trumped her fear when she decided to sneak out after curfew, but now she wondered if this hadn't been deeply foolish. Maybe she should have brought Thyme with her. A reanimated dead person had just tried to attack her, after all. But she was sick of dragging everyone she loved into danger. This time around, she'd do her best to handle everything by herself. Nevertheless, she shouldn't be wandering around alone at night.

"He's gone," she whispered to herself. "He can't hurt me any more."

She turned to go but stumbled over Bubbles. Adia shrieked as she tripped over him, expecting to land face-first in the dirt, but instead she found herself plummeting through the air, her torch falling from her hands. She instinctively released her power and called for a plant to help her. An agrias vine rushed forward, and Adia grabbed the thick vine as her feet dangled beneath her.

"What?" she gasped, turning to look down. There was just enough moonlight to let her see that she hadn't fallen into just a small crack in the ground. It had to be at least a mile deep. She clutched the vine harder as her panic rose. One slip and she'd be at the bottom of this bottomless ditch. What if a student who didn't have any powers to save them had been the one to trip into this? Or a helpless animal? If she hadn't been able to grab that vine, the drop would have killed her. Beads of sweat dripped into her eyes as her heart raced, making it hard to see. She shook her head to try to clear her vision, but the motion caused her glasses to slide off her face. She let out a swear word she'd heard Mbari once say as her glasses tumbled off her face and fell into the abyss.

"Climb," she said.

She propped her feet against the rocks and ignored the pain in her fingers as she used the vine to pull her way up. It was a painfully slow process but at last, her fingers connected with flat earth. She let out a sigh of relief once she was back on solid ground, but it turned to panic as someone grabbed her.

The flame from their torch was close to her face, the fire blinding her from seeing whoever had a tight grip on her arm. But she didn't need to see them to fight back. One dead person had already tried to attack her tonight. It wasn't going to happen twice. She shoved them off her as her mind desperately tried to connect with the spirit of the agrias vine, hoping it would do as she asked.

Tie them up.

Her would-be attacker yelped as the agrias vine shot out, wrapping itself around them and dragging them off her. She scrambled back.

"Adia, it's just me!"

Adia squinted in the dark, her night vision even worse without her glasses, but she could make out red-brown hair sticking out from the top of the vines wrapped around him. Of all people, why did it have to be *him*?

"Nami?! What are you doing here?"

"I was patrolling and saw you go into the woods. I wasn't going to bother you, but then I heard you scream. Can you let me out of this?"

Adia had half a mind to keep him tied up here all night, but she unclenched her fists, releasing her power and letting the vines fall to the ground. Nami gazed, open-mouthed, as they crept towards Adia before settling in a coil by her ankles. Another vine tapped her on the shoulder. She turned and saw that the plant had retrieved her glasses for her.

"Thanks," she said as the vine unfurled and extended her glasses out to her, taking them and putting them back on so she could stare Nami down.

"Wow," he whispered.

His shocked face made her realize he was now the only person other than Thyme and Darian who'd witnessed what she could do. Wonderful. She'd just given the least trustworthy person she'd ever known a first-hand display of her powers.

"How did you do that?" He stared at her in awe. "I've never seen anything like it."

Adia raised an eyebrow. "Why do you want to know? Do

you have someone in mind to sell my secrets to? Get yourself some coins at my expense?"

Nami went beet red. "I would never!"

"You would never?" She sputtered in disbelief. "*You* would never?!"

If there was a corpse in the vicinity, she'd just let it know where to come find her, but she didn't care. She was so mad, everything was coming out as a shout. "Why were you following me?"

"I told you! I heard you scream!" Nami ran a hand through his hair. "I thought you might be hurt. Orientation was weird enough with everyone passing out. That's why the Gold Hats are on patrol tonight to try to figure out what happened. *I'm* supposed to be here. But what are *you* doing wandering around the forest at night?"

Ugh. He had a point. But she wasn't going to admit it.

"That's none of your concern," Adia said, as haughtily as if she was Mallorie Amber. "I'll be going now. You can carry on with your Gold Hat duties."

"Wait," Nami said, bending down and grabbing his torch. He'd dropped it when Adia had tied him up. "You don't even have a light. I know you hate me but it's not safe for you to—Whoa." He took a step forward. "What is that?"

"Careful!" Adia said, grabbing his shoulder when he leaned too close to the edge of the chasm. "Are you trying to fall to your death?"

"Is this why you're out here in the middle of the night?" he asked in shock. "What happened here?"

"You tell me," Adia said. "You're the one who's supposed to be patrolling the Academy."

"Yes, but...we did drills in this area two days ago and this wasn't here. It's not like there have been any earthquakes or anything. Maybe there was some sort of rockfall or mudslide? Something that caused the ground to cave in? Or is it something else? Something, ummm..."

Nami wiggled his fingers and Adia narrowed her eyes at him.

"Something what?" she asked.

"I don't know!" Nami said in exasperation. "Something like whatever it was that happened to you and Darian. Or like how you just had a bunch of plants tie me up with a snap of your fingers."

Adia shook her head in disbelief. "Even if I did know what's going on, you think I'd tell *you*?"

Nami looked like he'd been slapped, but Adia refused to feel guilty. Good. Let him get a taste of how horrible he made her feel too.

They stared at each other for a few seconds before he sighed. "No. No, of course not. Look, whatever caused this, it's clearly not safe to be out here right now. Who knows if there's more of these cracks. I'll make sure the Gold Hats block this off so no one falls in tomorrow. But for now, we should head back."

She was about to tell him off for showing up and giving her orders when a whisper made her freeze.

"You woke her up."

"Adia?" Nami asked.

"Shhh," she hissed, turning back to the chasm. "Do you hear that?"

Nami stared at her in confusion, but he walked closer and held up the torch as she looked around nervously.

"I don't hear anything," he said. "Come on. Let's get out of here."

Adia blinked. She knew she'd heard it. And the eerie whisper had come from near the crack. She closed her eyes. Nami had already seen her power. There was no point in hiding it any more. She maintained her focus, ignoring his gasp when her hands began to glow. Maybe there wouldn't be any plant life that deep underground, but there would be roots. Her mind reached out until she connected with some. But the connection was weak. It was fading. Dying. Every root down there was dead, snuffed out by whatever had happened to create the crack. A normal earthquake wouldn't have done that. Some roots might have been ripped out from the force of that ground quaking, but all of them? And the energy around them felt exactly like the energy that corpse had given off.

Like death.

"Adia," Nami said, his voice insistent.

She swallowed and backed away from the chasm. Horrible Nami was right. It wasn't safe out here. And maybe Gini and Mbari might have an explanation for the chasm. Clearly it was linked to the corpse at orientation.

"You don't have to speak to me, I'll just walk you back. You don't have a light."

Adia gave him a curt nod and he held up his torch. She stared into the flame, then gasped and jumped back as a pair of eyes stared back at her. She closed her eyes and shook her head, and when she looked again, they were gone. Was she losing her mind? Whispers and eyes staring at her from inside a flame? Her brain tried to latch onto a rational explanation for what she'd just seen.

Maybe it had just been an owl flying behind the flame because, this time, she didn't see anything.

"Fine," she said, suddenly just as eager as Nami to get out of the forest. "Let's go."

"You woke her up."

Adia forced herself to remain calm and not let Nami onto the fact that she was currently hearing voices as she marched ahead of him while he lit her path from behind. She'd passed out after she'd destroyed Olark. Had she skipped off thinking her work was done when all along she'd accidentally unleashed some new horror into the world? Either this voice was trying to trick her, or it was trying to warn her that she'd done something terrible.

"Who are you?" she whispered quietly to herself so Nami couldn't hear. "Are you talking about the queen who wants my eyes? Who is *she?* When is she coming?"

A moment of silence followed by another eerie whisper.

"She's here."

CHAPTER 6

"Finally. You're awake."

Adia rubbed her eyes and glared. She was awake because Thyme was in the middle of target practice and all the noise had interrupted Adia's restless sleep.

"There was a note under the door from our illustrious new headmistress." Thyme dug around in her pocket and pulled out a small slip of paper. "Here."

Adia grabbed her glasses from her nightstand and read the note.

We've told the students and staff that a small earthquake released toxic gas into the air, causing a momentary bout of sleepiness. Just go with it. —G

"That's ridiculous," Adia said.

"That's Gini," Thyme replied. "I probably didn't pass out because I'm not from your world," Thyme mused. "Do you think your ability shielded you somehow?"

"I have no idea," Adia admitted. "But I need to talk to Gini."

She didn't want to worry Thyme with what had happened last night in the forest, but maybe Gini would have some answers. "And also say hi to everyone in the kitchens. Do you want to come?"

"No, they're your friends," Thyme said with a wave of her hand.

Adia frowned. "You'd like Maka and Lebechi," she said. "I don't want you to feel like you're only here to protect me. This is your school too. You should try to have fun and make friends." She was starting to get worried that Thyme was only her friend because they'd been through hell together. And because Thyme literally didn't know anyone else in the world. If they'd been normal girls who'd met in the Swamplands, she was pretty sure Thyme would have been the most popular girl in the village and would never have noticed Adia Kelbara sitting by herself.

But Thyme only snorted. "Having a front-row seat to Mallorie Amber's antics will be all the fun I need, don't worry. Go on. Go have your reunion."

"All right. See you later then." She'd have to work on convincing Thyme to expand her social circle later.

It took a few extra minutes to reach the kitchens. Every time she turned a corner one of Adia's new classmates would jump in front of her to ask about Darian and what she'd done to save him and if they could get an introduction.

"Note to self: use the passageways to get around," she said

to herself firmly. She almost crashed into a table in her haste to avoid Rusty when she'd noticed him barrelling towards her. She sighed in relief when she finally stood in front of the kitchen doors, which flung themselves open before Adia even had to touch them.

"I missed you too," she said with a grin as she walked into the chaos.

Maka was standing in front of a boy, dramatically pointing at a missed spot on a plate as the sloppy dishwasher barely held back his tears. Lebechi seemed to be doing a dance with a bunch of floating cloths, except judging from the furious expression on her face, the rags were having more fun with their game of tag than she was. And of course Bubbles was already down there, trying to snatch fish out of the icebox. Some things never changed, Adia thought with a sigh.

"I thought it would have calmed down in here," she said, announcing her presence.

"Adia!" Maka said, leaving the poor dishwasher to his weeping as she ran up to Adia and enveloped her in a huge hug. "Oh, sorry! I got your shiny new uniform dirty. Why didn't you come see us yesterday? Or are you too good for your old friends now that you're a student at the illustrious Academy of Shamans?"

Adia knew from the twinkle in Maka's eye that she was joking but she answered all the same.

"You know I'd rather be down here with all of you. How is

everything? How was your visit home?"

"It was—"

"It was nothing but gossip about you," Lebechi interrupted.

Adia took in her friend. As she ran to her station to stir her pots, she seemed as energetic as usual. No worse for wear after losing consciousness last night.

"You're all anyone's talking about," Lebechi continued. "A girl from nowhere saving the emperor? Our village is on the side that thinks you're some kind of saint who saved Darian with a divinely bestowed power. But the next village over thinks you're a witch who's controlling his mind. And the village over from that one thinks you're—"

"Lebechi," Maka said, giving a pointed look to everyone in the kitchen who was making a very poor attempt at hiding their eavesdropping. "Why don't we save this conversation for later? We're running behind enough as it is without you standing around yapping."

"Fine, fine," Lebechi said. "Don't suppose you want to stick around and help with breakfast, Adia? We had to clean up the mess in the dining hall after that dinner so now we're an hour behind on everything. Where'd you disappear to, by the way? Were you all right?"

Adia frowned. "Why? What do you mean?"

"The...toxic gas outbreak, of course," Lebechi said. Her tone made it clear that no one in the kitchen was buying Gini's excuse for a second. She ran to take a lid off an overflowing pot.

"Half the food wound up on the floor when everyone blacked out. I don't feel sick, though, do you?"

Adia shook her head, going along with Gini's lie. "No, no. I'm fine too."

"Yes. We're all fine," Maka said, giving Adia a look that said they were all most certainly *not* fine. "If you have time before you start classes, Adia, you might want to go look at the gardens. We've got some new plants you might be interested in. Lebechi, why don't you show her?"

"Oh, right," Lebechi said, her voice unnaturally loud. "The gardens."

Adia let Lebechi drag her outside. "Why are you all acting so strange?" she asked.

"It's this new council that's always lurking about," Lebechi said in disgust. "They were here even earlier than the Academy cleaners. They've been snooping around everywhere. Maka's on edge because she caught one hiding in the pantry when we all got here. He claimed he was checking supplies, but he was absolutely spying on us."

"Why would a council from the capital spy on a bunch of cooks?" Adia asked. "Unless they think you're going to poison the students."

"Hold your tongue," Lebechi said. "If the new headmistress hadn't saved us with that gas leak excuse, the kitchen staff's heads would be on spikes. We would have been the ones everyone blamed."

Adia knew Lebechi was right. Ridiculous as the toxic gas excuse was, it was better than blaming the cooks for food poisoning.

"And the council isn't interested in spying on us," Lebechi said as she marched purposefully to the back of the garden, which housed the cabbage patch. "They're interested in spying on *you*. They know you used to work down here and that we're your friends. Luckily Maka had only been yelling at us about a burned cake when we realized we were being spied on, so he didn't overhear anything he shouldn't have. Now, if we bring you up, we know to double-check there's no hooded figure lurking behind us. The gardens are safe, though. They're too open for anyone to sneak around without us noticing. Besides, I need to show you something in the cabbage patch. You still remember the layout, right?"

Adia nodded. She had mapped it all out the first time Lebechi had shown her around.

"Well, you won't remember this," Lebechi said, pushing tall stalks of corn out of the way as they entered the patch of green and purple cabbages. "Watch your step. It's not deep, but you're liable to twist your ankle. It's a miracle I didn't fall into it this morning."

Adia's jaw dropped. Before them was another massive crack in the ground like the one she had nearly fallen into last night. In the daylight, she could see it wasn't just split open, but also charred.

"Do you know what happened?" Adia asked, kneeling. "Was it struck by lightning or something?"

"It couldn't have been," Lebechi said, shaking her head. "I was here yesterday morning and everything was fine. And it didn't storm last night. Unless the weather turned for a few minutes while we were unconscious."

No, Adia thought. There hadn't been a cloud in the sky last night. Just stars and a full moon. She touched the scorched earth, letting the ash fall through her fingers. For centuries Olark and his followers had set fires throughout Zaria in his search for Imo Mmiri. Decimating forests and villages and ending countless lives, all in his desperate search for the mythical land that fire couldn't touch. And all that was left of the places he'd destroyed – collectively known as the burned lands – was black ash. This singed section of the gardens reminded her of them. Like a small burned land.

She'd only seen the one corpse at orientation. But what if there had been more? One sent to get her eyes, and another sent to burn down the Academy? If that was true, then it could still be here. Maybe this was why she was waking to a fire ability now. If she could tap into it, maybe she could use that connection to track down and stop whoever was crawling out of these cracks in the ground and setting these fires.

"Let me know if you find any other places like this," Adia said. Lebechi nodded.

A shrill whistle made them cover their ears.

Adia winced. "Where is that coming from?"

"The new headmistress must have had it installed." Lebechi grimaced. "She's really something."

"You have no idea," Adia said. She and the new headmistress needed to have a talk. But first, there was something she needed to ask her friend. When she was knocked out, Lebechi had been frowning in her sleep. As if she was in the middle of an unpleasant dream or nightmare.

"Lebechi," Adia said. "Do you remember what you were dreaming about when you were passed out last night?"

Lebechi rubbed her temples as if she had a headache. "Now that you mention it..."

"What?"

"It was dark. And I mean pitch-black. The air was stale and musty. It was hard to breathe..." Lebechi shuddered. "No wonder I forgot. I must have blocked it from my memory. I hate being in small, enclosed spaces. I felt scared and trapped. Like I'd been buried alive. I think I was trapped in a tomb."

Buried alive? Trapped in a tomb. *That's* what had been happening in Lebechi's mind as a corpse was trying to take Adia's eyes? Adia felt sick. The corpse had come for her, but others had suffered because of it.

Back when Adia had first learned about Olark's existence, Lebechi had been the first person she'd tried to tell about the demon's return to Zaria. But at the mention of Olark's name her friend had thrown a fit and clawed at her clothes, before forgetting everything Adia had said. That was the power Olark could command. He had made it so no one would believe you if you told them of his existence.

And now strong, cheerful Lebechi had once again had her mind and body taken away from her. Adia wasn't going to let this happen twice. If Adia had awoken this queen, whoever she was, then Adia would be the one to send her back to her final resting place.

"You don't have to try to remember any more," Adia said quickly. "That sounds horrible."

"Well, it's not like I was *actually* buried alive. It was just a dream," Lebechi said. She frowned. "It *was* just a dream, right?"

Adia stared at the ground for a minute before deciding to be honest.

"I don't know," she admitted. "I mean, no, of course you weren't buried alive. But I don't think it was a random nightmare either. Let me know if it happens again. And ask Maka what she dreamed about too."

"Pay attention to dreams and tell you if I fall into any giant holes in the ground," Lebechi said. "Got it. I should have known this wasn't going to be a normal semester. You woke something up."

Adia startled. "What did you say?" she gasped.

Lebechi tilted her head. "With your power," she said. "The Academy feels more alive than ever. Why do you seem so spooked? What's going on?"

Adia debated telling Lebechi about the corpse but, dream or not, Lebechi had been through enough. Telling her a walking corpse had been a few metres away from her sleeping body just seemed cruel.

"You mean what's going on besides the entire student body losing consciousness over dinner?" Adia said, going with the obvious. It worked because Lebechi sighed.

"Fair enough. Honestly...I thought maybe *you* did it."

"Me?" Adia asked, baffled. "Why would you think that?"

Lebechi looked embarrassed. "Well, you don't even know the full scope of your powers, do you? I thought maybe you'd lost control and did something to us. By accident, of course!" she added quickly.

Adia wasn't offended so much as concerned that two of her closest friends were slightly panicked at the idea of her not having control of her powers. Was it that obvious she didn't know what she was doing?

"It definitely wasn't me," Adia said firmly. "But I'm going to find out who it was."

CHAPTER 7

Adia didn't bother to knock before she flung open the door to Gini's office. The Academy's new headmistress was sitting in the middle of the room, cross-legged and levitating over a pile of letters.

"You really should lock the door if you're not going to keep your feet on the ground," Adia said, walking around the floating Alusi. A chair slid forward and Adia collapsed into it.

She glanced at the papers surrounding Gini.

"What's all this?" she asked. "Answers about what happened yesterday, I hope?"

"I'm afraid not," Gini said. "They were waiting for me in my office. Months of letters from a single man, demanding that the Academy send him money."

"All right," Adia said slowly. It must be the old headmaster, who Gini had clearly had fired. Fine. He did deserve some final payment. But she didn't know why Gini was focusing on that this morning instead of looking into who the High

Queen was. "And that concerns you because..."

"Because the man in question is your uncle."

"What?!" Adia shouted.

"And the money he's demanding," Gini said with a look of disgust, "is yours. Or, according to him, it's his. Seeing as you're a child and he and your aunt are your legal guardians, he insists that he be in full control of your money until you come of age."

Adia stared at Gini. "You can't be serious."

Gini shook her head in irritation. "He's also insisting on having a meeting with me to discuss your safety at the school."

"Well then, I guess Uncle Eric and I want to discuss the same thing because I'm also concerned about my safety at school. Gini, a corpse showed up at dinner! Do you have any explanation for that?"

"I've been trying to figure it out," Gini said with a frown. "All I did was lower the barrier between your world and the realm of spirit, and then that poor creature showed up."

"And there's no way someone could have come through without you knowing?"

"No," Gini said with a shake of her head. "Whoever, or whatever, was in control of that corpse is already here."

Adia shuddered. Just like the voice had said. *She's here.*

"But who else would be able to take over someone's body except..." Adia didn't want to finish the thought. She didn't want to speak his name ever again and give him any power, but she also couldn't ignore the gnawing feeling in her stomach.

"Except Olark. But he's dead," she continued quickly, refusing to even entertain that idea that he hadn't been truly vanquished. "And it's a queen who's after my eyes now. Which means…"

"Someone else is trying to find Imo Mmiri," Gini said bluntly.

"But how could anyone know that I can find it? That my eyes can see it!" Adia exclaimed. "That information should have vanished with Olark."

"I think that's the problem," Gini said. "Death isn't the end. It's just another state of being. Another realm – one that shamans can enter. Where they can listen to whatever the dead decide to tell them. But you're the last true shaman in Zaria."

Adia's eyes went wide.

"But that's not true," she said. "What about EJ and all the other kids Olark plied with Drops so he could steal their power?"

"Fragments of shamanic abilities," Gini said. "Your cousin and those other children will always be a little more in tune than everyone around them. Their dreams might occasionally come true, or maybe they'll see a spirit out of the corner of their eye. If they decide to train, some might even grow up to be excellent healers or wisewomen because of their heightened sensitivity to the realm of spirit. They'll be able to catch a glimpse of the other side every now and then. But you? You can walk between realms."

Adia frowned.

"If communicating with the dead is a shamanic ability, then I can't be the only shaman in Zaria because I can't do that."

"Can't you?" Gini murmured. "You spoke with Viona just fine, and she's been dead for centuries."

Adia opened her mouth, then closed it. Fair enough.

"But let's not get ahead of ourselves," Gini said. "A shaman might not even be involved in any of this. This could also be a result of you skipping around the astral plane without knowing what you were doing."

Adia flinched. The whispers had said she'd woken someone up. Of all the spirits in the realm of the dead, had she really woken a power-hungry queen?

"You've done too much without having any proper training and it's time we rectify that. You'll go to your classes with the rest of these children, but unlike your talentless classmates, *you'll* go through initiation."

"And what exactly happens during initiation?" Adia asked warily.

"Shamans aren't initiated by the living. You'll have to meet with spirits. *If* they decide you're worthy of seeing all the secrets of the spirit world, your powers will begin to open in new ways. They might give you a test, they might torment you to see if you can make it back with your sanity intact, or they may take one look at you and spit you right back out, telling you to try again in another decade. I have no idea what you'll be put through."

"I know you think this is important," Adia said, "but do you really think my initiation should be a top priority? What if everyone falls asleep again? What if it happens when someone is walking down a flight of stairs? Or in the bath. And have you seen the giant cracks in the earth all around the Academy? There's a huge one in the forest. If someone fell into it, they could *die*. I think we need to worry about that more than my initiation."

"I can worry about two things at the same time," Gini said. "The benefit of a superior mind. But don't think I'm not taking this seriously. Something happened when everyone fell asleep."

She picked up a piece of paper from her desk and handed it to Adia. "It came from the capital this morning. Delivered by a wild dog."

Adia took the paper. Wild dogs were incredibly rare and incredibly fast. A person was likely to get their hand bitten off trying to tame one, but a few of the wealthier residents of the capital had trained the beasts to deliver messages. A wild dog could make the journey from the capital to Chelonia in one night if it ran at full speed.

Dozens of fires last night in forests throughout Zaria. No one was hurt but a lot of earth was cracked straight through. Probably poachers trying to clear land. Were there any incidents at the Academy? Stay vigilant until we know what's going on.

—I

"'I'?" Adia said. "Ikenga's in Zaria too?" Horned Ikenga was Gini's other brother and the Alusi that Adia knew the least about. Which was fine with her. Whereas Gini and Mbari were always squabbling, Ikenga's expression was always so stoic she never knew what he was thinking. He was terrifying.

"Keeping an eye on the capital and Darian," Gini confirmed. "He can't say too much in writing, of course. Not when anyone could intercept it. But we all know this wasn't poachers."

So the capital was breaking out in fires too.

"Can't you do something?" Adia asked. "At orientation you put out every candle in the room. You can do the same with the fires."

Gini shook her head. "Notice that I put out those flames and then within seconds I relit them. There was no disturbance to the balance of your world. I didn't alter anything. And even that small display could get me in trouble. My only job here is to keep you protected. You know Alusi aren't supposed to meddle with the worlds we help create."

Adia frowned. Maybe Alusi couldn't meddle but *she* wasn't bound by their laws.

"What if I learned how to connect with fire? Couldn't I ask the spirits to help put out the fires?"

"If the spirit realm could exercise that level of power over a physical realm, it would no longer be a physical realm," Gini said. "The Academy is one of the few places in Zaria where things like that can happen. Imagine if everywhere in the world was like this building. With tables flipping themselves over because the tree they were made from had such a strong spirit inside, it could defy your laws of physics. The mortal realm wouldn't even exist. But all this is a moot point. You haven't started to manifest another ability. Have you?"

She hadn't wanted to tell Gini. If she said it out loud, that would make it real. But this wasn't about her and her growing panic about her lack of control over her powers. This was a matter of everyone's safety. It was time to tell Gini everything. She quickly explained about the chasm in the forest and that Nami had the Gold Hats surveying the grounds to make sure no student accidentally fell into the void.

"And...I keep hearing a voice. It says I woke someone up."

Gini rubbed her eyes. "I thought we had more time."

Adia stared at her. "What do you mean?"

"When I first met you, I was surprised that your affinity was for connecting with plant spirits. As I told you before, you burn hot. When I understood how much potential you had, I realized you probably would also manifest the ability to connect with fire one day. I just hoped it would be after you'd had time to properly train."

"What are you saying?" Maybe she'd been too hasty not blaming herself. "Are you saying this is my fault?"

"It might be, yes."

Adia lowered her head. She should have known better than to ask Gini a question she didn't want the answer to. Gini wasn't going to do anything but tell her the harsh truth. Even if it made her feel like crying.

Gini must have noticed her wilting in her chair. "Sit up straight. If you are the one causing this, it wasn't intentional. You have nothing to feel ashamed of. If you'd been born a few centuries earlier a wisewoman would have started training you in mind control from the minute you could understand speech. The blame lies with Olark, the missionaries, and the people from behind the Sunless Mountains who left you without access to your people's knowledge."

Adia wasn't sure if it made much of a difference whether she didn't mean to do it or that she hadn't been trained. But this wasn't the time to have a philosophical debate with herself.

"So what should I do?" It couldn't be safe for her to stay here when she might be the one who was waking the dead. "Leave school?" she asked, hopefully, but Gini shook her head.

"Let me talk with Mbari before we make any decisions." Gini glanced at her pocket watch. "For now, let's the two of us just make it through the first day of class. As you can imagine

I have a host of confused professors I need to speak with this morning."

"Yes, congratulations on your new post," Adia said sarcastically. "How are you supposed to be our new headmistress when you'll be disappearing after three months?" Alusi couldn't stay on the ground for more than three months at a time before they became completely untethered from reality. Mbari and Ikenga had to keep track of that for Gini because she had a tendency to forget when she was approaching her limits and needed to return to the stars.

Gini didn't seem concerned. "By then I'll have picked a suitable replacement to mind the place when I'm gone. You can even give me your opinions on the professors since you're going to have to take classes with them. I've taken the liberty of making your schedule myself."

Gini pointed at a sheet of paper on the desk. Adia sighed but picked it up.

Self-Directed Study
Herbology
Channelling
History of Zaria
Practicality (Waived)

"Self-directed study?" Adia asked, glancing up from the sheet.

"You'll have that right here," Gini said. "Your first class of the day will be in this office with me. I had thought we'd start working on bettering your control with plants, but I want to see what happens when you're around fire. I'd like to give you a bit of an assessment test right now."

Adia swallowed. "Do you really think that's a good idea with everything going on?" Adia asked. "For us to be wandering around in the spirit realm?"

"I think it's not only a good idea," Gini said with a frown, "but a vital one. You stormed in here wanting to find out more about the High Queen and that corpse, didn't you? Let's see if the fire gives you any answers."

With a wave of her hands, the coals in the fireplace sparked with embers, before exploding into a roaring fire. Gini pointed at a chair, and the chair dragged itself in front of the fireplace.

"Sit."

Adia eyed the fire nervously as she walked up to the chair.

"What am I supposed to do?" she asked, turning back to Gini.

"Relax, slow down your breathing, and stare into the fire. Don't try to force anything. Either something will happen, or it won't. Sit."

Adia sighed and sat down. Gini wasn't going to let her leave this room unless she did this assessment test, so she might as well get it over with. She breathed slowly, in and out, and did her best to let her mind go blank as she focused on the centre of the flame. After about a minute she sighed again.

"Nothing's happening," she said.

"Don't look away," Gini said. "Let your mind drift."

Adia pushed up her glasses and leaned forward. Another minute passed, but then she thought she glimpsed the silhouette of two figures – though whether they were human or animal, she couldn't tell. She was probably just imagining it.

"What do you see?" Gini's voice startled her. It sounded far away, yet so loud and urgent.

"I'm not sure," Adia said. "Two creatures, maybe? One of them looks like it has a hat on its head. No." She frowned and leaned closer to the flames. "A crown."

But as soon as she said it, whatever she thought she had seen vanished, along with the flames.

"Why did you put out the fire?" Adia asked.

Gini didn't answer. Adia was about to turn to look at her when the smoke from the extinguished fire rose up from the ashes, swirling and snaking around her. Almost like an agrias vine. Hovering in front of her, the smoke shifted as letters began to form.

"What do you see?" Gini asked again, her voice even more far away than before.

"Writing," Adia said, as the letters moved around, arranging themselves into words.

Adia shot up from the chair so quickly that it toppled over, before righting itself of its own accord. If what she'd just seen was real and not a figment of her imagination, then they had a lot more to worry about than reanimated corpses. All of Zaria was in danger. But no one was in more danger than her – and a boy in the capital.

"Darian," she whispered.

"Adia." Gini put her hands on Adia's shoulders and spun her around, staring down at her with an intensity that frightened her. "Tell me what you saw. Quickly. Before you forget it."

"I'll *never* forget it," Adia said in horror. "I never forget anything." She recited:

"Hear my words throughout the world
And read them in the skies.
Until this crown falls from your head
Your soul is bound to mine.
My every wish is your command
From now until you die.
And even in the realm of death
Our souls will be entwined."

CHAPTER 8

"Olark did something else to Darian." Adia was already halfway across the room. "Something we didn't know about to keep their souls tethered. I have to get to the capital. I have to make sure Darian is—"

"Calm yourself, child," Gini said, blocking the door. "Think. Is Darian the only person in your life with a crown on their head?"

"Of course he is," Adia said in frustration. "Do you think emperors and kings frequently visit the Swamplands? Do you think that queens – that queens…"

She blinked. Gini was right. She'd gone straight to worrying about Darian, but last night, someone *dead* had tried to steal her eyes. On behalf of a queen.

"You don't think this is about Darian," Adia said slowly.

"I don't know what to think," Gini said. "But I think it's more logical to assume that if a queen is commanding the dead, and you just saw a curse about the realm of the dead, then the very alive Darian isn't the only royal you need to be concerned about."

"Make another fire," Adia said, dragging the chair back to the fireplace. Terrified as she was that she'd had the strongest vision of her life through flames, not plants, she needed to dig deeper. "Maybe I can see more."

"Absolutely not," Gini said. "I wasn't expecting you to go that far. You're not to do that again until you've been initiated. Even I can't seem to stop the spirit world from rushing forward to send you messages. You need to have your own shields in place, and right now you're as helpless as a newborn lamb in there. Go to class. I'll talk to Mbari about what just happened, and we'll decide what to do from there. But for now—"

Bang, bang, bang.

Insistent pounding on the door interrupted them.

"I wasn't expecting anyone else this morning," Gini said with a frown. "Open the door."

Adia walked over to the door and pulled, but it wouldn't budge. Adia raised an eyebrow at Gini. Had their fire session conjured something up that the Academy was trying to protect them from? Gini held out her staff and nodded.

Adia swallowed and pulled again. This time the door groaned open. Actually *groaned.* But then she groaned too as she was greeted by the sight of angry blue eyes and bouncing blond curls.

"What a coincidence," Mallorie Amber said with a sniff. "I was just coming to introduce myself to the new headmistress and discuss a problem at the school, and would you look at that – the problem is standing right in front of me."

Adia took a deep breath. No way Mallorie was going to try to blame her for what happened. Not when Gini had given that excuse about a gas leak. "What problem are you—"

"You see, Headmistress Inika," Mallorie said, shoving Adia out of her way, "Adia has already broken an Academy rule. I have it on good authority that she has *a pet* in her bedroom."

Adia snickered. Mallorie *would* be mad about Bubbles.

"Mallorie, don't be so angry," Adia said, making her eyes wide and innocent. "It makes your skin get all splotchy. Are you running low on face cream?"

Mallorie froze. So far, the fact that she'd smeared Bubbles's vomit all over her face last semester was a secret only the two of them knew. Adia knew Mallorie would want to keep it that way.

"Students aren't allowed to keep pets!" Mallorie screeched, recovering from the shameful reminder.

"Is that so," Gini said, drily. "I'm sorry, I didn't catch your name, Miss..."

"Amber. Mallorie Amber. I'm sure you've heard of me." Mallorie didn't pause for breath as Gini gave Adia a bewildered look. Adia realized she'd never bothered to mention Mallorie to her.

"You're new, but *I'm* very well aware of the Academy rules,"

Mallorie continued. "My father is the school's biggest donor. Which makes me its wealthiest student."

"Yes," Adia said, unable to hide her irritation. "Which is why your room has about a dozen scented candles we're not allowed to have because of the fire hazard, your wall is full of holes where you forced the servants to hang all that ugly art you brought from the capital, and you waste the kitchen staff's time with your ridiculous demands. But you want to bother me about my cat?"

"You would know about what goes on in the kitchens, wouldn't you," Mallorie hissed, "seeing as how you still stink of onions and cooking oil. You're so quick to forget who you are and who *I* am. The most powerful student at this school. Which is why I get special privileges. Not that I mean to brag about money." She gave Gini what Adia assumed was supposed to be a conspiratorial look. "I'm just stating facts about whose family is the school's biggest donor."

"Yes, of course. And I see your point. The student who brings in the most money to the school *should* be allowed a few perks," Gini said in a calm voice as she picked up some books from her desk and took them over to a shelf.

"Exactly," Mallorie said triumphantly. "Which is why—"

"Which is why *Adia* will be allowed to keep her cat."

"I – I beg your pardon?" Mallorie stammered. Adia sighed, waiting for Mallorie to finally catch on to the fact that she'd just lost.

"Well, with Ms Kelbara's reward for saving the emperor's life..." Gini said, letting her voice trail off as Mallorie stared at Adia in disbelief.

"How much was the reward?" Mallorie asked, gaping.

"You can't seriously think I'd tell *you* that," Adia scoffed.

"As you were once the student in Adia's rather enviable position," Gini said, smoothly inserting herself between Adia and Mallorie, who both looked close to violence, "I'm sure you can understand why certain allowances must be made for our star pupil. The cat stays. Are we done here, Melanie?"

"It's Mallorie!"

"As I said." Gini shrugged and waved her hand.

"And no, we're not done," Mallorie said, completely at a loss about how this had all gone so badly for her. "I was doing my year of practicality with the old headmaster. I was training in leadership. Since he's gone I— I was hoping that I'd be transferred to you."

Gini rubbed her eyes. "I'm afraid I wouldn't have time for that. Go ask Professor Mbari," she said, looking a bit gleeful at the prospect of torturing her brother. "He's my right-hand man and will be an even better mentor for you. Tell him I sent you to him with the highest recommendation."

"But – but—" Mallorie stammered.

"You're dismissed," Gini said firmly.

Mallorie turned to leave the room, but even in defeat she still chose to be terrible. As she passed Adia she leaned in and whispered, "Don't think being the headmistress's pet is going to save you. See you in class." She bumped Adia hard with her shoulder then walked out the door.

Adia glared at Gini. "You shouldn't have provoked her. I can handle Mallorie on my own."

"Yes, I can see that," Gini said. "Being treated badly by someone who's known to be a horrible person doesn't sting as much as, say, being disappointed in someone you thought was a friend. But that's the very heart of betrayal, isn't it? That it was someone you trusted who broke your confidence."

Gini gave her a knowing look. They both knew who the great betrayer of Adia's life was.

"What does that have to do with anything," Adia muttered. Thyme knew not to mention Nami in her presence, but if Gini needed to be told she'd be happy to enlighten her.

"Oh nothing, nothing," Gini murmured, glancing at the clock. "It's time for you to get going. And good luck today. I'm sure you'll do well."

Gini gave her an encouraging smile and Adia nodded. She'd fought Olark and lived. How bad could her first day of school be?

Breakfast was almost over by the time Adia arrived at the dining hall, but she knew Thyme would save her something. She sighed in relief when she spotted her friend at a table by herself, waving Adia over. In the Swamplands, if she and EJ had different times for lunch, she had no one else to sit with, so she would just read a book as she ate. She was worried about Thyme not having any other friends, but she also couldn't pretend she wasn't happy to have someone other than books for company.

She expected Thyme to ask about her talk with Gini, but instead Thyme put a finger to her lips and tilted her head at a group of adults in long grey robes who were huddled in the corner.

"Who are those people?" Adia whispered. "New professors?"

"I'm not sure," Thyme said. "But they have everyone on edge. They keep snooping around the tables, clearly trying to listen in on everyone's conversations. So...don't say too much."

Adia nodded. She had to be careful. Thyme was right. For once, no one was paying any attention to Adia. Everyone was gawking at the strangers.

Adia squirmed when several members of the group fixed her with a steady stare. They had to be who Lebechi warned her about.

"I think I know who they are," she said. "It's—"

"It's the new council," Mallorie said as she walked past their table. "We all have to put up with babysitters from the capital after the mess you caused last semester. And don't try to tell me you just happened to save Darian's life. I know there's more to this story and I'll figure it out. But whatever it was that happened that night, we're all stuck with this council because of it. They're here to make sure the year goes smoothly. And they don't answer to anyone."

"You mean your family wasn't able to buy them off?" Adia asked drily, but her sarcasm was lost on Mallorie.

"And we offered so much!" Mallorie said, shaking her head. "If I wanted to be followed around, I would have stayed at home with my private tutors and my mother hounding me to practise piano. We're supposed to have more freedom being away from our parents. But you've ruined that too."

Mallorie flounced off, glaring at the council as she went, but most paid her no mind. A few even glared back at her. Adia guessed they'd already felt the brunt of Mallorie's temper. Nice as it was to know that even the Amber family couldn't get their way all the time, Adia *was* concerned that whoever this council answered to didn't care about money, and that was a rare thing for people from the capital.

"Capital babysitters," she repeated with a sigh. "Mallorie's right."

"Excuse me?" Thyme asked in a strangled voice.

"I mean she's right that this might ruin our freedom," Adia said. Much as she hated to agree with Mallorie about anything, this council could get in their way. "It's not going to be easy to figure out who was behind that corpse with watchdogs breathing down our necks. Oh no! One's coming this way."

"Ms Kelbara."

Adia took an involuntary step back as a man approached. He was one of the tallest people she'd ever seen. Taller even than her uncle. The council member's eyes were green compared to her uncle's brown, but still, he reminded Adia of Uncle Eric. Cold and cruel with a hint of anger brewing behind his gaze. Unlike the professors, who donned the traditional garb of Zaria in their attempts to claim shamanic power and an ancient lineage they didn't have, this man wore the style of the capital. He loomed in front of her now in his dark suit and waistcoat and white shirt with a high-winged collar.

"That's me," Adia said, then grimaced. Of course he knew who she was. Everyone knew who she was. And if they didn't, there was that giant new mural in the main hall with her face smack in the middle of it for all to see. Something about this man was making it hard for her to focus.

"I've wanted to meet you for quite some time. I'm Mr Chobly. I serve as one of Emperor Darian's advisers, as well as a member of the Academy's new council."

Back before Darian's letters had become cryptic, he'd mentioned his advisers. He hated them. Whatever reason these people had for being here, Adia knew it wasn't Darian's idea.

"Then shouldn't you be in the capital giving Darian advice?" Adia asked bluntly.

Mr Chobly laughed, but his eyes remained cold. Adia swallowed.

"What a charming young lady you are," Mr. Chobly said. "So blunt. I see why the emperor is so fond of you. Might we have a word in private?"

Adia turned to glance at Thyme, but she had vanished. Adia knew what that meant. Her friend was lurking somewhere, keeping an eye on Chobly, ready to incapacitate him if need be.

"Class is about to start," she said.

Chobly nodded, ushering her to the door. "I'll be quick."

When they were outside, all pretence of this being a friendly conversation dropped.

"The emperor has been quite different since your encounter. He's making decisions that have his advisers very concerned. Most worrisome is his decision to ban Drops."

"I'm not sure what that has to do with me." Adia hoped her face looked sufficiently innocent. According to EJ and Thyme, she was a terrible liar.

"Aren't you?" Mr Chobly asked, leaning closer. "It seems like it has a great deal to do with you."

Adia wanted to put more distance between them but something about Mr Chobly made her legs freeze. As if she had no choice but to stand still and listen to him.

"It would appear that unlike everyone else in the Swamplands, you've never taken Drops? The good Sister Claudia told us you got quite violent with her when she tried to give you your first dose."

The good Sister Claudia was a menace and a tyrant who ruled the Swamplands with an iron fist and a devotion to the Bright Father that few could rival. Not for the first time, Adia wondered if Sister Claudia knew that the Bright Father and Olark were one and the same.

Wait a minute...

"How do you know Sister Claudia?" Adia asked slowly.

Mr Chobly smiled. He was enjoying making her uncomfortable. Adia could feel it in her gut that he wanted her to be afraid. And if she was being honest, something about him *did* make her feel afraid.

"Oh, I don't know her personally. But I did meet with your uncle. A delightful man."

And with that, Chobly cemented his fate. Anyone who would call Uncle Eric *a delightful man* was her enemy. Adia glared at him as he kept going.

"You're lucky to have relatives who were good enough to take you in after your parents died. And you're not even a full blood relation, are you? Your mother and aunt didn't share the same mother. Your uncle was good enough to provide me with your medical records. Which is why I know about your refusal to take Drops."

The air around them rose a few degrees as Adia went hot with anger. Giving a stranger her medical records? Uncle Eric had no right. And knowing her uncle, he hadn't given that information for free. If someone offered him the right amount of money, he would sell Adia's soul if he could.

"So I couldn't help but think that if you told Emperor Darian about your aversion to Drops, well...could it be that he wants to ban them to make you happy? He wouldn't be the first young man to do something ill-advised to impress a pretty girl. But it's not in his best interest to fight this."

"Bold of you to question the decisions of an emperor known as the Warlord Child," Adia said, trying to regain some control over this conversation. Something about this man's voice was hypnotizing. It was hard for her to do anything but listen to him. "If Darian wants to ban Drops, I support his decision. They're terrible. All they do is make people easier to control."

"Oh, but they do so much more than that," Chobly said.

Adia's eyes narrowed. That was certainly true. How much did Chobly know about Drops?

"If you care about the emperor, it would be good of you to have a word with him and let him know you want him to do what's best for Zaria. He might have been the Warlord Child once, but there are whispers that he's grown weak since he met you. If he carries on the way he's going...well, who's to say he won't lose his crown?"

"You're right," Adia said. "It does seem like I need to have a word with Darian."

"Wonderful," Mr Chobly said, his smile genuine this time. "I'm so glad to see that you're a sensible young lady. And I hope you come to see the council as your ally. We don't usually make ourselves known, but our order is an ancient one. We help maintain balance in the empire, you see. Sometimes it's the throne that has too much power, sometimes it's the people. And at certain points in history, it's been the shamans.

"Which is why we'll be quite interested to observe your studies here at the Academy."

"She's not going to get any studying done if you keep her out here talking to you." Nami walked over to them and eyed Mr Chobly up and down. "According to my captain, the council is only here for a week to make sure the new safety measures are in place. What are you doing bothering the students?"

Adia stared at Nami in disbelief. Did he think she needed him to protect her? Although if she was being honest, he was a welcome intrusion. Nami's interruption had released her from whatever hold Chobly had over her. She took a step back just as a shrill whistle sounded. Everyone around them winced, and some students covered their ears.

"I need to go," Adia said.

"Of course, of course," Mr Chobly said, not bothering to acknowledge Nami. "And don't forget what we discussed. Enjoy your first day of school!"

Little chance of that, Adia thought as she rushed away.

CHAPTER 9

Adia's nervousness about her first day was now replaced with fear about Darian. Zaria had a history of getting rid of unwanted leaders in violent and permanent ways. If the council was this angry about his decision to ban Drops, they'd find a way to eliminate him too. Plus, while Gini was right that there was now another royal in her life, that wasn't definitive proof that Darian wasn't at the centre of this new curse. And in danger. She had to get a message to him as soon as she could to make sure he was safe. But first, herbology class.

Thyme was waiting for her at the door.

"I suppose you heard all that," Adia said as she opened the classroom door. Thyme went straight for a desk in the back. Adia quickly took the seat next to her. Their professor had already begun writing on the board.

"How worried do we need to be about Darian?" Thyme whispered.

"Gini says Ikenga is in the capital with him now. I'm sure

he'll be all right." She didn't know if she was trying to convince herself or Thyme about that, but worrying about Darian would have to wait. Class was about to begin.

Mallorie stormed past them but paused in confusion when she spotted Thyme.

"Wait a minute," Mallorie said. "Don't I know you? Aren't you a Hill nun?"

"I was," Thyme said, leaning back in her chair and putting her hands behind her head, as she gave Mallorie a smirk. "But they kicked me out. On account of my violent personality."

Mallorie gave her a horrified look before rushing to take a seat in the front. Thyme snickered.

"Why do you seem so happy?" Adia asked, baffled. This day couldn't have been more of a disaster than if Olark himself was teaching this class. There was nothing to be cheerful about. But she'd forgotten how twisted Thyme's sense of humour could be.

"Because this class is going to be like a free carnival act," Thyme said in delight. "I wish I'd brought snacks. Shhh."

"Quiet, please! We have some latecomers, I see," the professor said, frowning at Mallorie, Thyme and Adia. "Please don't let that happen again. I'll repeat my introduction. I'm Professor York, Master of Plants at the Academy. Now, I'm sure what you're all interested in is learning spells to turn rocks into gold, or how to create magical inks that will draw maps that lead to buried treasures."

Adia couldn't help the snort that came out of her mouth. "Of course. The rare shamanic ability of snapping your fingers and becoming rich," she whispered as Thyme snickered under her breath.

"But don't be quick to dismiss the healing power of plants," York said with a dreamy smile. "As a Master of Plants, I'm trained in floral arrangements and oil making. And if you pay diligent attention? Well, I imagine by the end of the year you'll also have a knack for making bouquets!"

"Bouquets?" Adia repeated in disbelief.

Professor York stepped aside and pointed at an admittedly beautiful floral arrangement.

Adia shook her head. "So by shamanic Master of Plants, she means she's a florist?" she whispered, but Thyme only hushed her again.

Mimi was sitting in front of them – the girl who'd had the sense to try to shut up her annoying twin Rusty at orientation. She turned around and gave Adia and Thyme a cautiously friendly smile. "Do any of our teachers actually know what they're doing?"

"Is there something the three of you would like to share with the rest of the class?" Professor York asked. Her eyes were cold.

"Sorry," Mimi said quickly. "I was just asking to borrow some paper. I forgot my notebook."

"I see. Well, since you're unprepared for class, why don't

you come up front and make yourself useful. You'll help me with a demonstration."

Adia and Thyme glanced at each other as Mimi slowly pushed her chair back and walked to the front of the room. Gini's "demonstration" had been bad enough. You would think the other teachers would be cautious about putting on any more displays.

"I have six ingredients on the table," Professor York said, walking behind her desk. Adia hadn't noticed the six small dishes with crushed plants when she'd walked into the classroom, but she studied them now in trepidation.

The professor bent down and pulled out a small plant that was covered in some sort of rot. It was very clearly dying.

"We're going to make a medicine to cure this plant. Using this treatment, you can be sure that your floral arrangements remain free of root rot."

"Is that true?" Thyme whispered.

Adia tilted her head. She didn't recognize any of the crushed plants, so she took a deep breath and tried to feel them instead. She shoved her hands underneath the desk to hide the telltale purple glow that came out when she used her ability.

"It's true," Adia said, blinking in surprise. Professor York's reasoning was a bit silly, but she was right. It would take care of the rot on that plant. "But only if you combine them in the right way. If you put in the wrong measurements, I'm pretty sure it would release something into the air that could cause blindness."

They watched tensely as Professor York instructed Mimi on the proper combination. Mimi snuck a glance at Adia.

"Two teaspoons of the red powder," Professor York said in a dreamy voice.

Adia swallowed back a yell. Professor York was definitely not preparing the medicine the right way. She shook her head furiously and lifted up one finger, hoping Mimi would trust her.

Mimi gave a subtle nod, and when Professor York turned to pull out the next tray, she grimaced and dumped the second spoonful on the floor.

"A pinch of the indigo powder," Professor York said, clasping her hands and giving Mimi an encouraging smile. Adia rolled her eyes. She had a feeling their teacher was just adding in colours she thought were pretty. Mimi looked at her nervously and Adia cupped her hand, hoping the girl would understand to dump as much of the indigo plant as she could in the glass. She sighed in relief when Mimi tossed the entire thing in. "And one spoonful of the green. That's the leaf of the beautiful wonderflower."

Chincherinchee, not wonderflower, Adia thought, sensing that the plant preferred to be called by the name the people in the south called it. That's where it grew. And she assumed that unlike Professor York, southerners knew not to touch such a toxic plant.

The other students were catching on that Mimi was following Adia's instructions instead of York's. Their heads swivelled back and forth between the two girls to see what Adia would tell her to do next, but Adia stayed focused, making sure Mimi didn't accidentally blind herself. She gave Mimi a thumbs up about the spoonful of green. One spoonful was fine now that the other proportions were correct.

"Give it a stir, and then pour it over the infected plant," Professor York said.

Mimi carefully picked up the glass and poured it over the rotting leaves. Everyone gasped as the plant began to bubble and gurgle. It was unpleasant to watch, but after a few seconds, the rot fizzled away.

The class began to whisper. The boy to the left of Adia leaned in. It was the annoying Rusty.

"Last semester we basically only learned how to grow a bean plant. You need to teach us how to do real stuff."

"I *need* to?" Adia repeated with a glare. York's instructions would have created a toxic gas that would have blinded Mimi and possibly everyone sitting in the front row, so Adia had felt a moral obligation to stop that. But that was as far as she would go to help them.

"Well done, well done," Professor York said, unable to keep the surprise out of her voice. "Yes, that was exactly as it should go. Thank you, Mimi. You may return to your seat. I hope everyone made note of the recipe!"

Rusty gave Adia a wink and a thumbs up and her head almost exploded. She was *not* on the same side as these people.

"Stop glaring. You wouldn't want them all going back to their dorms and creating a poisonous gas, would you?" Thyme said.

When Mimi was back in her seat she quickly turned to Adia. "What would have happened if I'd done it the way York said?"

"Don't ask," Thyme muttered.

Mimi's eyes widened then she gave Adia a nod. "Thanks, Adia. I owe you one."

"Don't worry about it," Adia said with a dismissive shrug. But she smiled to herself that she'd been able to help. It felt good. Satisfying. She knew that the ancient shamans of Zaria who'd specialized in plants were the healers. Maybe she would ask Gini if they could focus on plant medicines during her self-directed study once they figured out what to do about the rising dead. Her mood dropped. If there were even any plants left, given all the fires being set throughout Zaria again. Her classmates losing consciousness wasn't the only thing she had to worry about. All the plants and animals that lived in the forest were in danger of being burned to a crisp.

The rest of class was uneventful as Professor York mostly babbled about contrasting colours, so Adia used the time to write out a quick letter to Darian to warn him to watch out for his council. Then realized she needed to write to EJ too, now that Mr Chobly had let her know Uncle Eric was happily telling anyone who would pay all about her.

EJ would never knowingly do anything to harm her, she knew that. But she had to make sure her cousin knew not to repeat anything she told him to his wretched father. Besides, she was worried that she hadn't had a letter from EJ waiting when she'd arrived at the Academy. She'd written to him before they'd left the Horrorbeyond to let him know she was heading to school. And he'd been with her when Gini had told her she'd planned on having Adia trained. It wasn't like EJ to be so incurious about what was going on with her.

As soon as the lesson was over Adia tried to make a speedy exit to send off her letters, but was blocked before she could even make it out of her row.

"Tell us how you do all that stuff," Rusty said again. Mimi gave Adia a sheepish look, but she also didn't tell Rusty to shut up. Mimi wasn't rude like her twin, but she was clearly just as curious.

"Move it," Mallorie Amber snapped, pushing past them. She stormed out of the classroom, making it clear she wasn't going to join the parade of people wanting to talk to Adia. If she'd been expecting anyone to follow her – and Adia knew that was exactly what Mallorie had expected – she must have been disappointed because no one paid her any mind. Instead, the crowd pressed forward, trying to get closer to Adia.

Thyme stepped in front of Adia and stared down her nose at Rusty.

"I'm sorry, and you are..." she asked, pretending she'd forgotten his name.

He had the decency to look a little embarrassed.

"Rusty Darling, firstborn son and heir of—"

"Oh wait. I don't care," Thyme said. "You're at a school for shamanism, Crusty. Why are you bothering the new girl to teach you? Go ask a professor."

Rusty rolled his eyes. "Oh please. I'm not as clueless as these other kids. And it's Rusty, not Crusty."

Irritated rumbling started from the queue behind Rusty, but he wouldn't be deterred. "No one here is learning how to do anything because the teachers are useless. But Kelbara can really make things happen. So teach us some spells."

"Spells?" Adia sputtered. "Do you think I have a wand hidden in my sleeve and a broom under my desk?"

Rusty tilted his head. "Do you?"

"No!" Adia said, pushing him out of the way, dragging Thyme behind her. Mimi rushed after them too.

"Oh, come on," Rusty said, trailing after her. "Look, I get it." He lowered his voice so only Adia could hear, even though she knew Thyme's ears would pick up everything. "We didn't have abilities before. I know Mallorie's just trying to get attention. But things are different now. All of us from noble families were given a tonic last month when we were home waiting for the Academy to reopen."

Adia paused. "What are you talking about?" she asked. "What tonic?"

Rusty grinned, happy to finally have Adia's attention.

"It's been in the works for a few years, but they had to test it out on animals first to make sure it was fit for human consumption."

Adia stared at him. No. It wasn't possible. "Test what on animals?" she pressed.

"Whoa, why is it so warm in here all of a sudden?" Mimi asked. Thyme's eyes went wide and she moved closer to Adia.

"We should get out of here," Thyme muttered. "You're burning up."

"One second," Adia said. She needed to know about this *tonic*. "Go on, Rusty."

"It's called Liquid Gold," Rusty said. "Drinking it helps open us up to the spirit world. The last batch was extra potent. The people who make it changed the formula."

Adia wished the ground would swallow her up as she tried to contain her pulsing anger. Everything she'd done last year had been for nothing. So this was the workaround to Darian's ban. They might have changed the formula and they might have changed the name, but there was only one thing *Liquid Gold* could be. Not only had she not stopped Drops from being produced, now it had spread to all of Zaria. And with a new use. In the Swamplands, Drops had been given to open people up to the Bright Father's love. But people in the capital wouldn't go along with anything so pedestrian as that. For them, Drops were being sold as *power.* Liquid Gold.

"Let's go," Thyme whispered, grabbing Adia and shoving her through the crowd. "You're making the temperature rise." Mimi also inserted herself between Adia and the overeager students, pushing them out of the way and helping to clear a path. Beads of sweat were dripping down Thyme's face. Adia tried to get hold of herself – she was emitting too much heat.

"You'll tell me how you're doing this, one way or the other," Rusty called after them.

"Don't worry. He's more talk than action," Mimi said quickly.

"I'm not worried," Adia said. "Thyme and I have dealt with much worse than him. We'll be fine. But you shouldn't get involved with us." She winced when Mimi's face fell. "Not because we don't like you," she rushed to say. "We just tend to..."

"Cause chaos," Thyme said.

"Try not to sound so excited about that," Adia muttered under her breath. She cleared her throat. "I just don't want anyone getting hurt."

Mimi gave them a stiff nod. "Sure. I get it. See you around, then." She paused. "He's right about Liquid Gold, though. Last month missionaries showed up with vials and said it would give us strength and power. Now it's all the rage.

Apparently, it's an ancient, mystical formula created by some genius scientist that was recently unearthed. Thought you might want to know."

Adia stared after her. She'd never thought about who the original creator of Drops was. She'd assumed it was someone with a shamanic ability. But why not a scientist? They would have knowledge of poisons too. Mimi was right. She did need to know that. And she would have thanked Mimi for the information, but the girl was already gone.

"Maybe I was too harsh," Adia said, feeling guilty. "She was pretty nice. And helpful."

Thyme shook her head. "No. It was the right thing to do. You can't go letting everyone who seems nice in on your secrets." A stormy look passed over her face. "Speaking of..."

"Adia," Nami said. His face went red, and he immediately stared at the ground. "I just wanted to make sure you were all right. I didn't like how that council person was speaking to you. And we haven't really had a chance to properly talk."

Adia wanted to storm off, but something told her that if she didn't let Nami say whatever it was he wanted to say, she'd be cursed to see him staring at her glumly at every meal.

"Properly talk about what?" she asked coldly. "Go on."

"Er..." he said, eyeing Thyme's menacing expression. "Can we do this in private?"

This had better be the last request she had for a private talk that day. Adia nodded at Thyme. "I'll meet you in class."

Adia's expression was cold as she walked beside Nami. Students rushed across the campus, trying to avoid still being outside when the second whistle sounded, alerting them that class was about to start. Poison ivy, belladonna, devil's trumpet. Adia rattled off in her brain all the poisonous plants growing along the pathway to calm herself. So many ways she could render Nami unconscious with just a wave of her hand. The thought made her smile. She didn't need science. She was a poison master herself.

Nami gulped. Maybe her slightly evil smile was scaring him. Good.

"So what is it?" she asked, crossing her arms.

The words tumbled out of Nami's mouth. "I just wanted to say that I— I replay everything that happened that night over and over in my head. And it's like I'm watching it all from outside my body. Like I can't believe I really did that to you. That I sent Gold Hats after you and thought you could ever hurt anyone."

Adia didn't respond. Just gave him a stony stare.

"I tried to write to you when school was closed," Nami went on quickly. "I sent letters to your home in the Swamplands. Your cousin EJ sent them back. Well, he sent them back as torn-up pieces of paper, along with a note telling me that you weren't there, and to stop bothering him."

Adia refused to let herself laugh as she pictured how annoyed EJ must have been to see Nami's name on an envelope.

She'd never seen EJ get as angry as he had when she told him how Nami had betrayed her and almost got her killed.

"I wish you'd stop bothering me too." She didn't care if it was harsh. He didn't deserve anything but harshness from her. "Is that all you had to say?"

"No, but maybe it'll be better this way." Nami fumbled around for a second before pulling a folded-up piece of paper from his pocket. "I wrote one more letter. I figured there was a better chance of you reading it if I gave it to you in person."

"If I take it, will you leave me alone?" she asked.

Nami's shoulders sagged, but he nodded. Adia uncrossed her arms and took the letter by the tips of her fingers as if it was toxic waste so Nami would know how annoyed she was about this. But she tucked it into her pocket. She'd said she would take it, not that she'd read it.

"Thanks," Nami said, walking away. Peevishly, Adia didn't want him to have the last word. He always had the last word. The fact that he never shut up had always annoyed her, but in the end she'd put up with it, same as she put up with Thyme's clutter. Shrugging off someone's harmless, annoying habits seemed like a part of friendship. But those days were long gone.

"I play it over and over again in my head too, you know," Adia said. "And I also can't believe you would do that to me. I thought you were my friend. My *first* friend besides my cousin. Do you know how much that messed me up, Nami?

I don't know if I'll ever get over it."

Nami opened his mouth and let out a huge yawn.

"Am I *boring* you?" Adia asked in disbelief. Then she blinked as Nami's eyes began to droop. "Oh no," she whispered, flinging out her arms and catching him just as he blacked out. Across the yard, students toppled over as if an invisible hand had pushed them down.

She laid Nami down in the grass, immediately calling her power to her. She knew Thyme and Gini and Mbari were probably running from wherever they were to find her, but if this was anything like last time, something else was about to show up too.

The ground trembled, and Adia jumped back. She'd caused earthquakes before, but she would swear she wasn't doing it this time. In the distance, dirt and stones were kicked up in the air as the ground stirred. She was so focused on the sight that she didn't notice someone behind her until they touched her shoulder.

"Ahh!" She couldn't help the scream that came out of her. This corpse was older than the last one, with thin grey hair hanging down over its sunken cheeks. However this person had died, it had been after a long life. They should have been in their eternal resting place, wherever that was. Not staring down at her like a hungry ghost.

"Adia Kelbara," it whispered. "I need to bring the High Queen your eyes."

Adia shoved the corpse away, flinging out her arms and calling every plant she could towards her. Agrias vines crept forward faster than she'd ever seen them, like dozens of snakes rushing past her. They wrapped themselves around the corpse and dragged it over to the crack in the ground.

Adia hesitated for only a second before running after the retreating vines and the corpse. She needed to make sure it was taken care of. Thankfully, the plants once again helped the body decompose, turning the poor lost soul into dust before the vines crept away.

"Thank you," she said quickly. She and the agrias plant spirit were old friends, and she never wanted to take its help for granted. She knelt and touched the crack. It was hot. Scalding. She backed away and began checking on the collapsed students, making sure no one was hurt or in a precarious position. She was still running around the yard, dragging her classmates out of thorny bushes, or turning someone over who had fallen face down to make sure they could breathe, when a shout made her jump.

"Adia!"

"Thyme!" Adia rushed over to her friend. "Are you all right? Another corpse showed up. Same message about needing to bring the High Queen my eyes."

"Where is it now?"

Adia pointed to the chasm as Thyme rushed towards it with a drawn sword.

"These cracks in the ground," Adia said as she moved a second-year student out from under a tree. One strong gust of wind and a coconut could fall off a branch and break the girl's nose. "It's like the realm of the dead is breaking into the realm of the living. Like it's burning its way into our world."

"How is that possible?" Thyme asked. "And shouldn't everyone be awake by now?"

Adia wiped her forehead. Thyme was right. Last time this happened they'd woken up in a minute. Two minutes, tops. It had been almost twenty minutes now. She was about to tell Thyme to go find Gini when the students around them began to stir. Adia quickly ran back to where she'd left Nami and flung herself down next to him, closing her eyes.

"What the...? Adia!" Nami shouted, shaking her. "Wake up!"

"What?" Adia said, making her voice sound sleepy and confused as she stretched and sat up. "What happened? Why are we on the ground?"

Nami eyed her suspiciously. "I half expected you to tell me I got hit in the head with a pawpaw again. You really don't know what's causing this? Because I don't buy the headmistress's excuse about poisonous gas for a second."

"Adia!" a gruff voice called out. "Are you all right?"

"Hey! We *all* fell down," a nearby student wailed. "Or is no one important here except Adia Kelbara?"

"Er..." Mbari said, realizing he shouldn't be paying Adia

special attention. "She's just the first one I saw, that's all. Everyone, go to your rooms. We'll send a healer to check on all of you, but for now, classes are cancelled for the day."

At that, the annoyed student let out a whoop. Everyone jumped up, giddy at their unexpected luck.

"First day of school already cancelled?" the now-happy student said with a wink at Adia. "Guess you're not so bad to have around after all!"

This was no good. No one was buying Gini's earlier excuse about a gas leak. Everyone assumed this was all because of Adia.

And they weren't wrong.

"Adia," Nami said, but she held up a hand.

"I have to go. You should go lie down too."

"Adia," Nami tried again, but she let Mbari lead her away.

"Stay in your room with Thyme," Mbari said. "I need to talk to Ginikanwa. Lock your door and only open it for one of us."

"You don't have to tell me twice," Adia said, shuddering at the thought of another corpse hissing that it needed her eyes.

But as soon as Mbari turned a corner, Adia squared her shoulders. This had gone on long enough. She needed to find out everything she could about this High Queen that the dead clearly served. It was time to go back to the library.

CHAPTER 10

The last time Adia had been in the enclave that held the Academy's libraries, she'd found EJ and all the students Olark had kidnapped. If not for those horrible memories, it probably would have been the first place Adia came when she returned to school. As she walked down the dusty, deserted halls, she was sad to realize that Olark had ruined what had once been her safe haven. Being around books had always been where she felt the most comfortable. She wondered if she would ever manage to reclaim the joy libraries had once held for her.

"I'm not sure where to go or which section to look in," Adia said, touching the walls. "Any suggestions?"

She shouldn't have been surprised when a door flung open, but she was. Speaking directly with the Academy and having it answer back still took a bit of getting used to. And she hadn't even realized there was a door here. It completely blended in with the walls. There wasn't even a knob or latch.

No one was finding this door unless the Academy wanted them to.

Adia held up her torch and walked inside. It was a small room containing nothing but a small desk, two chairs, and a single bookcase. And to her surprise, every book on the shelf had a black spine.

"That's not ominous at all," she muttered. She looked around the room for somewhere to put her torch and spotted a sconce on the wall. As soon as she hung it, the door to the room slammed itself shut, as if some mechanism had been triggered to shut the door once the room knew someone was inside it. She ran to the door and pulled as hard as she could, but it wouldn't budge.

Adia swallowed nervously. If the Academy wanted her to stay in this room, then that *should* mean she wasn't in any danger. As long as it really was the Academy that was keeping her locked in here and not some other entity.

She turned back around to face the shelves of black-spined books. Her torch was smoking a lot more than it should have been and the fire was casting an eerie shadow around the room. No. Not a shadow. She took a step back. This was like in Gini's office when the smoke had spelled out words. Except the shapes she was seeing now weren't letters. It looked more like...a hand. She bit back a scream as the smoke's shadowy fingers crept towards her. But they brushed past like a warm breeze and floated along the walls before pausing in front of a row of books. The shadow hand pointed at a shelf, then disintegrated, returning to whatever realm Adia had accidentally pulled it from.

"Please be a friendly spirit," she said as she cautiously walked up to the shelf. She read the titles on the spines.

Necromancy

The Death Realm

Mind Training

Poison Studies

Reanimation and Limb Control

If Mallorie, Rusty and their minions knew that *these* kinds of books were tucked away in the library, maybe they'd leave her alone and come here instead in their quest to have magical powers. Adia pushed that thought away. She very much doubted the other students would be able to do anything with this information themselves, but they could make a mess with their false claims of power and knowledge. Just like the Academy's professors.

"Let's see what you have to say," she said, removing the copy of *Poison Studies*.

"YOU WOKE HER UP!"

It wasn't a whisper this time. It was a thousand voices screaming. Adia clutched her head and the book fell. It felt like her brain had just been pierced by a hot knife. As she lowered her hands, the pain faded as quickly as it had come but she wasn't interested in putting herself through that twice.

"What kinds of books are these?" Adia whispered. They were as alive as the Academy. And the Academy had opened this door and kept her stuck in this room for a reason. Sighing, she set aside her revulsion and picked up the copy of *Reanimation and Limb Control* and took it to the table and sat down. She wasn't even surprised when the pages started turning themselves. Slowly at first, then flapping so quickly they caused a breeze before slowing down again, settling on a page.

The ability to manipulate the dead was first discovered on the Dog Star. Those who dwelled there were consumed with the idea of a perfect mind – one that was in control of itself and its surroundings at all times.

Those who mastered the Perfect Mind practice were said to have extraordinary abilities, such as levitation, invisibility, imperviousness to pain, and even the ability to control the minds and bodies of others. The High Queen of the Dog Star was considered the greatest master of the Perfect Mind technique, as well as the last, as the Dog Star was annihilated during her reign.

Adia leaned back in her chair. The High Queen. A queen who had learned how to control the bodies of others, even when they were dead. But she was dead too. Or at least she should have been.

"But how did I wake her up?" Adia whispered. "I've never even heard of her."

But it didn't matter that she had no idea who this woman was. The High Queen knew who Adia was. And that she could find Imo Mmiri – find another home with the power of a star to replace the one the High Queen had lost.

Something creaked behind her. Turning, Adia gasped as the bookshelf moved away from the wall, revealing a hidden door. Who else but her knew about the Academy's secret passageways? She needed to get out of there. But it was too late. Someone stepped out of the passage and into the room. He wore green robes, a lopsided crown, and a worried expression, but his face broke into a huge grin when he saw her.

"Darian!" Adia shouted as she ran over to him, knocking him over with a hug.

Darian laughed and hugged her back. "Thyme said you were probably lurking down here. She's pretty mad that you didn't take her with you, by the way."

"Thyme's been through enough because of me," Adia said, feeling embarrassed that she'd just hurled herself at him. She pulled herself back and pushed up her glasses, hoping her hair wasn't full of orange cat fur. "I thought she could use a break."

"A break?" Darian asked, his expression confused. "Adia, we don't need a break from being your friend."

"Never mind all that. How are you even here? And how did you know about the passageways?" Adia asked.

"You always scribble maps on the backs of your letters," Darian said, pulling a carefully folded piece of paper from his breast pocket. "They're really good. I thought I'd have to search for a while but then a door in the wall opened all by itself. I guess the Academy thinks I'm a friend now."

She felt even more embarrassed that Darian had held on to her rambling letters. "Wait, what are you doing here? And why didn't you just walk in through the front gate?"

"I can't have anyone finding out I'm here," he said. "I wore a disguise the entire time I was travelling."

"Won't people notice the emperor has gone missing?" Adia asked with a snort.

Darian looked sheepish, but he grinned. "I left a note— Which was more than you did when you ran away. But I'll tell you about ditching the royal council later."

"You didn't ditch all of them." Adia quickly told him about Mr Chobly.

"I know him," he muttered. "He's the loudest person screaming about the Drops ban. I should have known he'd show up here to bother you too. But he's not our biggest problem."

"I know. The cracks in the ground and the fires. And...the corpses."

Darian blinked. "So it's true about the dead rising? I was

hoping it was just a rumour. I was in the capital with a Gold Hat who swore he saw a dead friend. But I was too busy looking at something else. Didn't you get my message? I sent it days ago. It should have been waiting for you when you arrived."

Adia shook her head. "No, there was nothing."

Darian frowned. "If Chobly's here, then he and the council are probably intercepting all your letters. It's fine. I phrased it in a way that no one except you or Thyme would have known what I was talking about anyway.

"Adia, I saw a message in the sky. The bottom part had already faded away, but it started like the last curse. *'Hear my words throughout the world and read them in the skies'.*"

Adia went cold at the familiar words. She'd been in the library the first time she'd heard them. The curse that had dragged her into all this. The curse that had made it so no one in Zaria knew that Olark had returned and was possessing Darian. She'd been so sure he couldn't be involved this time because it was a *queen* who wanted her eyes. But it would explain how the High Queen knew about her. If Olark had been sent to the realm of the dead, maybe he'd met up with some old and powerful friends and told them all about Adia.

"Maybe it's not him," Darian said, though his face let her know he was unconvinced. "Maybe it was some other celestial. One of the Alusi. But I was worried about you. Is there any way that – that *he's* back?"

Adia went from feeling overjoyed at seeing Darian to feeling guilty. She might not have spent as much time with him as she had with Thyme or EJ, or even horrible Nami, but she and Darian were forever bonded – the only two people in the world to have survived possession by Olark. Darian had a right to know what was going on. And he hadn't even been worried about himself – he'd run straight to the Academy to make sure she was all right.

"I don't know," Adia said. "But I know what the curse you saw was. I saw it too. Not in the sky. In a vision."

"A vision," Darian repeated. "You're having visions now?"

"Not always," she said quickly. "And only when fire is involved. I see things in the smoke and flames. At first, I thought what I saw was about you."

Darian took a deep breath. "All right. Tell me what you saw."

Adia knew how disturbing this would be for Darian, but he had every right to know. She wrung her hands and repeated what she had seen in the smoke.

Hear my words throughout the world
And read them in the skies.
Until this crown falls from your head
Your soul is bound to mine.
My every wish is your command
From now until you die.
And even in the realm of death
Our souls will be entwined.

"Darian?"

He had gone so still, Adia was worried he was in shock. A chair pushed itself forward and Darian sat down, seemingly unbothered by the sentient furniture. Or maybe he was too horrified to think about how bizarre it was that a chair had just slid towards him of its own accord.

"Who else could that be about but me?" he said, his voice solemn. "He's not finished with me. Our souls are entwined."

"No," Adia said quickly. "That's just it. I *do* think it's about someone else. Someone known as the High Queen. The dead serve her. And I don't think Gini believes me, but I think there's someone in Zaria communicating with her since she's in the realm of the dead. Another shaman."

She quickly told him about the corpses' mission. That they weren't just setting fires. Others were being sent to find her and bring her eyes back to the High Queen of the Dog Star.

"Darian, I'm worried I might be responsible for it – for all these cracks happening. I think I woke her up. And now she's clawing her way into Zaria, ripping the ground apart as she goes."

Darian looked at her sharply. He walked over and put his hands on her shoulders, staring into her eyes. She had to look up at him more than she used to. It had only been a few months, but he'd grown several centimetres.

"Adia, whatever's going on is not your fault," Darian said with a frown. "And so far no one's been hurt. Well, once one of my guards blacked out while he was going down the stairs. I tried to catch him, but I missed and he twisted his ankle. But he'll live. No one's been seriously injured. If they had been, I'm sure I would have heard."

"No one's been injured except the forest," Adia said glumly. "You have no idea how old those trees are, what plant spirits and wildlife might have been there and are now lost. I have to figure out how to stop this."

"Well, that we can agree on," Darian said. "But I don't see how you're going to do that here."

He was right. She'd learned more about the High Queen and that whoever she was, she had mastered the ability to control the dead. But books weren't going to save them or stop the High Queen from sending more corpses into the world of the living.

"If the fires are concentrated to one area, I think it's time we went out there and had a look around for ourselves," she said. "I just have to convince Gini to let me go."

Darian sighed. "She came to the capital to see me, you know. Flung paperwork at me to sign and stamp with the royal seal to make her the headmistress. Then took off."

"Ah. So I have you to thank for that," Adia said with a snort.

"Oh, come on. Like you would have been able to say no to her," Darian said, rolling his eyes. "We should go find her and tell her we're leaving. That is... Do you think she'll let you go? You're a student now."

"This is more important than school," Adia said, moving towards the door. But then she froze. Something Darian had said didn't make sense.

"Adia?" Darian asked with a worried expression. "What is it?"

"Shhh," she said, closing her eyes and letting her brain go over every single word they'd just said. Her eyes went wide.

"Your guard," she said urgently. "The one who fell down the stairs. You tried to catch him?"

"Of course," Darian said. "But I missed."

"Yes, but you were awake! Which means you're not affected either. When everyone passes out, you don't. Neither do I. And neither does Thyme."

"I – I didn't even think twice about it," Darian said. "With everything that's happened I've got used to witnessing the wildest things occur around me. I didn't realize you and Thyme weren't falling asleep either. But why?"

Adia frowned. "I thought it was my ability shielding me. And Thyme's not fully mortal so we thought maybe that had something to do with her being unaffected. But you're an outlier."

What do me, Darian and Thyme have in common that would make us all immune?

Her eyes went wide. It wasn't an immunity. They didn't have anything to be immune to because they'd never taken the poison.

"A student here said Drops are being given out everywhere in Zaria now," Adia said, remembering Mimi's information. "That it's a stronger version than ever."

"It's true," Darian said. "They don't even look like Drops any more. The colour isn't black, it's—"

"Gold," Adia said. *"Liquid Gold."*

"Exactly," Darian said.

"Even before this new and improved formula, I'd never been dosed. Thyme hasn't either. And it's not like Olark would poison his host, so you've never taken them either, have you?"

Darian shook his head. "Olark possessed me just before I turned thirteen. I wasn't old enough to take them."

"Then that's what the three of us have in common," Adia said. "That's why we stay awake when everyone else collapses.

"We've never taken Drops."

CHAPTER 11

"I'm sure Gini will understand that I have to go," Adia said as she and Darian reached the passageway that led to Gini's office. "And she'll be happy to see you too. Come on."

After she finished explaining everything, Adia waited for Gini to speak. About the whispers, about the theory that the High Queen was behind all this and that, somehow, Drops were once again involved.

"I do not understand why you have to go," Gini snapped. "And I'm very unhappy to see you here, Darian. What were you thinking? You can't just disappear from the palace. Your guards are probably hot on your heels. I'm sure Ikenga is already halfway to Chelonia by now."

"He came to warn us," Adia said, defending Darian from Gini's fury. "And that's not what you should be concerned about. Every student at the Academy was given Drops and sent back to school so that they could help Olark get to me. Someone deliberately looked up every student and made sure they were dosed enough to sleep and have their life force drained away so that the dead can rise."

Even as she said it, something tickled the back of her brain.

Why were Olark and the High Queen using this new energy source to send mindless zombies to set fires and hunt Adia down instead of just bringing Olark back himself? She shook her head. She'd have to figure that out later.

"I bet the second I'm gone everyone will stop losing consciousness. People are getting hurt because of me. Again," she said, her voice thick with shame. "The only way to keep everyone safe is for me to leave the Academy. Maybe go into hiding somewhere."

"And where do you think you can hide that would be safe?" Gini asked. "It's not like it's only the Academy students who are being drained. It's happening all over the world. And if you think you're strong enough to take this on all by yourself in your current state, you've woefully overestimated your abilities. This is some of the most powerful shamanic work I've ever witnessed. The realm of the living and the realm of the dead are on the path to a convergence. And if that happens, neither realm will survive the clash."

"But—"

"Gini's right," Darian said.

"Darian!" Adia looked at him in shock. She thought that if anyone could understand what she was feeling right now, it would be him.

"And so are you," he said quickly. "Every student here has been given Drops. Or Liquid Gold as they're now calling it. That's not a coincidence. Somehow Olark knew you'd be here and, yes, he sent all these students back here as some sort of trap. But that means someone is reporting your movements to him. Maybe a spirit you can't see is following you around and somehow sending messages to the dead? If that's the case, there's nowhere that's safe for you right now."

"Or it's another shaman," Adia said, giving Gini a pointed look. "How else could Olark have known I'm a student at the Academy instead of home in the Swamplands? And someone in Zaria had to give him a list of every student's name and make sure they were given Drops."

Gini had acted like it wasn't possible there was another shaman in Zaria, but she had to realize now that it was more and more likely.

Gini stared at her for a few moments before speaking.

"Darian, wait outside. I need to talk to Adia alone."

"Not if you're going to yell at her," Darian said, shocking both Adia and Gini. But his expression was firm. Sometimes Adia forgot he was only a year older than her. He might not have wanted to wear that crown on his head, but she had to admit he wore it well.

"I won't yell," Gini promised with a nod.

"I'll let Thyme know what's going on," he said to Adia.

"Be careful," she said. "If the council spots you—"

"I know," he said. "I'll stay out of sight, don't worry."

As soon as the door closed, Gini turned back to Adia.

"We've put this off for too long. I'm sure by now you've figured out that these voices you're hearing are spirits reaching out to you. You're even starting to see them in the fire. And shadows picking out books for you! Do you know how lucky you are that whoever that shadow was, it was someone trying to help you? What would you have done if it wanted to harm you? You're so untrained you can't shut them out or even tell who's speaking to you. They're in control now, not you."

Adia didn't want to admit Gini was right. "I've survived so far, haven't I?" she muttered.

Gini narrowed her eyes and strode over to her. Adia cowered in her chair. She was so used to Gini now that she'd forgotten the goddess could probably turn her into a puddle of goo if she wanted to.

"Don't be so cocky. You've made it this far on natural talent and sheer luck, but you'll completely flame out before you've touched even a fraction of your power because you haven't been initiated. I know you're scared to face your power, but I can't let this go on any longer. You'll hurt yourself at this rate. And, yes, it's possible that somehow there's another shaman in Zaria right now who's communicating with Olark and this pet queen of his. But you'll be no match for any of them. Not until you've gone through your initiation."

Adia froze. Viona had mentioned this to her in a vision right before she'd defeated Olark. She said she'd almost lost herself because she was skipping around the astral world completely untethered and uninitiated, and that what she was doing was dangerous. That usually the first time an apprentice journeyed, they'd go in with their teacher to guide them. But Adia hadn't had a teacher until now.

"So you're going to lead that for me?" Adia asked.

"Can you ask for a better guide than a goddess?"

"No, of course not," Adia admitted. Although there was a fifty-fifty chance Gini would get distracted by something shiny halfway to wherever this journey was supposed to lead them. "What exactly happens in initiation?"

"I'm afraid I can't tell you that."

Adia closed her eyes. It was time to be honest.

"Gini..." She paused, unsure how to continue. "I don't know if I want to go through with this."

Gini nodded. "I know what you're thinking."

"I doubt it," Adia muttered, but she sighed and let Gini continue.

"The Underworld can be frightening. Even dangerous, but it's not a hell dimension or a place of evil. I've told you before, there's no such thing as good or evil."

"How can you still say that?" Adia scoffed. "After everything we've been through. Everything we're *still* going through!"

"Olark is unevolved. And I say that with no malice," Gini

said, her voice sombre. "Some of us are simply further along in terms of our soul's evolution. And maybe we won't all be free until the last of us is free. Perhaps Olark is the last of us. Maybe this will keep playing out for us over lifetimes and different incarnations until he's finally freed from his insanity."

Adia stared at Gini. "I don't understand."

"That's all right," Gini said. "It's not for you to understand yet."

Adia stood up and walked over to the fireplace. She stared at the coals and flames for a minute before speaking. "Can you at least tell me how the Underworld is different from the realm of the dead?" she asked quietly.

Gini smiled. "It's a world of primal energy, not death. A world of life and spirits from all over the universe. From the past, from the future, and everywhere in between. Beings and animals and plants that you couldn't imagine in your wildest dreams. Many of whom hold deep knowledge and wisdom about the universe. You have nothing to be afraid of. The dead can't hurt you there."

That did sound less terrifying than what she'd imagined, but Gini had misunderstood. Adia wasn't afraid of going to the Underworld. She was afraid of going any further down this path – corpses, fires, demons and the dead all wanting her eyes. It wasn't like she'd asked to be the last descendant of the people of Imo Mmiri. None of this was her choice; it was just her burden because of her blood. Because of her eyes.

Maybe it was selfish, but right now all she wanted to do was disappear and never have to deal with any of this again.

Gini frowned. "Look, Adia, you don't have to practise shamanism if you don't want to," she said.

Adia turned to her in surprise. Maybe Gini *did* understand.

"Just because you have a gift doesn't mean you're obligated to use it. It's your choice. But you do have to be initiated for your own protection. Especially now that malevolent spirits know who you are and that you have an ability. Your name is being whispered on the wind, and the wind travels."

"You're sure it's completely safe?" Adia asked.

"It is when you have a proper guide who knows what they're doing. And when the apprentice is worthy. You know I would never let you go through with this if I couldn't guarantee your safety. You'll be fine."

Adia wanted to believe Gini, but after the year she'd had it was hard to trust her. Would she ever *really* be safe? But she knew that whether she decided to carry on with shamanism or not, she would need to go through her initiation.

"All right, then. Take me to the Underworld."

Adia thought she knew every centimetre of the Academy's grounds, but Gini was taking her deeper into the forest than she'd ever gone. They'd been walking for so long that the sun had now set.

"Is this still part of the school?" she finally asked when Gini showed no signs of stopping. "The boundary on the map ends with the crypts, and we passed them twenty minutes ago."

"Your maps only tell half the story. The Academy of Shamans is vaster than you realize. Although," Gini paused, "a few decades ago it got so mad at the students that a quarter of the campus ran away. Nevertheless, it's still much larger than you know. But all its sections aren't always visible."

Adia snorted. "I'm sorry, but how does a *school* run away? Wouldn't people notice a building running down the road?"

"I imagine it ran when most people were tucked into bed, fast asleep," Gini said with a shrug. "But thankfully the initiation room stayed put. And here we are."

Adia turned her head to where Gini was pointing her staff.

Maybe this had been a room long ago, but Adia could only describe what stood in front of them as an abandoned ruin. Nothing more than seven stone columns surrounding a grey stone floor and piles of rocks. As decrepit as the ruins looked, though, the power coming from this spot was so strong it made her feel dizzy.

Gini stuck out her staff and Adia grabbed it to steady herself.

"Breathe, child," Gini said.

"What is this place?" Adia asked. She let go of Gini's staff. She was still shaky, but she could stand on her own now.

"I supposed you could call it the Academy's heart," Gini said.

That made sense. The energy Adia felt here was pulsating, steady. Like a drumbeat, but a heartbeat worked too. The land the school was built on really was alive.

"I've never seen stone like this before," Adia said as she took a cautious step towards the ruins.

"You wouldn't have." Gini touched one of the pillars. "These pillars are made from some of the oldest stones in Zaria. By now any other kind would have broken down into dirt and sand."

"So this is where initiations used to happen?" Adia asked as she climbed onto the ruins.

"In the beginning there were dozens of initiates," Gini said with a fond smile. "But as the missionaries came from behind the Sunless Mountains, the number grew smaller and smaller. You'll be the first apprentice to go through initiation in centuries. I'll leave you now."

Adia spun around in surprise. "Leave me? How can you be my guide if you're leaving? I don't even know what to do. How do I start?"

"It's already begun," Gini said. "Be a good girl and try not to die."

"Try not to *what*?" Adia shouted, but Gini just gave her a wave and disappeared.

Adia sat in the centre of the ruins, drumming her fingers

against her lap as Bubbles ran around chasing things she couldn't see as the minutes went by. Nothing was happening.

"How long am I supposed to sit here?" she said with a bored sigh.

When even Bubbles stopped chasing things and fell asleep, Adia decided it was time to call it quits. They'd been here for almost an hour.

"I give up," she muttered, getting to her feet and shaking out her stiff legs. "Wake up, Bubbles. I can't go through initiation if no one tells me what I'm supposed to do."

A few minutes later she walked back into the Academy, slightly worried that initiation had been a complete bust. Maybe the spirits who were supposed to show up had taken one look at her and said, "Never mind." Maybe they'd sensed that she still wasn't entirely sure she *wanted* these powers, and her indecisiveness was enough to make them decide to not even put her through a test.

"Adia, where have you been?" Thyme slid up next to her, munching on an apple. "I just finished a night run. You want to come play cards with me and Lebechi and Maka?"

Adia felt a pang that her friends had been about to go have fun without her. No. This is what she wanted. She wanted everyone else to be happy and have normal lives and not get caught up in the misfortune she seemed to bring with her wherever she went.

"I was in the forest doing absolutely nothing," Adia said.

"You go ahead. I need to find Mbari and ask him about..." Adia's voice trailed off as she glanced at Thyme. "Whoa! What's going on with you?"

Thyme raised an eyebrow. "Going on with me? What are you talking about?"

"Thyme! You're glowing!"

Thyme blinked and held up her hands, moving them back and forth.

"What are you talking about? There's nothing happening. Are you sure you feel all right?"

Adia was so fixated on the very real and distinct glow coming off Thyme that she didn't notice the person in front of her until she crashed into them.

"Sorry, Adia," Nami said, quickly stepping back. "Umm... so we've checked the grounds and there are a few more chasms. None as big or deep as the one we saw, but it's still pretty dangerous. We've blocked everything off and we've reported it to the council and the professors and..." Nami paused and glanced at Thyme.

"Is she here with us or in a trance?" he finally asked.

"I'm not sure," Thyme said slowly. "Adia? What's going on?"

Adia knew she must look strange right now, gaping at them and not saying a word, but she wasn't sure what was happening. Thyme's glow almost hurt her eyes. What was coming off Nami hurt too, but in a different way.

Random streaks of light jumped up and out from his body – and coming out of Nami's chest was a grey hand, reaching for the light. Sometimes the hand would sag when it missed catching a wisp of light, and other times it would clench and fling itself forward in a punch, angry at not being able to touch the rays of fragmented sun. But more often than not it would just droop down. Like a puppy who wanted a pat on the head but was being ignored. Adia let out a shaky breath. It should have been scary, but she mostly just felt sad whenever the hand gave up, wanting to be in the light but not strong enough to reach it.

Something *had* happened to her at the ruins. It was as if she'd been walking through life wearing the wrong pair of glasses. So used to everything being slightly out of focus that she'd never realized she wasn't seeing the full picture. *This* was how the world was supposed to look. At least to her. Her brain was meant to see the world like this, with a vision and clarity that was so heightened she could see beyond a physical body to a person's energy.

Was this what it was like to walk around with your shamanic ability turned on all the time? To see everyone's pain?

"Is she having some sort of fit?" a shrill voice asked.

Adia turned her head slightly and almost gagged at the murky colours swirling off Mallorie Amber. Even Nami had streaks of light around him, but Mallorie's energy was so dense and thick with shadows that no light was penetrating through. She had no idea why Mallorie Amber was rotting away at the age of thirteen, or how Thyme, who'd been through so much, could still have such goodness in her that she shone brighter than everyone. But still...Adia wanted to believe Mallorie wasn't a lost cause. No one should have to live like that. Maybe there was a way to fix her.

She tilted her head as she had a random thought. "Maybe this is what it's like to be a surgeon. When you cut someone open, to everyone else it just looks like a pile of blood and guts and organs, and you wouldn't know what's what. But a surgeon knows exactly what it's supposed to look like in there and can tell when something is smaller or bigger than it should be or when it's been pushed into the wrong place."

"And now she's standing in the middle of the room talking to herself."

Adia winced. She hadn't meant to say that out loud. Frowning, Adia reached out her hand. Mallorie's energy was foul, but she could help clear it up. At least a little.

"What are you doing?" Mallorie shrieked, jumping back.

Adia blinked. Mallorie's friends were staring at her with expressions ranging from terror to pure awe.

"Did – did you see something, Adia?" one of them asked tentatively. "Are you having a vision? Can you tell us?"

Not only had she seen something, she'd had an internal understanding about how to fix it. It wouldn't be a permanent fix, but she could clear out some of the dark fog that engulfed Mallorie. Not much, but enough so that a bit of clear light could pierce through. Maybe enough to show Mallorie how it felt to *not* behave like a monster. But even if Adia did try to help, it would be the same as attempting to clean Thyme's messy bedroom. Adia could straighten up temporarily, but Thyme would just throw dirty clothes right on top of the newly cleaned spot if she didn't care enough to keep her room clean herself. Adia could help, but Mallorie would have to be the one to do something with the gift she gave her.

But Mallorie wasn't looking grateful that Adia had been about to give her this gift. She looked more terrified than Adia had ever seen her.

And she had every right to be.

If a dentist realized you had a tooth that needed to be pulled, they would tell you and ask if you wanted to have it pulled. They wouldn't strap you down and shove pliers into your mouth to extract the rotting molar as you screamed. This *was* like surgery. And Adia couldn't do that to someone without their consent.

Adia said two words that she had never expected to utter to Mallorie Amber.

"I'm sorry."

She stepped forward and paused. Had Mallorie done something different with her hair? Something about her was off. Adia blinked. Actually...something about the entire dining hall was off. She was so accustomed to hearing the subtle hum of every plant around her that she usually didn't even pay attention to the noise. But now the plants in the dining hall were completely still. And in Gini's office, Darian had said he was going to go find Thyme. So Thyme shouldn't be going off to play cards with Lebechi and Maka as if everything was fine. She should be with Darian trying to figure out how the High Queen was using Drops to reanimate the dead.

Adia furrowed her brow in confusion. "Wait. How did I get here..."

She had been tired of sitting in the ruins, waiting around for initiation to start as if nothing had happened. So she'd grabbed Bubbles and left...but she couldn't remember climbing down the steps or walking back through the forest. One minute she'd decided to leave, and then the next she'd been back at the Academy. But she couldn't remember anything in between.

"This isn't real," she whispered.

CHAPTER 12

Adia landed with a thud.

"What?" she gasped.

The dining hall was gone. Mallorie and her friends, Thyme, Nami – they'd all vanished. And Adia was now sprawled out on the cold stone slab floor of the ruins. She'd never left. She was still in the middle of her initiation.

"An illusion?" she said in disbelief. It was the only explanation, but she couldn't believe an illusion could be that realistic.

Maybe nothing that had just happened had been real, but the lesson was true enough. She had no right to manipulate people's souls and energy if they didn't want her to. If she did, she would be just as bad as Olark possessing people. Mallorie had been terrified. Maybe almost as terrified as Adia had been in those few seconds when Olark took control of her body. In that moment, Adia was Mallorie's demon.

It didn't make it better, but Adia understood Mallorie's

hatred of her a bit more. While the other kids were faking having powers for the fun of it, Mallorie's fear proved she knew just how powerful a true shaman could be. She wasn't just jealous of Adia's power. She was terrified of it. And she had every right to be.

"Was that a test?" Adia wondered.

"Yes," a voice said.

Adia gasped and scrambled back.

"Who's there? What did you just do to me?"

The seven pillars that held up the ruins vibrated and hummed. They still looked like pillars, but they somehow also looked like people too. Everything was so hazy. It was hard to hold on to what she was seeing.

"Who are you?" she asked.

A lone voice answered her. "We're the founders of the Academy. We guide all initiates through this experience. You have passed your first test. The spirits trust that you understand that just because you have great power, it doesn't mean you should use it however you want. And now, if your vision has truly been opened, you'll be able to enter the Underworld, where you will be offered a gift. If it hasn't, you will not be able to see what's coming next."

"See what?" Adia asked. "What's coming next? Are you shamans then? What's your name?"

There was no response. Adia blinked, wondering if she'd imagined it, as everything around her shimmered in and out.

It was getting too hard to hold on to reality. All she could do was let go.

She waved her hand and watched as a trail of energy followed the movement of her fingers. But it wasn't just that everything was visually distorted. She closed her eyes, trying to make sense of what she was feeling. She imagined this was what the inside of a tree felt like. Water running like rivers up and down her spine. It was as if she could feel an entire universe in her body.

"Primordial energy," she said. Gini was right that she'd needed to do this. It felt like a part of her that had been asleep was waking up. As she let the energy of the Underworld wash through her, she felt as if she was being recharged. Like a wilting plant getting hit with a dose of sunlight.

Drumming in the distance made her open her eyes. She walked towards the sound, purple light sparking up from the ground with every step she took. Soon the music was joined by laughter and singing in languages she'd never heard before. It should have been a cacophonous mess, but somehow everything was in harmony.

Spirits winked in and out of view as Adia walked into a lively festival. Colourful streaks of light cut through the darkness, occasionally bursting above them like fireworks as people cheered. She jumped out of the way as a group of small children ran past her chasing after a bright blue butterfly as big as a dog. She turned to stare a little longer at the giant butterfly. But it and the children winked out of view.

"What—" Adia gasped.

To her left, a girl sat on a bench, hunched over a large barrel of water. She caught Adia's eye and beckoned her over.

"It's your first time here, isn't it?" she said, giving Adia a grin. "You have that look in your eyes."

"First time," Adia confirmed. "Did you see those kids chasing the butterfly? They just vanished."

"Don't worry. That's just what it's like here," the girl said. "We're only here in our spirit form, so it's not uncommon for people and animals to disappear right in front of you. They'll either go back to their bodies or skip off to another realm. You get used to it. Look in here." She moved aside and made space for Adia at the barrel of water. "It's like a mirror. You'll see how you look to me, and I can see what I look like to you. When you're down here, everyone looks like something familiar to you. Like your own species, or an animal from your home world. I suppose it's easier to process a sight you're used to. Less terrifying. But I always like to see everyone in their true form."

The girl leaned down and frowned, tapping her teeth.

"Is this how you see my mouth?" she asked curiously. "I actually have two long fangs where these things are. And you really don't see my feathers?"

"No, sorry," Adia said, wondering where the feathers would go. To her, this girl looked like a Zarian. Brown skin and wide eyes. A teenager, maybe around Maka's age.

"Pity," the girl said. "I have the prettiest plumes. So what are you called? Name and species?"

Species? Adia didn't know how she would ever process this. A year ago she'd thought the Alusi were nothing more than a myth. Now she was in a spirit realm with creatures from all over the universe that could travel through space and time with nothing but the power of their minds. And she was one of them.

"I'm Adia," she answered. "And I'm, ummm, a mortal girl from Zaria."

"Adia the Mortal. Pleased to meet you. I'm Sabo. I don't know the word for what I would be in your world, but I'm a flying species."

"So my mind is making you look like something I recognize?" Adia said, fascinated.

"More than that," Sabo said. "You're not even speaking your language right now. You're speaking in vibrations. But it's a language that everyone who journeys here should intuitively understand."

"How is any of this possible?" Adia said, blinking.

"You're in spirit form, remember? Your cat is too. When we're in our bodies we only have access to the eleven senses."

"Five," Adia said.

"What?"

"Mortals only have five senses."

Sabo looked at her in pity but then gave her an encouraging

smile. "Well, some species are more limited than others. I'm sure you have other gifts."

Adia tried not to roll her eyes. Sabo and Gini would get along.

"When you're in spirit form," Sabo continued, "you can access more of your senses. And the ones you already have are heightened. Like seeing colours your eyes aren't capable of seeing when you're in your body."

Adia glanced down at Bubbles. That explained how he'd followed her down here – it was just his spirit form. She should have known cats could travel between dimensions. It explained his nightly screaming at ghosts or whatever it was that riled him up when she was trying to sleep.

"If you can make it down here, it means you've lived a lot of lives. You've probably even been here before. The more you visit, the easier it gets to remember. That's why I like coming here. There's a past life of mine that I like to remember. And when I'm here…it's like it all happened yesterday."

"That's incredible," Adia said. She would need more time to consider that she'd been here before. *Lived* before. "So were you rich and powerful in that life you like to remember?"

Sabo closed her eyes and rubbed her forehead. "Something like that," she finally said.

"You don't sound happy about it," Adia said slowly.

"That world was destroyed," she said. "Because of one person's greed and ambition. I didn't realize how amazing that life was until it was all taken away. So as painful as the memories are, I come here whenever I can. To make sure I don't forget who I was."

"I'm so sorry," Adia said. While she couldn't fully understand what people like Sabo and Thyme had been through, having their world annihilated, she understood how one person's greed could destroy a kingdom. "Someone is trying to destroy my world too. Maybe every world has some monster like that. I'm sorry your world didn't survive yours."

Sabo didn't speak for a few seconds, just looked at Adia sadly. "It was hundreds of years ago," Sabo finally said. "I shouldn't have brought it up." She pointed at the barrel of water. "Go on. Take a look. You can see what you look like to me."

Adia could tell Sabo wanted to change the subject. So she climbed over the bench and peered into the barrel.

The water bubbled and turned into a thick, dark green liquid for a few seconds, then went back to being clear. Now when Adia looked at her reflection, she was dark blue with tusks coming out of her mouth and feathers on her shoulder.

"This is..." She wasn't sure what to say. Amazing? Terrifying? But Sabo only laughed.

"It's fine. You shouldn't think too hard about any of this your first time. I don't think I even remember half of what I see when I'm journeying. No one does."

Adia looked around her. It would be interesting to see

what she remembered later. After all, she was cursed with a brain that never forgot anything she saw even once. Books, every detail of a painting, every twist and turn in a forest. And, to her horror, even conversations. She could still replay every horrible thing Mallorie and Nami and Olark had ever said to her. Now *that* was something she wished she could get rid of. That would be a true gift.

"I'm not sure where I'm supposed to go," Adia said, but the girl shook her head.

"Don't worry about that. Honestly, it's easier if you just relax and don't try. What you need will find you here. And it's never what you expect."

Adia sighed. What she needed was answers to all her questions about the High Queen. Specifically, how to stop her. Another round of disembodied whispering began. Adia shuddered. It was all so eerie.

"Who is that?" Adia asked. "The whispering. I can't make out what they're saying."

"I can't hear it," Sabo said. "I only have visions. That's why I'm always drawn to power objects that let you *see*. Like this barrel."

Adia nodded. It was starting to make sense now.

"I'm starting to have visions when I'm around fire. But for the most part I hear things," she said, tugging an ear.

"Ooooh, that's what you should do!" Sabo said.

"Huh?" Adia asked.

Sabo pulled a quartz from her pocket.

"Me and my sisters carry around crystals to help with our vision. But people like you who hear things put them in their ears."

"You mean earrings?" Adia asked. "I'm not allowed."

"Not allowed by who?" Sabo asked curiously.

Not allowed by who, indeed. Adia frowned. "Well, there's this group of people who infiltrated my village. Missionaries. They told us we weren't allowed to wear our own jewellery. My aunt even handed over her wedding ring when they showed up."

Sabo stared at her in confusion.

"People came to your village to steal your jewellery?"

Adia rolled her eyes.

"They came to steal everything," she said. "Our land, our money, our way of life. The jewellery thing didn't even seem like that big a deal since I didn't own any in the first place. But I wasn't allowed to pierce my ears. They said that doing so would tarnish you in the eyes of the Bright Father."

But Adia was free of all that now. Why shouldn't she pierce her ears? Now that she thought about it, maybe it wasn't as random as she'd once thought that Olark's missionaries had also taken away their jewellery. Sure, gems were worth money. And she'd assumed that's why they'd wanted them as well as the tithe they collected from everyone in the Swamplands. But if the stones could also give someone with shamanic potential a boost of power, of course Olark and his minions would have been sure to remove them.

"Where do I go to get my ears pierced?" Adia asked.

"Nowhere," Sabo said. "It's all energy down here. Your ears won't be pierced up there," she said, pointing above her head. "But maybe you can receive a power object that will become a part of your soul. No one else will be able to see it, but you'll be able to feel it just as if it was a solid object. Close your eyes and let your mind go blank and ask if you can have one."

Adia closed her eyes, sceptical. But almost immediately she flinched when an invisible hand brushed the nape of her neck.

"What is that!" she said, opening her eyes and staring at Sabo in panic.

"Stay calm," Sabo said sharply. Adia forced herself to be still despite the eerie feeling of being touched by something she couldn't see. "And keep your eyes closed."

Adia nodded and squeezed her eyes shut.

Two hands were placed on her shoulders, and the noise of the spirits in the festival went silent. The hands moved up her neck before touching her ears. Two small pricks made her inhale sharply. Then she felt something heavy in her earlobes, touching her shoulders. And even though she couldn't see the earrings, she knew they were long and black.

She opened her eyes and stared at Sabo in shock.

"I can feel them!"

"Congratulations!" Sabo said, clapping her hands in excitement. "You just got your first power object."

For a moment, it felt as if her eardrums were full of water. She swallowed hard and the pressure popped, and suddenly it felt like her hearing was clearer than ever before. But then she heard something she didn't expect.

"Gini! Her ears. She's bleeding. You said she couldn't be hurt wherever she was. It's been three days and now she's bleeding. We have to get her out of there."

"Thyme?" Adia said, frowning in confusion.

"Time?" Sabo snorted. "No one keeps track of time down here."

"No, I thought I heard someone," Adia said. "My friend." She tried to focus but Thyme's panicked voice didn't speak again. That couldn't be real. She'd only been down here for maybe an hour. Not three days.

"Your hearing is heightened now," Sabo said. "It's possible you heard someone who's close to wherever you left your physical body."

Adia went cold.

Sabo continued talking, not noticing Adia's dread. "You should pierce your ears when you're back in your body too."

"Wait," Adia said, shaking her head and snapping out of the dreamlike state the spirit realm had put her in. Instead of finding out about the High Queen she'd been sitting here chatting with a bird person about jewellery. "If what I heard was real, my friend just said I've been down here for three days, but I swear I only left an hour ago! And my teacher wouldn't have sent me down here for three days. Well, technically she's a goddess but she's also literally my teacher. My headmistress. No way she'd let me skip around the Underworld for three days when I should be in class."

Sabo gave her a look of concern. "Give me a second."

Adia's mouth fell open as Sabo's eyes moved rapidly, rolling back into her head until all that showed was the whites, then settled back down.

"There's someone else's energy mixed in with yours. It's like a leech sucking you dry."

Adia blinked. "But I feel completely fine."

"You're in spirit form. I'm guessing that your body is *not* fine. Your friends are right. You've been down here longer than an hour. I think someone is keeping you down here on purpose so they can drain you."

Drain her? Was this another test? She'd been so distracted by all the sights in the Underworld that she'd again forgotten she was in the middle of initiation. She held out her hands and called her power to her. She gasped when nothing happened. No rush of heat through her body, no purple glow.

Sabo stood and moved closer to her. "Breathe. Try again. Your power is yours alone. If someone is trying to take it, stop them."

Adia swallowed and tried again. She could feel it now – something holding on to her power in a tight and greedy grip. But whoever it was, they hadn't realized that she was aware of their presence now. She could almost feel their surprise when she grabbed her power back. But she didn't know if she was strong enough to hold them off if they tried again.

She took a step back. "I have to get back to my body."

Sabo nodded. "Come with me. I think I know a way out."

"Gini, there has to be some way to bring her back. It's been five days."

Adia stopped short when Thyme's panicked voice came through to her again. She'd been following after Sabo for close to an hour. If she was really hearing Thyme, that meant that every hour she spent in the Underworld was closer to two days in Zaria. But Gini absolutely would have told her if time moved differently down here.

"The girl is too strong, Ginikanwa."

Mbari. His deep voice was thick with concern. It was all so real. Adia looked around frantically, half expecting to see everyone there, but it was just their disembodied voices.

"I should have been able to pull her back, but she refuses to budge," Mbari continued, his voice far away. *"I've never seen an initiation go on for this long. We can keep her body alive for a while longer, but if her spirit doesn't want to return…"*

"Trust her," Gini said. *"She's strong enough to break free of this."*

Adia clutched her head. Whoever the spirit trying to siphon off her power was, they were also messing with time. But what kind of spirit could have the power to manipulate space and time like this and keep her trapped here?

"Hey!" Sabo grabbed Adia's shoulders and peered into her eyes. "Are you still with me? Come on. We're almost there. You have to keep moving."

Adia didn't protest as Sabo propped her up and helped her limp down the hill.

"Why are you helping me?" Adia asked sluggishly. Her body was getting so heavy. Even her tongue felt like it weighed a ton. It was getting hard to speak. Sabo didn't answer.

"I hear someone again." Adia closed her eyes and focused, wincing as Nami's voice floated through the air. Even when his voice was disembodied it was still so *loud*.

"What do you mean she's journeying? Journeying where? She looks dead! Adia, wake up!"

If Adia could whack Nami on the head, she would. Who'd invited him? Someone needed to throw him out of whatever room they were all in back in the physical world. Another voice spoke and said exactly what she was thinking.

"Maybe she doesn't want to wake up to see your face staring down at her."

Darian. His voice cut through Adia's fog like a knife. A bolt of energy went through her, and she took a deep breath, trying to get her thoughts to focus.

"Are we close?" she asked as Sabo barrelled ahead.

"It's just through these caves. Quickly now."

Adia followed her inside and was immediately engulfed in darkness.

"Don't we need a torch?" Adia asked. "It looks pitch-black in there."

"You don't want to use fire right now," Sabo said. Adia couldn't make her out in the darkness, but her voice was annoyed. "Hurry up already."

Adia came to an abrupt stop. Sabo's sudden impatience made her nervous. What was she doing? Trusting this stranger who had just lured her into a dark and isolated cave.

"Sabo...does anything live in these caves?"

"Live?" Sabo repeated. "Oh no. I wouldn't say anything in here is *living*."

Adia had had enough. She no longer felt safe with this strange bird creature girl.

"I think I'll find another way," she said, hoping she sounded casual and not desperate to get away from Sabo. "Thanks for the help." She spun around to go back the way she came but she couldn't find the entryway. She stuck her hands out, but they only met solid rock.

"Once you enter you can only go in one direction," Sabo said.

"That's ridiculous," Adia said, frantically grasping at the cave wall, searching for the exit.

"We can't stay here, Adia. It's not safe."

"I'm starting to think that *you're* not safe," Adia said. "I'm getting out of here."

She closed her eyes and called her power to her, hoping that there was some plant life somewhere nearby for her to connect to. She opened her eyes and smiled triumphantly when her hands glowed purple. Her powers still worked. It had been foolish to trust Sabo so quickly, but at least she wasn't helpless. She held her hands up and the cave was illuminated with purple light, finally letting her see her surroundings. And what she saw made her let out a terrified scream.

Sabo was gone, and where she had once stood was a creature with two arms, legs and eyes like a mortal, but she was well over two metres tall, with skin as black as obsidian and feathers that spilled out and around the giant gold crown on her head.

"If you want to make it out of here alive, you'll do as I say. Starting with shutting up!"

Adia hadn't even been this scared in the Horrorbeyond. Back then, even though she'd been lost, she'd known that Gini was somewhere in that cursed land too. But now? She was all alone with an onyx bird woman wearing a giant crown.

"I told you the Underworld lets us see each other in a form that our brains are more willing to accept. You already saw a glimpse of my species in the barrel, remember?"

Yes, but a small image in a barrel of water a few centimetres deep hadn't done Sabo's flying species justice.

"Then why am I seeing you like this now?" Adia asked.

"Because we're no longer in the Underworld. We're in a Hollowgate. They were created as a way to escape the Underworld if it was ever under attack. They only stay open for a few minutes once you step inside. To make sure an army can't use it to come through. But creatures from other realms can access it. Not too many know about Hollowgates, but those who do use them as a meeting place."

"Why wouldn't they just go straight to the Underworld to meet?" Adia asked.

"Because not everyone is welcome there," Sabo said. "Now let go of that wall and follow me. If you don't move, you're going to end up stuck here until someone else comes through. And they might not be as friendly as me."

Adia couldn't tell if this was a trap, but Sabo was now marching forward, more concerned with getting out of here than attacking her. Adia followed but made sure to keep a healthy amount of distance between them.

"And put out that light," Sabo snapped.

"Oh." Adia had forgotten her hands were still brightly illuminated. She quickly pulled her power back, but she let one finger glow, pointing it forwards like a thin beam to light her path.

They'd been walking for a few minutes when Sabo suddenly spun around and shoved Adia. Hard. Adia fell into a hole in the wall, her shoulder jamming into stone and bringing tears to her eyes.

"What's the matter with you?" she gasped. Sabo put a finger to her lips. Her face was so tense that Adia closed her mouth.

"Don't move until I give you a signal," Sabo said. "When I do, crawl through this tunnel. There's a short drop at the opening. You'll land close to the shore. But for now, don't make a sound."

Adia felt around her. Sure enough, the hole Sabo had rudely shoved her into was the opening to a small, cramped tunnel. She'd have to crawl through it on her belly. Something furry touched her leg and she went tense, but then Bubbles's familiar rough tongue licked her. She was about to ask Sabo what the signal would be when her body went hot.

Not now, she thought in horror. She tried to slow her breathing to calm herself, but it didn't help. She knew she was giving off the heat of the sun right now. But why was she burning up? The only time she overheated to this extent was when she was so angry that her entire body wanted to combust. And there was only one person – or she should say, one demon – who made her that angry. Who made her blood and the blood of her ancestors boil over in white-hot rage.

"Don't...make...a sound," Sabo said. "He's coming."

Adia shook her head. It couldn't be him. It wasn't possible.

"I thought I saw a light," a deep, gravelly voice said. "But you can see in the dark and so have no need of a flame. I thought perhaps you were here with someone."

Adia held her breath. If she didn't, she would scream. And you can't scream if you can't breathe, she told herself as she trembled in fear. In the darkness, a metre or so in front of her, stood her worst nightmare.

Olark.

CHAPTER 13

In her heart, Adia had known Olark wasn't really gone. The nightmares that had plagued her since he'd possessed her. The feeling she couldn't shake that he was now a part of her. The dread she felt every morning as soon as she woke up and at night before she fell asleep that she would never truly be free of him. To have her worst fears confirmed was heartbreaking. The monster who had almost ruined her life stood just a metre or so away from her. And if Olark learned that she was here, just a few steps away, she knew she would never make it out of here alive.

"I thought I felt your presence," Sabo said.

Adia hoped the loud thumping of her heart wouldn't give her away. She wished she could see them, but she'd be risking her life if she made a sound. Sabo had told her to hide here. Which meant that for now, whoever or whatever Sabo was, she wasn't planning to give Adia up.

"But I wasn't expecting you tonight. What happened to your messenger?"

"They're currently occupied," Olark said. "Which means I have to risk travelling here myself to find out why the new formula still isn't right. Why has it taken you so long to make a slight modification?"

"A slight modification?" Sabo snapped. "Creating a mind-controlling substance is one thing, but to make something that drains everyone's life force and raises the dead is another. And you know what the agrias vine is like. I have to change the formula every few days because the plant doesn't *want* to be warped into a poison – into Drops. I'm doing my best."

Adia's eyes went wide. *Sabo* was the mastermind behind Drops and Liquid Gold? She'd hoped the Underworld would lead her to answers, but not like this.

"Stop lying to me," Olark said, his voice low and dangerous. "I know you're holding back. You work your sorcery—"

"Science—" Sabo snapped.

"—but it's still not enough energy to let the dead return to life for long. If you sent me up there now, I'd only have a few hours on Zaria before everyone woke up and I got spat back down to the realm of the dead. Plus, I would need to use more power than a corpse that still has a physical body or skeleton to return to."

So that's why Olark hadn't been one of the dead who'd returned. He was waiting for Sabo to come up with a formula so strong that the dead – even a being like him who'd never had a mortal body in the first place – could exist in the realm of the living for ever. Meaning everyone in Zaria would stay asleep for ever. No, Adia thought. Not sleep. Die. Their lives in exchange for his.

"I don't see how any of this is my problem," Sabo snapped. "I've told you over and over again that I want no part of this."

"Want?" Olark said. "Come now, Sabo. You know what you want doesn't matter. And I would think you'd be happy to see me. After all, my arrival in the realm of the dead is what woke you up. The bond between our souls."

"I was at peace," Sabo said. "And as for who woke me up, I'd say credit lies with the one who sent you to your death. Adia Kelbara."

Adia recoiled in horror. *You woke her up.*

"I suppose that's true," Olark mused. "Even if she had no idea what she was doing. Or that I would have such a prize waiting for me in the death realm."

No, Adia thought in dismay. She'd had no idea what she was doing. She never did.

"I've lived many lives since we last met, doing what I could to fix the damage we caused."

Adia didn't know if Sabo was putting on an act for her, Olark, or her own self, but Sabo's voice was thick with remorse and exhaustion.

"Damage?" Olark said with a laugh. "Spare me your shame.

You knew what you were signing up for. I gave you a crown in return for your soul. High Queen of the most powerful star besides Alusia."

"And what use was a crown when you massacred every living creature on the star I was supposed to rule, and stained my home with the blood of my people," Sabo said.

Adia couldn't help a sharp intake of breath. She already knew from the black-spined book in the library why no one had ever heard of this scientist queen who had mastered limb control and reanimation.

That she wasn't a Zarian queen, but a queen from a star. What Adia hadn't known was that the High Queen was from the star Olark had massacred, leading Gini to expel him from the skies.

Sabo was High Queen of the bloodstained star.

"It's your fault for not specifying the terms of our bargain," Olark said. "I gave you the crown you so desperately wanted. It's not my fault you failed to mention *where* you wanted to rule. I couldn't very well have you ruling over a star I planned to take for myself now, could I?"

Sabo didn't respond for so long, Adia wondered if she had walked away. But then the High Queen spoke again, her voice smaller now. "I should have died with my people."

"Die with your people?" Olark repeated. "I would never let a mind as incredible as yours be obliterated. That's why I made sure you were gone when I did what I had to do. Why

I bound your soul to mine. Besides, you betrayed your people. That's what they called you, you know. Sabo the Betrayer."

She's here. Adia startled as the whispers sounded through her head. *The Betrayer. She's here.*

Could these whispers be the spirits of everyone who'd once lived on the bloodstained star before Olark murdered them? It would explain why these voices had always felt more familiar than terrifying. Adia had spent weeks in the presence of the stone that contained the last fragments of their world. She'd thought she had delivered justice for those lost people when she'd defeated Olark the first time. But had their souls travelled to Adia through space and time to warn her that their betrayer queen was another person she needed to defeat before they could finally rest in peace?

"It hardly would have been fair for you to die with them," Olark continued. "Don't you think you deserve an eternity of suffering?"

"I used to," Sabo said. "But I guess the universe disagrees with me. I'm allowed in the Underworld, while *you* can only make it as far as a Hollowgate for a few minutes before you're dragged back to the realm of death. I felt remorse. I've lived many lives since then trying to fix what I'd done. This was supposed to be my final rest. Because my soul grew. While yours rotted into this."

"I don't see what you're complaining about," Olark said, his voice low and cold. "You've had five hundred years and lived how many lives since then. While I was trapped between time and space because of that bald-headed Nrian girl. But now that I'm back, you're bound to me. Or do you forget the words of our contract?"

Adia closed her eyes as her vision in the fire finally made sense. She let the words she'd seen in the smoke run through her mind.

Hear my words throughout the world
And read them in the skies.
Until this crown falls from your head
Your soul is bound to mine.
My every wish is your command
From now until you die.
And even in the realm of death
Our souls will be entwined.

Gini was right. This had never been about Darian. They were Olark's words, yes. But this curse was Sabo's. She was bound to Olark. His eternal servant, even in death.

"How could I forget. But you're quite clumsy with Words of Power, you know," Sabo said in a mocking tone. "This crown literally welded itself to my hair. Cutting the strands didn't even work. My hair became hard like metal wherever it touches the gold. Forever forged together. Even when I lived, I had to sleep with this thing on my head. A permanent reminder of how foolish I was to make a deal with you."

"That's right," Olark said. "A deal. A binding contract. Not a curse. You willingly chose to work for me. And you will until you bring me what I need. Be grateful this experiment wasn't a complete waste of time. Our new servants can carry on setting fires and trying to get Adia Kelbara's eyes. But my patience is running thin, Sabo. The next formula had better be the one that lets me return to Zaria permanently. I don't care if every last mortal on Zaria has to die for you to do it. Get it done. I'll let you get back to work."

Adia leaned back, making herself as small as possible so Olark didn't notice her as he made his exit.

"Maybe the delay isn't on me," Sabo said.

Adia almost groaned in exasperation. He'd been about to leave. Why was Sabo trying to pick a fight with him?

"I just give you the formulas," Sabo continued. "It's your shaman up above who twists my science into something foul. Uses my techniques to raise the dead. Maybe *they're* the one you need to summon."

Adia covered her mouth with her hands. She knew it.

There were three of them. Olark was in charge, the High Queen was the scientist coming up with the new and ever-changing formula for Drops, and there was a shaman in the realm of the living carrying out their plans. Sabo might be the one who figured out who to do it, but it was Olark's shaman in Zaria who was enacting the demon's mission.

"You worry about making a stronger formula, I'll worry about my servant in Zaria."

"As you command, Master," Sabo said, her voice dripping with hatred. She walked away from Olark, but paused when she reached the spot where Adia was hiding. Adia held her breath as she stared at Sabo's back. Was the High Queen going to give her up? Why go through the trouble of hiding Adia if Sabo was going to let Olark have her? But Sabo didn't look in Adia's direction. "Just send a signal whenever you need to talk."

Signal. Adia understood. As quietly as she could, she flattened herself onto her stomach and started to crawl through the tunnel. It was time to get out of here.

"After all," Sabo said, "we don't want this to take much longer. It might give someone enough time to find the cure for Drops. And if that happened...well. You and your shaman would never be able to use it to siphon off anyone's energy ever again."

Adia went still. A cure? Her heart raced. There was a way to stop this? *Give me more, Sabo. What's the cure?*

"It's not like I would ever create a mind-controlling substance and not create an antidote for myself."

So the antidote *did* already exist. *Where?* She willed Sabo to give her the final key. To at least point her in the direction she needed to go.

"And I'm grateful you had the foresight to do so," Olark admitted. "I might have need of the antidote one day as well. But no one will ever find it. How could they? I buried it with you. And no one will ever find your tomb."

* * *

The "short drop" that Sabo had told Adia would be at the end of the tunnel turned out to be a never-ending free fall. Adia didn't know how she managed to hold in her scream as she tumbled through the air for what seemed like an hour before landing hard in the cold water. She kicked frantically, gasping when her head broke through the surface. A horrible wail from above made her glance up.

"Good grief!" she said as Bubbles somersaulted down after her. She quickly swam forward and managed to catch him just before he face-planted into the primordial ocean of the Underworld.

Bubbles frantically crawled up her face and dug his claws into her hair in a panicked attempt to not have any water touch him. "Stop that!" Adia snapped, treading water as she tried to shake the terrified cat off her head so she could see. "Your body isn't even real right now. Who cares if you get wet!" But there was nothing to be done about getting Bubbles to swim on his own. She pushed forward and swam them towards the shore, refusing to let this all be for nothing because she'd been drowned by a cat.

Adia swam so fast and for so long she knew it was only a matter of time before her limbs and lungs gave up on her. It didn't seem fair that she still felt pain and exhaustion when she wasn't even in her physical body, but she ignored the cramp in her leg as she pushed forward. She was fuelled both by her fear of Olark, and by a fear of sharks and whatever ancient water spirits might dwell in the deep. Rocks scraped against her legs, causing her to grit her teeth so she wouldn't cry out. But the rocks meant she had finally reached the shore.

She stood and waded through the rest of the water, sighing in relief when she was on dry sand again. Shaking Bubbles off her head, she spun around. There was nothing as far as the eye could see except water. She took a deep inhale, breathing in the salty sea air, and allowed herself a minute to catch her breath and gather herself.

She'd just been centimetres away from not only Olark, but the creator of Drops; the High Queen of the bloodstained star. But if High Queen Sabo was to be believed, she wasn't Adia's enemy. Sabo had made sure Adia knew there was another shaman working in Zaria and that there was a cure for Drops. And since Adia had no idea how to free Sabo from her curse, she was going to have to find that cure. Which meant she would have to find Sabo's tomb. If Adia found that, she would be able to stop everyone from falling asleep. From dying. She just had to figure out how to get back to Zaria first.

Her vision opening and allowing her to see into everyone's spirit body had been the first test of initiation. Being able to enter the Underworld must have been the second.

"Maybe figuring out how to get back into my body is the final thing I need to know?" she wondered. But she was at a loss.

Gini's speech at orientation floated back into her mind. That getting stuck between worlds was one of the most dangerous things that could happen to a shaman. Adia understood now. Her body might be alive back at the Academy, but her soul wasn't in it. Which meant both her body *and* soul were in danger right now. Look at Sabo. She'd had lifetimes of atonement, and her soul was still trapped. At least Gini, Thyme and Darian were with her body and could keep it safe. But she and her soul were on their own. She wasn't even sure if she was still in the Underworld or if she'd fallen into another realm where there was nothing to the left or right of her other than dark waters. The only light came from the stars above.

She glanced up then paused, needing a minute to understand what she was seeing. The sky above her was a *Zarian* night sky. She could see Alusia.

"Wait. Am I home?" she gasped. But when she glanced at Bubbles, she saw that he was currently experimenting with making himself grow as big as a tiger. Her shoulders drooped. "Nope. Still in spirit form." But these were Zarian constellations, just not the ones that should be in the sky right now. These were winter stars.

"Did I travel through time?" she wondered. That was the only explanation she could come up with why she was staring at stars that shouldn't be visible yet. Either that or she was in a part of Zaria that she'd never heard of where these constellations were visible this time of year. She frowned and studied the stars, burning them into her brain like they were a map. As she took it all in, she paused. That was a star cluster she'd never seen before. Not in the sky, not in a book. She traced her fingers along it. The shapes curved up and down, like waves in the ocean.

Adia slowly lowered her hand.

"It can't be," she whispered, turning back to the water. She took a deep breath and opened up her vision as she let her power spark from her fingertips. Purple light rushed forward to the ocean. And the ocean answered back. The darkness of the sea gave way to bioluminescent waters.

Adia jumped back as, all at once, spirits in beautiful blue robes that flowed in the breeze appeared around her. She knew she should be afraid, but she wasn't. She knew these people. And her blood knew this land.

Gini and Sabo had said she would find what she needed here. She'd thought what she needed was to know about the High Queen. And she did. But there was something else she needed. And she might have just got it. Somehow her astral body, her soul, was standing in Imo Mmiri.

One of the spirits raised their hand and pointed at the sky. Adia's eyes followed the gesture as she looked up again at the stars. She nodded.

It wasn't an exact map, and she didn't know if one lifetime was enough to search the world looking for a single constellation. It wouldn't be just a matter of location, but a specific time when the stars were in this exact place in the sky – still, it was more information than she'd ever had before. If she found the place in Zaria where the stars looked like this, and where she could see this constellation, she would find Imo Mmiri.

She lowered her head to find that she was once again standing on an empty beach in front of a vast, dark ocean. No spirits in sight. She wanted to call out to them to come back. These were her ancestors. Her family. If she stayed with them, maybe for the first time in her life she would be in a place where she felt like she belonged. But she knew she couldn't stay here, lingering in a spirit world. And maybe *that* was the final test. Knowing that even if she found a beautiful realm, even if her spirit felt like it was where she belonged, she was still a mortal girl of Zaria. She'd been given her ability to help other people. Not to use it to escape a world full of ugliness and misery by spending her days living in a trance. It was time to go home and figure out the way to the High Queen's tomb.

"Come on, Bubbles. We're getting out of here."

She picked him up and took a deep breath. She knew what she had to do. In some ways, she might have always known how to get back into her body. It was just that she was scared to do it herself. She hated to admit it, but being in Olark's presence again was how she'd figured it out. It all came back to the curse he'd put on her bloodline. The one that had ended up being his undoing.

For a brief moment, Adia felt the deepest sense of relief as she realized that her greatest fear would never come to pass. The fear that held her back from embracing her powers. From wanting to open herself up to the shamanic world. The fear that if she did, she would lose control and be possessed again.

Olark *couldn't* possess her again. No one could. Her name was all she needed to say to cast out any spirit who tried. And the reason why Olark had chosen to use the realm of the dead to hunt her down was perfectly clear.

Her name will be a Word of Power in a world of lies.

And anyone who brings her harm will be the one who dies.

These reanimated corpses were the perfect army because they had immunity to her Word of Power. Her name. They could harm her all they wanted without fear of dying. They were already dead.

She didn't know if Thyme or Gini had realized that in the months since she'd been possessed by Olark, there had been one word she'd never said. Her own name. The Word of Power that had expelled Olark from her body and flung him into darkness and death. Adia had taken to imagining vines holding her name in place before she ever spoke it out loud. So much that it had become an unconscious habit – and a self-inflicted binding of herself. But now, she let the vine that held her name in place go.

Because she knew without a doubt that this was her final test. The way back to her body. The way to make sure she never got trapped in between worlds. As long as she held on to a Word of Power, she would always be able to find her way back. She closed her eyes.

"I'm going back to my body now. It's time to wake up... ADIA."

CHAPTER 14

Adia opened her eyes to find Gini's anxious face peering down at her.

"How long was I out?" she asked.

"Six days," Gini said. "I wasn't sure if you'd ever come back. I'm so sorry. I thought I'd taken every precaution, but it was like someone had your soul held in a vice and there was nothing I could do to break you free."

"I know." Adia winced as she sat up. Her body had never been this stiff in her life. So she really had been unconscious and lying in a bed for a week. "Someone was trying to keep me down there to steal my power. At least that was Sabo's theory."

"Who's Sabo?" Darian asked.

"The High Queen," Adia said.

Everyone shouted all at once, but Adia was too distracted by all the new sensations that had come with passing initiation to answer the questions they were flinging at her. Thyme was glowing the same way she had in her vision. But Adia didn't understand what she was seeing with Darian. His energy was just as bright and pure as Thyme's, but there was something else to it. It wasn't quite the same as Gini's or Mbari's, but silver dust floated all around him. Stardust? No, that didn't make sense. She rubbed her eyes. It would take her a while to understand what this new, second sight actually meant.

"Maybe we should give her a minute," Darian said with a frown.

"No, I'm all right," she said quickly, feeling herself flush at how long she'd been gawking at him.

She quickly told them about Sabo. The misguided queen who'd sold out her people to Olark and let him turn her world into a bloodstained star. But she decided to keep the information about Imo Mmiri to herself for now. She trusted everyone in this room with her life, but she'd been trapped in the Underworld for almost a week. For all she knew, a spirit was lingering around this room right now, relaying information to the other shaman. Because who else would have the power to trap her soul in the Underworld? Who else would even know that the Underworld existed, let alone that she had journeyed there? She would tell them about the constellations of Imo Mmiri when she was sure no one else was listening.

"I always wondered how he conquered the Dog Star so easily," Gini said. "It never occurred to me that he had inside help. All that destruction because Olark wanted to be an Alusi and Sabo wanted to be a queen."

"Well, as far as I can tell," Adia said, "Sabo's quest for power ended ages ago. Nothing like watching everyone you ever loved get wiped out by a power-hungry monster to make you feel instant regret. But she's still bound to him, even in death. Though she's been at peace, I think. In the realm of the dead."

"So when you sent Olark there…" Thyme said.

"I accidentally woke her up," Adia finished. "And now he can control her again, per the terms of their agreement back when he made her a queen. She has no choice but to keep working on new variations of the Drops formula for him. The agrias vine is fighting back now, so Sabo has to make a new formula every few days to keep draining people enough to reanimate the dead. But since they're both dead spirits now, Olark's had to work with someone here in Zaria to get the Drops produced."

"Yes, of course," Thyme said. "The missionaries, the palace, any vendor trying to make extra coin. We already knew that."

Adia shook her head frantically.

"No, it's not just them. It wasn't some random spirit who messed with my initiation and tried to keep me trapped in the Underworld. It was another shaman. I heard it straight from Olark's lips. What I can't understand is why the shaman didn't let Olark know I was there. Sabo might be trying to help me, but that shaman was trying to steal my power without me noticing."

"Isn't it obvious?" Thyme said. "Olark might have tracked

down another shaman, but he's being double-crossed. By them *and* by Sabo. It sounds like Sabo just hates him and wants to be free of him, but whoever this shaman is, they probably want to find Imo Mmiri just as much as Olark. Why be the henchman when you can be the master? Which means that right now, a demon, the dead and a shaman are all after Adia."

Adia couldn't handle this any more. Initiation was just supposed to be about opening her powers and being blessed by the spirits, not this. She felt like she couldn't breathe. "I think I need some fresh air," she said. She stood up, but immediately her legs gave out. Darian grabbed her before she could fall.

"That's a good idea," Thyme said. "Go walk it off."

"I think she needs to rest, not walk it off," Darian said, glaring, but Thyme shook her head.

"We were moving her arms and legs around for her but she's still stiff as a board. She hasn't used her legs in a week and we've been forcing juice down her throat so she didn't starve."

"Thyme is right," Mbari said. "We've had to keep you quarantined. Or at least that's what Gini told the professors. For better or worse, everyone's missed so much class from losing consciousness that you being out for a week didn't seem that strange. Yesterday everyone was asleep for almost half the day."

Adia closed her eyes. Sabo was getting close to perfecting her new Drops formula then. It might be only a matter of days before people never woke up again. She needed some air.

"I'll be back in a few minutes."

"No, no," Gini said. "Let's call it a night. You need to move your body, get some proper food *and* rest. This conversation can wait till tomorrow. Let's give Adia some room to breathe." Gini gave her an awkward pat on the head. "Glad to have you back. Darian, come with me. I'll make sure you get to my office without anyone seeing you. You've been sleeping on the floor next to Adia and that will no longer do. You'll stay in my office until I can get you back to the palace."

Darian nodded but turned to Adia, who was trying not to die of embarrassment knowing that he had camped out by her sickbed for six days. "Be careful, Adia," he said. "We've had to deal with at least half a dozen corpses while you were unconscious, and fires being set everywhere."

Adia tried not to wince at how stiff she was as she walked around the yard. The sun was setting so this would have to be a quick walk, but thankfully her muscles were starting to loosen up. She bent down to stretch and touch her toes but an annoying voice made her pop back up.

"Kelbara," Rusty said, jogging up to her. "So you're still here? Mallorie told everyone you'd been kicked out again."

Adia frowned. She didn't mean to, but she could see an aura around him. Rusty's energy was interesting. It was almost split in two. As if there were two sides to him that were in constant battle to be in charge. It would be an easy thing for her to fix. All she had to do was merge the two together. But she remembered her lesson from initiation. She had no right to play around with someone's astral body. She shook her head, bringing herself back to the conversation. What had he just said? Oh. Some silly rumour Mallorie had started.

"And you believed her?"

"Not for a second," Rusty said. "I know she's out to get you – of course she'd make up a lie. So what really happened?" He leaned close, clearly eager to get the gossip and spread the word that Adia was back.

"Nothing interesting," Adia said with a sigh. "I was just sick and in quarantine. It was highly contagious. Still might be." She gave a few coughs for good measure and smiled as Rusty quickly covered his nose and scurried away, giving her a backwards wave. After a few minutes, she was still sore, but she had control of her legs. She turned to head back to the library but tensed when she saw a pair of boots sticking out from behind a tree. Had someone blacked out?

Adia rushed over to the tree. Nami. Fast asleep. But she spotted a group of Gold Hats walking over. No one was unconscious. Nami had just fallen asleep at his post. And would probably get punished if she didn't do something.

"Gran," he mumbled in his sleep. "Gran, what is it?"

She sighed. *Why do I even care?* she wondered. But she gave Nami's leg a hard nudge with her boot.

"Nami, wake up," she snapped.

He jumped up so quickly he almost knocked her over.

"Gran!"

Adia rolled her eyes.

"Do I look like your grandmother?" she asked with a glare, but she softened when she took in his expression. His eyes looked haunted as he stared at her. It seemed to take him a minute to know who he was looking at.

"Adia!" he gasped. "You're awake! And sorry, I— I was just with my grandmother. I mean, not really *with* her. That wouldn't be possible. She died two years ago...but it felt so real."

Adia's eyes narrowed. Lebechi said her dream about being buried alive felt real too. Maybe some part of these dreams *were* real.

"Did she speak to you?" Adia asked.

Nami shook his head. "No. It was more like I was watching a memory. But it wasn't *my* memory. She was talking to my mother, except Mom was younger than she is now. Only a few years older than us. She had a bag and was trying to leave home, but Gran was trying to stop her. She said my dad would gamble away every last cent of my mother's inheritance and she'd end up penniless and begging to come home."

Adia frowned. She knew the part about the gambling was right. Nami had told her that his dad had lost everything and they had no friends left to ask for help.

"But my mom stormed out of the house. I tried to go after her, but I couldn't move. My grandmother sat down and started to cry. I walked up to her and put a hand on her shoulder, and she jumped. She stared right at me. I think she was trying to say something. Her mouth was moving but I couldn't hear it. And then you woke me up."

Nami turned red and ruffled his hair.

"Sorry, I know it sounds ridiculous. It was just a dream."

But Adia shook her head.

"It doesn't sound ridiculous," she said. That was the troublesome part.

"I wish you'd tell me what's going on," Nami said quietly. "I saw you this week. The headmistress told everyone you were sick but that's not what it was at all. You were in some sort of trance. And no one could figure out how to wake you up. I mean, everyone's passing out for longer and longer now. Yesterday we were all out cold for twelve hours. We didn't even see the sun. It felt like an endless night. But you were asleep for days."

Adia closed her eyes. She knew she didn't owe him an explanation, but he looked so panicked that it felt wrong not to say anything.

"I'm not sure what's going on," she admitted. "But I think

what you saw was real. I think— I think these cracks in the earth are more serious than anyone could imagine. I think they're not just cracks in the earth, but cracks between our worlds."

"Our worlds..." Nami repeated. "You mean—"

"The realms of the living and the dead. I think our worlds are converging in on each other. I don't think you were dreaming about your grandmother – I think she might have really been here somehow. At least for a moment."

Nami stared at Adia. He was quiet for so long that she started to get concerned.

"Nami?" she said.

"Sorry. I'm trying this thing where I think before I speak," he said with a self-deprecating laugh. "Is this what was going on with Darian when you helped him? Something otherworldly that only you could see?"

"Something like that," Adia admitted.

"And instead of helping you I acted like you were trying to hurt people. I wonder about that a lot. What would have happened if you hadn't managed to get out of the dungeon. How'd you do that anyway?"

"Maka slipped me a key when she brought food to my cell," Adia admitted.

Nami looked even more defeated. "Well, I'm glad someone had the sense to help you."

Adia was too tired and sore to be mean to him. Suddenly

being mad at Nami felt like a waste of energy when she had very little energy to spare. Maybe this was what forgiveness was. Something that happened when you realized being angry about the past only kept it alive and bled your soul dry. Her anger towards Nami was starting to feel like she was walking around with her own personal Energy Thief lodged in her chest. And she was sick of it.

She shrugged. "I never told you what was going on. You weren't really hit on the head with a pawpaw on the island you followed me to, you know."

"I knew it!" Nami said. Adia couldn't help but grin at seeing some life come back into his eyes. "What really happened?"

"Something other-worldly that only I could see," she said, wiggling her fingers.

Nami grinned, but his eyes went sad again. "You did try to explain, though. And I cut you off and called the Gold Hats. I'll never do anything like that to anyone again. And I want you to know...if there's any way I can help you now, I'm here. Speaking of you needing my help..."

Adia grimaced as Mr Chobly barrelled down the path.

"Ms Kelbara," Chobly said. "How fortuitous. I was just coming to get an update on your illness and here you stand, alive and well."

Adia almost asked if he was disappointed, but she decided not to antagonize him. Chobly wasn't even trying to appear friendly any more. No fake smile graced his lips, just prolonged eye contact that made her feel like a zebra being stared down by a lion before it attacked. She tried to see his aura like she had with everyone else, but the second she tried, pain shot through her head, making her pull back. She frowned at him. Maybe it was easier to see Thyme's and Darian's auras, and even Mallorie's, because she knew them. Or maybe she was too tired to use an ability she'd only just acquired. She hoped that was the case. And not that Chobly had some way of blocking her powers from affecting him.

"The council will be so happy when I tell them the news. It will lift their spirits. Everyone's been quite upset these past few days over the distressing news. We've received word that the emperor is missing."

Adia tried to move aside but just like the last time she'd been near Chobly, her feet were frozen to the ground. It wouldn't take him long to figure out Darian was here with her and hiding out at the Academy. But she feigned confusion.

"Is that so?" she asked.

"Yes," Chobly said coldly. "It is so. Even his mother doesn't seem to have any idea where he's disappeared to. Captain Perpetua assures us he's fine and taking care of something that requires the utmost discretion, but my council members in the capital say she was just as shocked as everyone when she found out he was gone."

Adia gave him a blank stare as Nami whipped his head back and forth between them.

"Does the emperor need to explain his business to you?" she asked.

"No, no," Chobly said with a smile. "Of course not. But since the two of you are so close, I'd only wondered if you might have some idea as to where he could be."

Adia stood there awkwardly, not sure how to get out of this.

"Everyone from the council is down at the staff library," Nami suddenly burst out.

Chobly fixed him with a withering look, as if he'd only just noticed Nami's presence. "Excuse me?"

Nami cleared his throat. "I'm just making sure you're not forgetting about a meeting you needed to attend."

"Your concern for my work schedule is touching," Chobly said drily. "Mr Watson. That's your name, isn't it? Nami Watson. Son of Kevan Watson. Your family certainly has had a lot of troubles."

Nami didn't answer, but he took a step closer to Adia.

"And how is your father?" Chobly continued. "I heard he had to spend three months in debtors' prison. That must be quite difficult for you and your mother. She has a weak constitution, does she not?"

Adia hadn't known that. She'd known a lot of Nami's actions last semester had been because his father's gambling was about to put his family in the poorhouse, and he was desperate to help his mother. He'd been on a mission to befriend the rich and powerful so that he could get a good job and take care of her. A fact she liked to forget. He might not have had purely selfish reasons for selling her out, but he still could have got her killed.

"I'm sure it doesn't help that your father gambles away money that could go to buying her medicine," Chobly said.

Adia grew more and more nervous about what Nami was about to do. It was clear where this was going.

Chobly leaned down and gave Nami a conspiratorial smile, putting his arm around his shoulder. "You know," he said, "as a senior council member, I could do quite a lot to help you, Mr Watson. Getting your mother the medicine she needs, sending a proper, capital-trained physician to your home. I'm very good to my friends. And I'd like us to be friends."

Adia's stomach dropped. Uncle Eric had already sold her secrets to this man. Nami had an even better reason to give Chobly what he wanted. His mother was sick. A flash of guilt ran through her. She was as rich as the emperor himself, yet all her money was tucked away in a hollow tree in the Horrorbeyond when she could be using it to help people. But when had Nami become someone she wanted to help?

Nami glared and shrugged off Mr Chobly's arm. He took a step closer to Adia.

"I'm glad to hear you're so good to your friends," Nami said. "I've been terrible to mine. But I'm trying not to make the same mistakes twice. As I said, the council is in the staff library. I wouldn't want you to miss an important meeting."

Chobly gave them both a contemptuous stare.

"I'm sure you wouldn't. Well then, I'll be on my way. And you two should be on yours. It's never good for children to be lurking about in the dark. These are dangerous times we're living in. So why don't you go tuck yourselves safely into your beds." He locked eyes with Adia. "Have a wonderful sleep."

Adia stared at his retreating form. Again, something about this man had made her feet freeze to the ground. And again, Nami had been the one to help free her from her stupor. And what had Chobly meant by *Have a wonderful sleep*? Was Chobly Olark's servant in Zaria? Sabo, forced to help him in the realm of death and Chobly up above to carry out Olark's plans in the physical world?

"Be careful around him," Adia said slowly. "I think that man is more dangerous than we think. And...thanks for not telling him anything about me."

Nami turned red. "It's not like I have anything to tell," he said, shuffling his feet.

Adia wasn't sure if she should ask, but she wanted to know. "Your mother. She's sick? Is it serious?"

Nami looked at the ground. "I'm not sure what's wrong with her. Chobly was right. We can't even afford a good doctor. But don't worry. She'll be all right."

Adia nodded. "She will be. I'm going to send a doctor to your house."

"What?" Nami gasped.

"And whatever medicine she needs will be taken care of."

"Adia, what are you talking about? You can't do that."

"Of course I can," she said with a shrug. "I got a reward for helping Darian. I have more money than I'll be able to spend in a lifetime. Helping my—"

Adia closed her mouth. What had she been about to say? Helping my *friend?* Since when had she begun to see Nami as a friend again? She cleared her throat.

"Helping a sick woman seems like a good way to start spending my coin."

But Nami was shaking his head furiously.

"I don't want your charity," Nami said loudly, then turned even more red when Adia just raised an eyebrow.

But Nami was still shaking his head in protest.

She had to say something to get him to accept her help. She almost snorted to herself. If anyone had told her a month ago that she'd be out here making up reasons to *help* Nami Watson, she would have assumed they'd eaten a poisonous mushroom and had lost touch with reality. She forced a harshness into her voice that she didn't feel.

"Who said anything about charity," she snapped. "It's for my own peace of mind. I know you won't sell me out if you're not worried about your mom."

Nami flinched and straightened his shoulders.

"I see," Nami said. "Well...it would great if she could see a real doctor. And if it'll make you not worry about me telling Mr Chobly about your powers or anything else about you."

"It would," Adia said quickly. "That's settled then. Well, I'd better get going. Neither of us should be out at night if we can help it. Chobly's right about one thing."

Nami stared at her in surprise. "What's that?"

Adia looked up at the rising moon. "Nothing is safe any more."

"Wait a minute," Nami called out. She turned back around. "What would happen if the realms converged?"

Adia stared at him. It was time to face how serious this all was. What would happen if Olark finally got his way and entered their world, and the living never woke up again? If she didn't find Sabo's tomb and stop all this?

"We all die."

CHAPTER 15

Adia couldn't believe she'd been ordered to return to class after only a day of rest. You would think being trapped in the Underworld would warrant a week off from school. Honestly, that she still had to bother with school was ridiculous. She really wished Gini would get her priorities in order. Sure, they were all going to meet in the headmistress's office later that day to come up with a plan, but why carry on with class when what Adia really needed to do was find the High Queen's tomb?

She'd rushed out of her room before Thyme could stop her. Thyme, Darian and even Nami had spent the better part of a week glued to her bedside. Adia didn't care what Darian said. They all needed a break from being her friend. (Or in Nami's case, her tolerated acquaintance who *maybe* she was considering becoming friends with again.) She had self-directed study this morning anyway. So she'd decided to skip breakfast and self-direct herself to Chobly's quarters to do a bit of snooping. She knew there was another shaman in Zaria thanks to Sabo and, right now, all signs pointed to him.

The council's temporary quarters were adjacent to the Gold Hat barracks. She'd never walked through this side of the Academy. At first because the Gold Hats terrified her, with their machetes strapped to their waists. And then because she wanted to avoid running into Nami. Sure enough, she spotted him doing drills with a few other kids who must also be working with the Gold Hats for their year of practicality. They would have their own teachers here since they still had to do schoolwork too.

Before, she would have glared and walked right past him, but now she nodded her head discreetly. Nami's eyes went wide. He said something to the other trainees and walked over to her. It was clear he was trying to look casual, but he was barely keeping himself from running.

"What's the matter?" he asked. "Are you all right?"

"Do you know where Chobly's office is?" she asked.

"Second level. That room there." He pointed to a window that would have a view of the courtyard. "Why?"

"I need to get into it," Adia said.

Nami stared at her. He looked like he wanted to say something, but then he nodded. "Come on."

She followed as he led her into the council's quarters.

"They all took off a few minutes ago," Nami said, "but I wouldn't linger for too long if I were you."

Adia nodded. "Can you stand guard and give me a signal if anyone is coming? Cough loudly or something if anyone comes and I'll jump out the window."

"It'd be a pretty long drop," Nami said with a snort.

"Just give me some sort of heads-up," she said. "I'll be quick."

Chobly's room was at the end of the second-level hallway. The door was ajar, and Adia opened it slowly, gaping at the state of his chambers. She'd expected someone as severe as Chobly to be the picture of organization down to having his socks neatly arranged by day of the week. Instead, dirty cups and plates sat in piles on the table with flies hovering around them, and papers were flung all over the place. Chobly might be even worse than Thyme in terms of messiness.

She took a step forwards but froze when something crunched beneath her feet. Shattered glass was all over the floor. That's when she noticed the cracked mirror hanging on the wall. As if Chobly had smashed it in a fit of pique. But most disturbing of all was what else was on the wall.

Dozens of papers were nailed into wood panels, some with angry red circles or arrows around certain things. And at the centre of it all was a sketch of a girl with long, thick hair and large round glasses that couldn't hide how big her eyes were.

Adia touched the sketch of herself.

"What is this?" she whispered in horror. She lowered her hand and took a step back. Next to the sketch was a map of the Swamplands, with her aunt and uncle's house circled in red. She leaned forward to read the small note underneath it.

Epicentre of the Swamplands Earthquake. First display of power.

Everywhere she looked there was a paper detailing some part of her life, down to her medical records and end-of-year exams. She read a note on her last exam.

Teachers, missionaries, aunt and uncle all confirm that AK possesses an eidetic memory. She only needs to see something once to memorize it. Council must be warned.

"Warned?" Adia murmured. This entire thing made her sound like a dangerous criminal who needed to be apprehended with the utmost caution. She examined document after document about her life, until one made her heart stop.

Mother, Zina Kelbara. Death due to sleeping sickness (allegedly). Fire channeller, according to village accounts.

"Fire channeller?" Adia whispered. Village accounts? She'd never thought about returning to the village she was born in to ask about her parents. To ask about her mother, who should have been here with her as one of the last two descendants of Imo Mmiri, instead of Adia being the sole survivor of their bloodline. But Chobly had. And he'd found out things about Adia's mother she'd never known.

"He's obsessed with me," Adia said slowly.

Chobly *had* been here when the corpses started arriving.

And as a member of the council he would have had access to the student roster and known who to give Drops to. Adia was about to leave the room when she saw a pile of letters with familiar handwriting on them.

"EJ," she gasped, rushing over to the table and grabbing the letter on the top and quickly unfolding it. Darian had been right. Chobly had not only been intercepting her mail, he'd been reading it.

"How dare you," Adia whispered in fury. She quickly opened the letter in her hand and skimmed it as fast as she could.

Adia. You should be at the Academy by now. I hope you're all right. Something weird is happening in the Swamplands. Are you hearing about people losing consciousness? There's also reports of the ghosts of people who died being seen not far away from the villages where everyone is fainting. You might want to look into it. I'm not sure what's real or not any more.

But more importantly, people from the capital showed up asking questions about you. Once they offered Dad money, he told them everything. I'm so sorry, but I've been giving Mom updates about you. Not much, of course, but she knew you were heading back to the Academy and that you'd be a student this year. Which means Dad knows too and, now, so do these capital people. They call themselves the council. One of them kept asking if your apprenticeship would include initiation. But Dad had no idea what they were talking about. Mom got annoyed with all the questions and threw them out of the house. She's been trying to keep everything that happened to us quiet, but you know Dad. He'd do anything for money.

Just be careful. Write to me as soon as you can so I know you're all right. Say hi to Thyme and Bubbles for me.

—EJ

Adia was going to be sick. No wonder Chobly had made sure she never saw this letter. She put it down to grab the next one but a commotion outside made her freeze. Nami's voice cut through the air, unnaturally loud.

"I was checking to see if there were any gas leaks in your quarters," Nami practically shouted to someone.

Adia clenched her fist in frustration. She couldn't take the letters with her or Chobly would know she'd been in his room. But luckily they were already burned into her memory, since Chobly's intel was right and she only needed to see something once to memorize it. She had to get out of there. She carefully stuck her head out the door and seeing no one, made a run for it, barely turning down a hallway before someone came up the stairs.

"Someone needs to do something about that little Gold Hat," Chobly was saying to another council member as they disappeared into his room. Adia could only hope she had left his mess exactly the way she found it.

Nami sagged in relief when he saw her. She let him grab her arm and rush her outside.

"Did you find what you were looking for?" he asked.

"I'm not sure," Adia said.

She hadn't found any definitive proof that Chobly was working with Olark. But according to EJ's letter, Chobly had asked Uncle Eric if she was going to be initiated. If he knew enough about shamanism to know she would be put through initiation, then he also could have known that she'd be in the Underworld at some point. And he could have been waiting for her there. Then again, he also could just be a government official who was keeping tabs on everyone he thought had influence over the emperor. All she knew was that whether or not Chobly was a servant of the dark or a greedy government official, there was something about him that was different from anyone she'd ever met. She didn't know what kind of power he had, or where it came from, but there was an otherworldly strength to him. And until she figured out who or what Mr Chobly really was, she needed to keep as much distance from him as possible.

Adia was quiet for the rest of the day as she thought about what she'd discovered.

"I wish you'd tell me what's going on," Thyme said. "And don't say it's because of corpses and Olark. Something happened today that you're not telling me."

"It's nothing worth mentioning," Adia said, pushing the door open to Gini's office. She wasn't ready to tell anyone else how much of a mess her life was. "And we definitely have other things to worry about. Like finding the High Queen's tomb."

"But where is this tomb?" Darian asked. He was standing next to Gini and Mbari. Thyme and Adia had been the last to arrive. "Is it part of the crypts that house Zaria's rulers?" He shuddered. "My mother showed me where my plot would be."

Adia sighed. "I was hoping one of you would know." She turned hopefully to Thyme, but the warrior girl gave a bewildered shrug.

"Gini?" she tried. "Mbari? Any divine insight?"

"Even if we were back home in Alusia, you'd be asking us to locate a needle in a haystack," Mbari said. "We know the locations of everything we created for you – the mountains, the deserts, the seas. But we don't keep track of every structure you mortals build, let alone the graves."

Gini nodded in agreement. "What about those maps you're always poring over, Adia?" she asked. "You've never seen mention of it?"

"Nothing," Adia said, defeated. How was she supposed to find one woman's grave in all of Zaria? Sabo hadn't even specified if her tomb *was* in Zaria. There were seven other kingdoms in the world. Eight, if you included the wasteland behind the Sunless Mountains.

Adia realized this must be the same frustration Olark walked around feeling. Needing to find something that was hidden. Maybe his agony was even worse than hers – he actually *had* a key that would open the gate to the utopia he so desperately sought, except the key refused to turn for him. Or rather, the key refused to let a demon gouge out her eyes. He at least had a way to get to Imo Mmiri. Adia had nothing to show her the way to what she needed.

"How do we know this isn't a trap?" Thyme asked, interrupting her thoughts. "Everyone I've talked to sees a tomb in their dreams when they lose consciousness. You said Lebechi saw it too. Or felt like she'd been buried alive in a tomb. Maybe this is a trap to lure us there since they can't reach us in our dreams."

"Sabo doesn't want to work for Olark," Adia said. "I'm sure of it. She's bound to him."

"Sabo's been dead for centuries," Gini said. "And she entered into a bargain with Olark willingly. She isn't like Darian. He was an innocent. A hapless baby who let himself be possessed."

"Thanks," Darian muttered.

"Gini," Thyme said with a pointed look, "just because something is true doesn't mean you need to say it out loud."

"You're not helping, Thyme," Adia muttered, but Darian only chuckled under his breath. "And all right, she made a bad decision."

"*A bad decision?*" Thyme sputtered. "She sold her soul, created a mind-controlling substance, handed it over to a demon and got her people killed. Whether she meant to or not, this all started with Sabo and her greed! She basically made Olark what he is today."

"I know," Adia said, "and it's all so horrible that it's almost impossible to wrap my head around the destruction she caused, all because she wanted a crown but...I don't know. Her soul is for ever bound to the demon who killed everyone she ever loved. She's literally spent lifetimes trying to atone for her mistakes. And she could have given me up but instead she hid me and told me where to find the cure. Should one horrible decision decide the fate of your entire *existence* when you're genuinely sorry and trying to make it right? Don't our souls get to evolve if we really try to be better?"

Thyme snorted. "You say that, but you look ready to smash a vase over Nami's head every time you see him. He's falling over himself to apologize to you and make things right. So does his soul get to evolve too?"

Adia's mouth fell open. "I can't believe you're defending him. You can't stand Nami."

Thyme held up her hands. "Don't get me wrong. I'm not saying he deserves a second chance. Far from it. I'm just trying to put things in perspective. You won't trust Nami ever again because he betrayed you and that's more than fair, but you'll trust the High Queen? Someone who did something a whole lot worse?"

Adia fell silent. She didn't want to admit that Thyme had a point. Maybe she was being a bit of a hypocrite to act like everyone who genuinely felt bad about their terrible choices deserved forgiveness except for the people who had wronged *her*. She supposed it was a lot easier to be forgiving when you weren't the person who was harmed.

"All right," Darian said, sensing Adia's turmoil. "Let's leave Nami out of this conversation for now. Sabo may have her own reasons for helping us, but the fact is, she wants to be free of Olark's control. Which means that, by default, she's on our side."

Thyme pursed her lips but gave him a begrudging nod. "The enemy of my enemy is my friend."

"So if we can find her tomb and somehow cure everyone who's ever taken Drops, Olark won't be able to siphon off the energy of the living and return to Zaria," he said. "Except no one has any idea where Sabo is buried."

"And it's not like there really is magical ink that can draw you maps that lead to treasure," Adia sighed.

Gini startled. "What did you say?"

Adia rolled her eyes and waved her hand. "Nothing important. It's just something ridiculous Professor York mentioned on the first day of class."

Mbari stood abruptly and rushed over to Gini. The Alusi began whispering furiously to each other. It went on for several minutes before Darian cleared his throat.

"Anything you two would like to share?" he asked.

"I don't know how Professor York learned about it, but she's not wrong. That ink is real," Gini said. "I've never mentioned its existence because I knew Adia would spend the rest of her life obsessed with finding it. But there's a method of creating maps using ink made from the bones of a bird that no longer exists."

Adia and Thyme looked at each other in shock.

"We thought York was just talking nonsense. You mean it's real?" Thyme asked eagerly. "What kind of bird would have bones that could do something like that?"

"It's quite real," Gini said. "The bones are from a black owl that was known as the greatest oracle of any species to ever live. Highly revered. Killed in a senseless tragedy."

"What happened?" Adia asked.

"Children playing football accidentally whacked her out of a tree with their ball."

Thyme snickered. "The greatest oracle in the known world, killed by a wayward ball?"

"Yes, Thyme, a ball," Gini said with a glare. "Even the greatest of us don't always manage to go out in a blaze of glory."

Thyme's ears bent down in the way they did when she felt chastised. But Adia knew they'd point back up soon enough.

"They were going to cremate the owl and give her a sky burial," Gini continued, "releasing her ashes from the summit of a mountain. But the night before the burial, a sangoma – those are healers and prophets with immense power – in the village received a vision, telling her to crush the owl's bones and mix them with ink. For years the bottle of ink stayed in that elder's hut, until she received another vision telling her to make a map with it."

"So where would this ink be?" Adia asked. "I don't suppose it's as easy as buying it from a market."

"If only," Mbari said. "The person protecting it isn't some vendor doling out trinkets. She's a bone thrower."

"What's that?" Darian asked.

"Throwers can read messages in bones," Adia said, recalling something she'd read in the library last semester. "They throw the bones and see messages in the patterns that fall. Right?"

"That's correct." Gini nodded. "The current guardian is a descendant of the sangoma who received the vision. No doubt she would have grown to be a great one as well if she'd had a teacher, but the Bright Father's missionaries burned all their books and destroyed their teachings long ago. She lives by herself now. Near the Mbari Mines. We keep an eye on her from Alusia."

"Why?" Adia asked.

"She has the greatest collection of power objects in the known world," Gini admitted. "Thankfully Olark has never found out about her. Probably because she does nothing with the vast amount of power in her hut. She seems content simply to keep the objects safe. I imagine she won't be happy to see you or to learn that someone knows her whereabouts, but getting her to make a locator map is our best chance of finding the High Queen's tomb."

"If she's so protective of these objects, what makes you think she'll be willing to help?" Adia asked. "She doesn't even know me."

"She doesn't need all the bone to produce a map," Gini said. "Just a pinch mixed into the ink would be enough. But even that pinch will cost you a fortune. And since you left all the money I gave you in a hollow tree in the Horrorbeyond—"

"She did what?" Mbari sputtered.

"—we'll need to give her something that's worth an equal trade," Gini continued. "Mbari, a gem from your staff should do the trick."

"No," Mbari said, backing away from Gini nervously. "I'd never seen a stone this colour in any of my mines. Which is why I kept it for myself. Give her one of your flowers."

Gini held her flowering staff behind her. "Don't be ridiculous. My flowers are alive. Your stone is just a hunk of rock. Stop being so selfish."

As Gini and Mbari argued, Darian turned to Adia.

"How are you going to explain being away from school for that long? Gini might not care if you take off, but the council will. They're watching your every move."

No kidding, Adia thought, remembering Chobly's chamber of horrors. "Getting out of here won't be a problem," she said. "Trust me. I got expelled my first week at the Academy last year without even trying. Imagine how much faster I can get kicked out when I make an effort."

CHAPTER 16

"You look great, Thyme," Adia said as Thyme adjusted a knife strapped to her ankle. "But I still say you could have added more weapons if you tried."

Thyme gaped at her. "Adia, if even *I'm* telling you to tone it down, you've probably gone too far."

"We have to get thrown out or we'll never make it to the bone thrower for that map," Adia said. "It's our only hope of finding the tomb. Which means there's no such thing as going too far right now. Where's your battleaxe? You're going to have to really cause a scene. I'm talking about beating up three Gold Hats, minimum."

"As long as I can start with Nami," Thyme said with a grin.

Adia opened her mouth to make a similarly snarky comment about Nami, but she realized her heart wasn't in it any more. He'd helped her more than once this semester and was showing zero signs of planning to betray her again. Maybe she was being foolish, but she was warming up to the idea of giving him a second chance.

"Why can't Gini just give us...I don't know. Some sort of field assignment or research that we have to do off campus?" Thyme whispered as they walked into class and took their seats.

"I thought about that too," Adia said. "But Gini said the council would just assign one of its members to come along as chaperone. We have to cut all ties to the Academy so they have no legitimate reason to follow us."

"All right, so I'll start a fight," Thyme said. "But what's your plan?"

"If there's one thing I'm good at, it's getting into trouble. I'll just look at Mallorie wrong and she'll throw a tantrum and accuse me of something. The manipulator shall become the *manipulatee*."

Thyme rolled her eyes. "That's not a word. And you may be good at getting into trouble but most of the time it's by accident. I've never met anyone less likely to pull off a scheme than you. Your face will give everything away. You can't lie to save your life."

"I can do it," Adia said stubbornly. "Just watch."

"Yeah this is going to go terribly," Thyme muttered as Adia rushed into the classroom and made a beeline for Mallorie's desk. Mallorie's jaw dropped as Adia slid in next to her.

"Mallorie. I'm so glad to see you!"

"I – I – what do you want? This is where Wren sits. Wren?!" Mallorie said in a high and panicked voice.

Adia turned around and saw one of the girls who was usually attached to Mallorie's hip staring at them from the back of the room, unsure of what she was supposed to do.

"Oh, I'm sure she'll be fine," Adia said. "It's not like we have assigned seats in this class. Professor York doesn't care."

"You're going to tell everyone about the cat vomit, aren't you?" Mallorie hissed.

"Not if you stop trying to get my cat thrown out of the school," Adia said. "I'm more than happy to keep that incident our little secret."

Mallorie crossed her arms. "What are you up to?"

"Absolutely nothing," Adia said. And she meant it. All she had to do was glue herself to Mallorie's side, sit back and relax, and by the end of the day Mallorie would find some reason to get Adia suspended. It was the perfect plan. Her existence alone was enough to send Mallorie into a rage.

"Good morning, students," Professor York said. "For today's lesson, you'll be working in pairs."

Adia beamed at Mallorie, who scooted her chair away several centimetres.

"I don't want to work with you," Mallorie moaned under her breath. "You're going to put a curse on me."

Adia sighed. "Mallorie, I'm just trying to get through class. Besides, I don't know how to put a curse on anyone. Now pay attention. We're missing the instructions."

Professor York gave them another wrong formula for a tonic to help the symptoms of a cold, and it once again included the tricky to work with Chincherinchee plant, but at least this time York's formula wouldn't harm anyone. Of course, it wouldn't help anyone either. It would just taste disgusting. Mallorie reached over for one of the vials on the tables, then immediately dropped it into her lap.

"Look what Adia did," she wailed.

Normally Adia would be furious, but today it was all she could do not to pump her fist in the air. Mallorie was nothing if not consistent. She seemed confused when Adia didn't point out that she hadn't done anything.

"Mallorie, what are you talking about?" someone behind them whispered. "We all saw you drop it. We're watching Adia so we can copy what she's doing for the assignment."

Adia frowned when she realized every student in the class had their eyes trained on her. She also grimaced when she realized she had instinctively gone for the correct vials and was producing an excellent cough medicine.

"What's this?" Professor York said, her voice clipped. "Adia, are you helping students cheat?"

Adia's jaw dropped. Letting Mallorie throw a tantrum to get her expelled was one thing, but to be accused of helping *these* kids cheat was too much. Her pride couldn't take it.

"Of course not," she said.

But Professor York gave her a stern look. "We'll discuss this after class. Meet me in the headmistress's office. Cheating is a serious offence."

"So the people who were cheating off Adia *without* her permission aren't in trouble?" Thyme said in annoyance from the back of the room.

Professor York pretended that she hadn't heard Thyme and clapped her hands. "All right, everyone, back to work. And eyes on your *own* ingredients."

Adia tossed Thyme an exasperated look as Mallorie leaned back in her chair with a smug expression.

"You might have money now," she said, "but you still don't belong here. Why don't you go back to where you came from and leave us in peace?"

This hadn't gone the way Adia had wanted, but since she was arriving at her intended destination all the same, she held back from pointing out that it was Mallorie's people who'd stomped into Zaria from behind the Sunless Mountains. Mallorie was the foreigner here, not the other way around.

The pair sat in furious silence for the rest of the lecture, and the second class was over, Mallorie stormed out of the room.

Adia paused by Thyme's desk. "Pack your bags if you haven't already. We should be out of here in a few hours. I'll act like a brat in front of Gini and Professor York and make sure Gini has no choice but to suspend me."

"Good," Thyme said. "I'm ready for an adventure. We've been stuck at school for long enough."

Adia nodded, then squared her shoulders as she made the short walk over to Gini's office.

Professor York was already waiting.

"Ms Kelbara," Gini said, her exasperation clear. "Professor York has been giving me an account of today's lesson. I must say, it sounds unbelievable."

"I know, headmistress!" Professor York said.

"No," Gini said. "I mean *your* account sounds unbelievable."

"I— WHAT?" Professor York quickly recovered and gave Gini a placating smile. "Headmistress. You're new here and might need to learn how things go. You see, we professors must stick together. An unshakeable unit in the face of the enemy— I mean, the students. And Ms Kelbara is causing a disturbance in my class."

"In what way?" Adia asked, forgetting for a moment that she *wanted* to get thrown out.

"She's shown a wanton arrogance," Professor York sniffed. "I've been hearing whispers of her holding her own tutoring sessions where she undermines everything I've taught."

Adia gritted her teeth to stop herself from snapping. Underground tutoring session? When all she'd done since she got here was try her best not to engage with any of her classmates? The lies this woman told.

"It's dangerous!" York's voice was full of passion and

theatrics. "These plants are more than just pretty flowers."

Adia couldn't help laugh at that. "You spend half of class making floral arrangements!"

"Plants are where poisons come from," the professor continued. "And who knows what she's creating with her— Her concoctions! She could hurt the other children! I'm afraid there's only one course of action left here."

Adia swallowed her pride. *This is what you wanted*, she reminded herself, even though she could feel herself heating up at the indignity of having to watch a *teacher* behave like such a bully.

"And what course of action is that?" Gini asked, right eyebrow raised.

Adia and Professor York spoke at the same time.

"Suspension!"

"A parent–teacher conference!"

"A *WHAT*?" Adia gasped in shock.

Professor York glared at her. "A parent–teacher conference," she said slowly, as if Adia just hadn't understood the words. "If anything, it's an oversight that we've never met the girl's guardians," Professor York said, eyes gleaming now. "I know Adia came to the Academy under unusual circumstances – though no one can seem to get a straight answer about what exactly it was that she did for Emperor Darian – but it *is* standard practice that we meet the families of our students. So I assume an invitation will be going out to Adia's parents?"

"Her aunt and uncle," Gini said, "not parents."

Gini couldn't be serious. The air left Adia's lungs and all that came out of her mouth was a strangled "guhhhhhhhh" sound.

Professor York scrunched up her face and Gini tutted.

"Good heavens, Adia. What an ungainly sound. Stop that this instant."

But the moan wouldn't stop. Adia flopped over in the chair, the life sucked out of her body.

"Er, Professor York, thank you for your recommendation," Gini stammered as she ushered York out of the room, realizing that Adia was officially useless. "I'll continue disciplining Adia and I'll get back to you about that conference."

When Gini turned back, Adia had grabbed an Academy map off the desk and put it over her head. Maybe she could will herself to vanish underneath it.

Adia had never been so horrified in her life, and she'd spent the last few months in the literal Horrorbeyond. "Gini, you can't invite my uncle and aunt here," she said, her voice small and muffled under the paper.

"Do stop the theatrics," Gini said drily. "It will be inconvenient, to be sure, but I can't pretend I'm not curious to meet whoever raised you. Make sure it wasn't raccoons." She snatched the map off Adia's head. "Besides, it should only delay you by a few days."

"What if we don't have days?" Adia asked. "What if the next time everyone falls asleep is the last?"

"If Olark was that close, we would know. An army of the dead would be at our doorstep. More of them are showing up, yes, but he hasn't amassed enough strength yet or he would have hit us harder," Gini said. "Besides, we can use the time before your family arrives to work on your training. I watched you almost walk into a door because you were staring at one of your classmates' auras."

Adia opened her mouth to protest, but realized she had nothing to say. Gini must be talking about when she'd been staring at Mimi's aura last night at dinner. It had been a nice soft pink and felt playful. For a capital girl, Mimi's truest self appeared to be incredibly kind. And yes, Adia had been so surprised that the capital could produce someone so gentle that she'd almost crashed into a wall. So, fine, maybe she did need to learn how to not walk around seeing everyone's auras.

Gini nodded in satisfaction when she saw that Adia realized she was right.

"We'll figure out another way to get you off campus. Your aunt and uncle might even be useful in that regard. Your punishment for offending York can be suspension. The council won't be able to stop that, and you'll be able to get off the Academy grounds. This might have unintentionally all worked out in our favour, so I don't see what the fuss is about."

"You don't see what all the fuss is about?! One," Adia said, "the Academy is probably going to start tossing forks and knives at Aunt Ife's head the second they step on the grounds. Two, my family are devotees of the Bright Father and are going to call everyone here heretics. Three, Thyme will probably attack them. Four, it'll take days for them to get here and by then the dead might be our new professors. Five—"

"All right, all right," Gini said. "I hear your concern. I'll make sure the Academy is on its best behaviour. As for the rest, well, we'll put out those fires when they arise."

Adia realized there was no point in arguing. It didn't matter what she said. Gini had already decided this was the best course of action. Which meant like it or not, Aunt Ife and Uncle Eric were coming to the Academy of Shamans.

CHAPTER 17

Adia spent the next three days wanting to jump out of her skin, she was so impatient for her aunt and uncle to arrive. She'd channelled her frustration into her training with Gini, and now knew how to control her breath and slow her heart rate down so that she wasn't seeing auras everywhere she looked. But she was still annoyed by the delay. A suspension would have meant getting out of the Academy right away. Instead she had to spend three days watching everyone collapse all around her.

Yesterday had been particularly terrifying. Everyone had fallen asleep in the middle of breakfast and hadn't woken up until almost bedtime. She'd had a deep moment of panic when she'd thought this was it – that the convergence of the realms of the living and the dead was upon them and they would never wake up again. Olark was getting too close. She'd been so happy when she'd heard Mallorie Amber shrieking, she'd almost given her mortal enemy a hug.

So when Lebechi sent word that she'd seen Adia's aunt and uncle's ship docked in the Macobar Jetty when she'd been gone that morning to pick up the Academy's fish delivery, Adia had rushed to Gini's office. She tapped her foot impatiently as she waited for everyone to arrive.

She shot up when the door finally opened and a Gold Hat entered.

"I'll find the headmistress and let her know you've arrived," the Gold Hat said, moving aside so that Adia could see her aunt and uncle. Uncle Eric was the first one in. Adia took a step back in confusion as he charged at her with open arms.

"Beloved niece," Uncle Eric bellowed, engulfing Adia in the world's most awkward hug. Her arms hung limply at her sides as she peered around his shoulder. Aunt Ife was giving her husband a cold look, but she plastered a smile on her face when she saw Adia.

"Adia," Ife said, walking over to her. Adia hesitated for a second but decided to return her aunt's hug. Uncle Eric had already proven he'd sell all her secrets for the right price, but Adia knew Aunt Ife would try to protect her if it came down to it. Not out of any fondness for her, but unlike Uncle Eric, the blood connection with her half-sister's daughter did seem to imbue Aunt Ife with some level of familial obligation not to feed her to the wolves.

"We're so excited to see you and hear how you've been doing. A bit surprised you're not wearing a fancier get-up,"

Uncle Eric said, frowning. "All that money the emperor's given you, I thought you'd buy yourself some nice clothes."

"It's a school uniform," Adia said slowly as she realized why Uncle Eric was suddenly so friendly.

The money. He wasn't going to leave her alone until he had control of it.

"Oh, of course, of course," he said. "Ericson and EJ could use new uniforms too. I wish we could afford to get them some. Money's been tight, what with paying for repairs to the house after you destroyed..." His voice trailed off as he gave Adia a sly look. "After that earthquake last year destroyed the roof."

Adia wasn't going to let Uncle Eric see that he was rattling her. All right, maybe she *did* owe them some money for repairs. But she'd be handing that money over to Aunt Ife, not him.

"And where is EJ?" Adia asked, quickly changing the subject. "He didn't come with you?"

"No," Aunt Ife said. "I didn't want to leave him at home, but given what happened to him here, we thought it might upset him to come along."

"Yes, terrible misunderstanding that," Uncle Eric said, ignoring Aunt Ife when she glared at him. "Of course the missionaries never meant to take EJ or declare him dead. And they paid us compensation for our pain and suffering while he was gone."

"So why is the roof still a mess?" Adia said bluntly, but as always, Uncle Eric pretended she hadn't spoken.

"It all worked out in the end," Uncle Eric carried on. "We got the boy back, didn't we, Ife? Best to leave the past in the past. And he needed to toughen up anyway. The whole ordeal seems to have made him a bit stronger at any rate."

Adia caught her aunt's stormy expression. It seemed her relatives weren't on the same page about what had happened to EJ. Or at least they disagreed about what they were going to admit out loud. But she couldn't imagine Aunt Ife still held the same high opinion of the missionaries once the son they'd declared dead had turned up over a year later after being held captive.

"Shame it took you so long to invite us here," Uncle Eric said, looking around.

"I didn't invite you and you didn't even want to let me come here," Adia said, exasperated. "Why would I invite you when I had to run away to attend in the first place? Besides, you hate shamans."

"You're not a shaman," he said, finally losing the fake smile. "You think I don't know what this school is? Capital brats who want to be special, and I guess you want that too. The shamans were thrown out of Zaria ages ago, and good riddance. It's time to move into the future with the rest of the world. But if the nobles have decided the old customs are 'magical'," he said, waggling his fingers, "then by all means let them have them. It's not like they have any of that power in their blood. No more than you do."

"Eric," Aunt Ife said in a clipped tone. "Why don't you go see if you can find Headmistress Inika and tell her Adia is here. Or alert some teacher to our presence. You said we'd be here no more than two days. I don't want to leave EJ on his own for too long."

"What?" Uncle Eric said. "Oh, right. Guess we should get on with it. But, Adia, we'll need to have a talk. You're far too young to manage all this money I hear you got for whatever it is you did for the emperor. We're going to have to make sure this is done through the proper channels and that your guardians are the ones in control of your fortune. To make sure you're protected, of course."

With that, he left Adia alone with her aunt.

"Are you safe here?" Aunt Ife said briskly. "You're not being harmed in any way?"

Adia blinked but quickly shook her head.

"No, it's all right, I'm safe," she said. "Well, as safe as I can be."

"And your abilities? Are you able to control them?"

Adia fell silent, and Aunt Ife sighed. "I'd hoped I was just imagining it. For your own sake. But I knew you were like your mother the first moment I laid eyes on you."

Adia's heart skipped a beat. Aunt Ife never talked about her mother. And since she'd died when Adia was barely two years old, she didn't have any of her own memories to go on.

"What could she do?" Adia asked.

Aunt Ife swallowed and walked over to the desk, touching a melted candle.

"Zina could look into a flame and start telling you things no one had any right to know about a person. But it only happened when she had access to fire. It was like she was reading the pages of a book. She'd get this dreamy look on her face and her voice wouldn't even sound like her own... Half the time she didn't even remember what she'd said."

Adia was startled. So Chobly's research was right.

"Zina was always an odd fish," Aunt Ife said, "but she was kind. Kinder than I ever was. And so clever. I resented her for it. Strange as she was, everyone liked her. Except my mother. Zina's mother – your grandmother – was our father's first wife and she died giving birth to your mother."

Adia listened intently. This was more information than Aunt Ife had ever given her about her family. She was afraid to interrupt with questions and risk annoying her aunt and making her stop.

"He married my mother a few months later. She raised Zina since she was a baby but never treated her like a child of her own. Especially not after she had me. In the end Zina did exactly what you did."

Adia frowned. "Did what?"

"Ran away," Ife said, her expression surprisingly sad. "She sent me letters, though. Not a lot. She told me when she got married. Wrote to me when you were born. And sent one final letter when she realized you were most likely going to be orphaned after she and her husband, your father, caught the sleeping sickness that was running rampant through their village. I arrived too late. I didn't get to say goodbye. I was in time to stop them from carting you off to an orphanage, but I didn't do right by you, did I?"

Adia wasn't going to lie to assuage whatever guilt her aunt was currently feeling. No, Aunt Ife hadn't done right by her. She hadn't treated Adia like one of her own. Same as her mother must have been made to feel like some unwanted stepchild. But Adia wasn't heartless, and she could tell Aunt Ife's regret was genuine.

"You kept me alive and fed," she said with a shrug. "Not everyone's half-aunt would have done that."

Aunt Ife gave her a dejected look. Not exactly a high compliment for a woman who'd once prided herself on being the picture of piety.

"I overheard some of the Gold Hats talking about students losing consciousness. It's been happening in the Swamplands too. No one really believes what they're saying about toxic gas. I don't suppose you know anything about that?"

Adia hardly considered Aunt Ife a confidante, but maybe there was some chance of salvaging their relationship one day, if they both reached out a hand to try. And it felt like Aunt Ife wanted to try.

"Not really," Adia said, unwilling to say too much. "But our headmistress is incredibly powerful. She thinks there's a cure and...and she's got people working on it. I have faith that this will be over pretty soon."

Aunt Ife frowned. "I hope you're not one of those people working on this. You're just a child, Adia. Leave finding a cure to the physicians in the capital. What exactly does this headmistress of yours have you doing at this school? I assume she knows you have true power. You need to be more careful. People will want to use you for their own gain."

Before Adia could respond to what she had to admit was a practical warning from her aunt, Uncle Eric burst back into the room, followed by a very annoyed-looking Gini.

"Ife, this is Inika, the headmistress. We had a nice chat on the walk over."

Ife stood up. "Has everything been cleared up?" she asked.

"Oh yes," Gini said. "I've assured your husband that soon enough, he'll get everything that he deserves."

Uncle Eric was too clueless to notice Gini's sarcastic phrasing.

"We'll be leaving straight away on tomorrow's ship then," he said. "You've seen that the girl is all right, Ife. And Headmistress Inika, it was wonderful getting to know you.

I look forward to my reward for being the guardian of the girl who saved the emperor."

Adia couldn't help snorting in disgust. She didn't know what Gini had said to make Uncle Eric think he was getting any sort of reward and she didn't care. As long as he got her out of there.

Aunt Ife looked just as relieved. "That's good. I want to get back to EJ as soon as possible."

"Oh, stop worrying. We left Ericson in charge."

"That's what I'm afraid of," Aunt Ife snapped as Adia raised an eyebrow. Maybe after the trauma of losing EJ for a year her aunt had finally decided to do something about her other son's relentless bullying. Just because Ericson was EJ's brother and Adia's cousin didn't make him any less their tormentor. And his parents had never said a word about it as he shoved EJ and Adia around and punched them in the arm for no reason when no one was looking.

"You go on ahead," Eric said. "There's someone else here I need to speak with."

Adia glared at him. He was probably going to find Mr Chobly next to see what he could get out of the council member. Uncle Eric went to open the door and frowned in confusion when it opened by itself. Then sniffed when he saw Thyme standing there. "Another delinquent, I assume," he muttered as he walked by, Aunt Ife trailing after him.

Thyme scrunched up her face as she stared after Adia's

unfortunate relations. "He seems nice," she said, her voice dripping with sarcasm.

"Indeed," Gini murmured. "I must say, it was a fascinating experience. My brief conversation with your uncle appears to have given me my first headache. I'm always fascinated when this body feels things the way a mortal would. Did you just walk around with your head in pain for the first twelve years of your life?"

"I found ways to avoid being home for too long," Adia admitted. "Was he that bad?"

Gini gave a dry laugh. "Professor York happened upon us and gave him her version of the story. The way she was carrying on you'd think you stabbed a student with a pencil. I can't believe this is who your people allow to be teachers. That bully of a woman is angry because you intimidate her."

Adia was surprised. She'd assumed that was why York hated her, but she hadn't expected a grown-up to admit that sometimes a teacher was the worst bully a student had to deal with. But Gini wasn't exactly a grown-up. She was a goddess, and an honest one at that.

"But your uncle was more concerned with me writing a statement about you being an incompetent and disturbed child to support his case that he be allowed full control of your money."

"Of course he was," Adia said drily.

"But it's all worked out. You have a ticket on tomorrow's

boat. You won't have me or Mbari to protect you, but I threw Thyme out too, so she'll be on the boat with you. Your uncle's agreed to watch her on the boat and hand her off to her parents. I'm sure she'll figure out a way to slip away before that point."

"It won't be necessary," Adia said. "If I know my aunt and uncle – and I do – they won't be paying any attention to her either way. When do we leave?"

"Tomorrow morning on the first ship," Gini said. "I hope I'm making the right decision letting you go alone."

"I don't need Alusi babysitters, you know," Adia said. "Not that I'm not grateful, but you can't spend the next eighty years taking turns coming to Zaria just to be with me."

"We won't do this for ever," Gini agreed. "Just until Olark is officially wiped from existence and you're safe. Now go pack."

As Adia headed back to her room to pack, she was surprised to feel a twinge of sadness at leaving. She didn't know when it happened, but the Academy felt like her home. Even more so than the Horrorbeyond.

She walked a little off the trail so she could say goodbye to the forest behind the school. She hadn't planned to go too deep, but a movement caught her eye. There was a chasm up ahead. She hoped it was just an animal, rather than a corpse or student who'd fallen in. But on the off chance it was the latter, she quickened her steps and went to check. When she saw who it was, she immediately froze and ducked behind a tree.

When Uncle Eric had said he needed to speak with

someone else, she'd assumed he was going to find Mr Chobly to sell more of her secrets. So why was he out here in the forest all by himself?

"What's going on?" someone whispered behind her.

Adia spun around and slapped her hand over Nami's mouth. His eyes went wide, and he nodded. She slowly lifted her hand, praying he'd be able to keep his mouth shut for more than thirty seconds. She ducked back down and had no choice but to let Nami duck beside her. What was her uncle doing? She tried to open her new vision but nothing happened. Maybe she needed to be closer to someone to get a read on their aura. Every time she'd done it before she'd been within an arm's length of the person.

Barriers were placed around the crack that now ran through the Academy grounds to stop any unwitting students from falling into the newest chasm. Uncle Eric paced up and down along the crack.

Adia bent the branches of the tree down, further hiding her and Nami from view. Nami gaped as he realized she, and not the wind, was making the tree move, but he managed not to squawk about it. She peered between the brown and red leaves and watched her uncle. He glanced around him, and when he was satisfied no one was watching, he ducked under the rope and moved closer to the chasm.

A bench uprooted itself, looking as if it was about to hurl itself at Uncle Eric's head.

"Hang on," Adia whispered urgently, hoping the bench would calm itself.

She fully understood why the Academy would attack Uncle Eric just as it attacked the students, but she needed to see what he was up to without any antics from the school. She almost swore she could hear the bench sigh in annoyance, but it lowered itself back to the ground and made itself look like the inanimate object it was supposed to be.

Uncle Eric was none the wiser that a piece of outdoor furniture had almost knocked him out as he knelt and touched the ground. He picked up a handful of dirt and let it fall through his fingers, whispering something as he did. Then he lifted his hands up above his head before clasping his palms together as if in prayer. Just when Adia thought this couldn't get any stranger, he took a small vial out of his pocket. Adia was close enough that she could see gold liquid. He spilled the Drops into the chasm, then touched his lips to the ground before rising to his feet and heading back off the trail.

She held her breath as her uncle walked past their hiding spot and didn't breathe again until she was sure he was out of earshot.

"What was that?" Nami said, aghast. "It was like he was doing some sort of ritual. But he's not a professor. The Gold Hats memorize the faces of every teacher and student here so we can spot intruders and I've never seen him before."

Adia cautiously walked over to the chasm, Nami annoyingly close on her heels.

"He's my uncle," she said as she ducked under the rope to stand where Uncle Eric had just been. She rolled her eyes. Of course Uncle Eric had left the vial on the ground instead of throwing it away. On top of being the worst, he would also think nothing of polluting a forest. She knelt down and picked up the small bottle. It was still half full. This was the first time she'd seen Drops in its new form. She'd have to examine it later.

"That doesn't explain what he was just doing," Nami said.

No. It didn't. Putting the vial in her pocket, Adia leaned forwards on her hands and knees and stared down into the chasm and thought about everything she knew about her uncle, but quickly realized that wasn't much. He had a temper, her violent cousin Ericson was his clear favourite, and she and EJ had never been treated as anything more than annoying bugs he was forced to live with. He did as the missionaries said but had never been as pious as Aunt Ife. He even grumbled at the end of every week when the missionaries showed up to collect their tithe for the Bright Father.

Could Uncle Eric really have hidden something like this from all of them? That he was a disciple of Olark?

She supposed it was possible. There were seven hours of the day when she and EJ and Ericson had been in school. Who knew what messes adults got up to when their kids weren't around. And Aunt Ife spent a lot of time with her church friends gossiping about everyone, so it wasn't like she and Uncle Eric spent every second of the day together. It was more than possible that he had a secret life.

But dabbling in the dark arts?

Maybe she was jumping to conclusions, but everyone else kept a healthy distance from the chasms. Uncle Eric looked as if he was worshipping it.

"Adia?" Nami said, interrupting her thoughts.

"I have to go," she said, pushing herself up and dusting the dirt off her hands. This wasn't safe. She didn't know what she was dealing with, but who knew what Uncle Eric would do if he caught her spying on him. And Nami didn't need to be involved in this any more than Thyme did. He might not be her friend any more, but she didn't want him, or anyone, to get hurt.

As soon as she was sure Nami wasn't following her, Adia squared her shoulders. She had one more night left at the Academy and she knew how she was going to spend it. If Uncle Eric was communicating with the dead, it was time she did too.

CHAPTER 18

Adia didn't know the first thing about how to hold a seance, but she knew now that she could call spirits to her through flames. Which meant building a fire was the first place to start. The site of her initiation seemed like the best place to do it since it seemed to be an easy access point into different realms. So she'd made the long walk back to the ruins. She was putting logs in a pile when footsteps crunched behind her.

"Darian," she said. No matter how hard she tried to sneak off by herself, either her friends or an Alusi always seemed to track her down. She didn't have to look around to know this was Darian. At first, post-initiation, Adia had thought she could only see people's auras. But she was starting to realize that she could also *feel* the presence of the people she was closest to. That must be how she'd still been able to hear them in the Underworld. Although...Nami had been one of those people she could feel too. She shook off that thought as

Darian sat next to her. She didn't look at him. Just kept on putting logs into a pile as he gazed around at the ruins.

"How'd you know it was me and not a corpse?" he asked.

"Remember what I told you about seeing an aura when I look at people now? It was something like that."

Darian looked at her curiously.

"So what do you see when you look at me?"

Adia hesitated. She shouldn't have brought this up. Darian's aura *was* different. She just didn't know how he'd handle hearing about it.

"Well..." she began. "It's like everyone else's but...there are also specks of stardust falling off you, like Gini's."

Darian didn't say anything for a minute. He just stared down at the logs. Adia was about to ask if he was all right when he seemed to recover his voice.

"Do you think it's because of Olark?" he asked. "He may be a demon, but he *is* star born."

"That's what I was wondering too," Adia admitted.

A flash of anger went through Darian's face. "So there is some part of him that still lives in me," he said in disgust.

"We can't be certain that's what this is," Adia said quickly. She hated seeing Darian so upset. Something in her voice must have made him worried because his expression immediately went from disgust to concern.

"I'm not the only one he possessed," Darian said, gesturing to her. "What about you? Can you see your own aura?"

She shook her head. "I'm just myself when I look in the mirror. No otherworldly hazes around me." She took a deep breath. Maybe she couldn't see it, but who's to say Olark hadn't done something to her and Darian's souls? Warped them in some way. "Have you felt different in any way since the exorcism? Anything strange?"

Darian looked solemn.

"Yes," he said slowly. "But I think it'd be stranger if we didn't feel any different after going through something like that, don't you?"

She did, but she also couldn't shake the fear that one day, the side effects of their possessions would come out.

"We'll figure it out," he said. "We're going to be all right. One of these days we'll be all right."

Adia stared at the ground.

"I hope so," she said in a small voice. But then she cleared her throat and straightened her shoulders. There was no time for this. "You should head back."

"Not until you tell me what you're doing out here," he said gently.

Adia stopped fiddling with the logs. "I'm going to journey again. I'm going to try to call Sabo's spirit to me." She quickly told him about Uncle Eric's strange behaviour. "I doubt she's ever seen Olark's shaman face to face, but maybe if I describe Uncle Eric she'll know if it's him. And I'm still not sure about Chobly either. I need to know which one of them I'm dealing with. All I know is that I'm being watched and followed, and even if I make it to Sabo's tomb one of them will probably be right on my heels and destroy the cure before I can get to it."

Speaking of the cure...Adia remembered the vial in her pocket. She pulled it out and opened it, taking a sniff. She made a face at the foul odour and grimaced as some of it got on her fingers. "Do you have a handkerchief?"

Darian made a sound of disbelief as he dug around in his pocket. "The last time you went to talk to spirits you almost didn't wake up. And you came out here for round two? By yourself?!"

"It won't be like last time," Adia said with a calmness she didn't really feel as she wiped her hands. She tried to give the handkerchief back to Darian but he shuddered.

"Just burn it," he said.

Adia tossed the cloth into the logs. "I know how to get out of it now. Olark's shaman won't be able to trap me down there again. You can stay or leave, but I'm doing this." She struck a match and lit the kindling she'd stuffed into the pile of logs, but the wood must have been damper than she realized because the fire wouldn't catch. She tilted her head. At orientation Gini had had fire spirits blow out the candles. She closed her eyes and reached out the same way she did when she connected with plants – but this time, she called to the spirit of fire. A wave of heat washed over her. Unlike the times when she'd overheated because she was angry, this wasn't an uncomfortable heat. She took a deep breath as she felt some of her stress and panic burn away. Maybe fire could be cleansing.

Darian gasped as flames began to crackle.

It was working! Adia let her power come to her hands, holding up her fingers as purple sparks flew from them. She swallowed and stuck a digit into the smoke. It swirled around her finger, faster and faster. It was a hot, humid night, and she was sitting directly in front of a roaring fire, yet wherever her hand was, it was cold. One part of her body was in another realm.

The thought made her pause. If she ever saw a hand floating in the air her first inclination would probably be to fling a knife at it. But just as she moved to pull herself back, her finger brushed up against something. Some*one*.

Adia gasped as she felt dozens of hands grabbing at her and heard multiple voices murmuring. All speaking at once, trying to get her attention. It was overwhelming. Somewhere in all the noise, she heard Darian's voice too, but he sounded so far away. Everything fell away, and she found herself sitting in a dark and empty void. She had done it. She was in the realm of spirit. But this time, she could still feel the earth beneath her. She was walking in between two realms. Her soul was somewhere else, but unlike last time she was still aware and somewhat in control of her body.

"A little shaman," one whispered. "So much power." She slapped that one away. Not all the spirits flinging themselves at her felt malevolent, but that one had.

"Get away from me," she said, hoping her refusal to speak to it would get the spirit to leave her alone – but another soon replaced it. This one was just a roar in her head, like an angry lion. Several others were speaking in tongues she didn't understand.

It was too much. "I can't help all of you," Adia said, pulling herself back, terrified of these hungry spirits. Her soul flung itself back into her body with so much force that she would have toppled over if Darian hadn't caught her.

"What happened?" he asked anxiously. "Did you...stars save me!"

Adia followed his horrified stare. The ground was splitting open. He grabbed her and dragged her back as the small crack quickly grew and a hand rose up from the earth. Adia gasped as she realized what was happening. Darian pulled out his sword, but Adia put a hand on his arm.

"Wait," she said, staring intently as the corpse crawled its way up to the surface.

"Adia Kelbara," the corpse whispered.

Adia refused to be afraid. If she needed to, she would call every plant and root in the area to her to drag this body back into the ground.

"We need your eyes. The High Queen needs..."

The corpse glanced at Adia's hands, tilting its head at the purple glow and giving her a look of understanding.

"You summoned me," the corpse said in shock. "You're in control this time, not the other one. Very well. How do you command me, Master?"

"How dare you," she gasped. "*I'm* not your master."

"You summoned me," the corpse repeated, climbing up until it was on the ground with Adia. "Same as the other one. I don't come to you freely. Duelling shamans, disturbing the dead to use us in your war. The other one wants me to gouge out your eyes. What do *you* want? For me to bring you the other's tongue?"

"Duelling shamans?" Adia repeated in disbelief. "I'm not duelling with anyone and I'm not after anyone's appendages. I'm just trying to stay alive and keep *you* dead."

The corpse glared at her, its disbelief plain. Adia's first reaction when she'd seen this person was terror and anger, but now she was filled with pity. The dead wanted no part in this. They were being used as puppets, just as Darian had been when he was possessed.

"Who is the other shaman who summons you?" Adia asked. "I promise I have no interest in being your master or disturbing your peace. I'm trying to stop this. So if there's anything you know that can help me..."

The corpse considered her for a moment then nodded. "I don't know their name," the corpse said. "But four months ago a great darkness entered the realm of death. You know the darkness of which I speak. It's touched you, I can see it." The corpse seemed to delight in trying to scare her, but Adia wasn't having it. She might have been touched by Olark's power but she had never stopped fighting to make sure she was the one in control of her soul.

"How can I stop it?" she asked. "I want to help you."

"Then wake everyone up. When they sleep, we rise. We feed from them. Right now, dozens of the dead just rose because you put everyone to sleep."

Adia recoiled in horror. "That's not possible. I don't have that kind of power."

"Maybe you don't, but the High Queen does. And you used her formula to call me."

"Used her formula?"

The handkerchief. She'd added Drops to the fire. Everyone at the Academy was probably passed out right now because a corpse had been reanimated. And this time, *she'd* done it.

She ran forwards and stomped out the flames. "Wake up," she whispered. "Everyone, wake up."

She turned back to the corpse. It was staring at its hands, which were quickly turning into dust. But it spoke one last time.

"He knows you spoke to the High Queen. If you want any chance of saving us, you must get to the cure before he does."

"Go in peace," Adia whispered as the corpse disintegrated.

Darian walked over to the pile of dust. He stared down at it before looking up at Adia, but she couldn't meet his eyes. She had just reanimated the dead. Which meant that whoever Olark's shaman was, she was rapidly beginning to catch up to them in terms of power. And she didn't like that one bit.

CHAPTER 19

By the time they got back to the Academy, everyone was up and wandering the halls in confusion. Adia guiltily avoided making eye contact with any of her groggy schoolmates. Darian had taken a hidden passageway to get to Adia and Thyme's suite, but she didn't think anyone would have even noticed if the emperor was suddenly a part of the student body. That's how chaotic the Academy was right now.

Adia knew Darian would be waiting for her and that Thyme would be frantic when he told her what Adia had just done, but she couldn't face them just yet. Or their disappointment that she'd been so reckless. She was disappointed too. It was officially embarrassing to realize she had no control over what she was doing – to the point that she hadn't realized she'd caused hundreds of students to lose consciousness. But at least she'd been the one in control this time and only raised one corpse. And when she'd got rid of it, everyone had woken up within minutes instead of being knocked out all day.

"I've had enough!" Mallorie Amber screamed, forcing Adia to look up from the floor. It's not like anyone could ignore the sound of Mallorie's high-pitched, nasal voice. "Where's the headmistress? I'm sending a message to Daddy and telling him to get me out of here. If there really is poisonous gas, then we need to be evacuated. If the capital knew what was going on they'd level this school to the ground. I'm getting out of here before I end up dead."

Adia winced. Mallorie wasn't exactly wrong. No, it wasn't poisonous gas, but they didn't know that. For all intents and purposes, the Academy looked like it had gone from flinging students out of chairs to outright poisoning them. She had to find Gini. The Academy wasn't to blame for any of this; she didn't want it to be marked for demolition because it was deemed a toxic site. Speaking of toxic...Mallorie smelled absolutely awful.

She began to speed-walk, passing Mallorie as quickly as she could, to get away from both the sound of her voice, and also from the incredible odour coming off the Academy's resident spoiled princess.

"What are you doing, Kelbara?" Mallorie snapped, breaking into a run, leaving Adia no choice but to do the same.

"I'm doing the same as you," Adia said, dodging Mallorie's arm as the blond girl tried to elbow her out of the way.

"I need to talk to the headmistress."

"If you think you're getting out of here before me you're mistaken," Mallorie said, moving to stomp on Adia's foot.

"Mallorie, I swear to the stars I will rip your hair out," Adia said, jumping out of the way of Mallorie's pointy boot.

"Headmistress Inika!"

"Gini!"

Both girls banged on Gini's door for only a second before the door opened on its own, forcing them to tumble inside the room, one on top of the other.

"So unseemly," Gini said with a sniff as Adia and Mallorie clambered over each other trying to stand up.

"Headmistress, I demand that a letter about the unsafe living conditions at this school be sent to my father at once," Mallorie said, shoving Adia aside. "Do you hear me? I said at once!"

"I heard you," Gini said drily. "The dead probably heard you. Miss Amber, I assure you your parents have already been notified that there is a situation at the Academy and that we're putting every possible safety measure in place."

"Safety measures? Do you know where I just woke up? I went to the stables to make sure my horse had been brushed before bed and next thing I know, I'm lying in the middle of a pile of...a pile of..." Mallorie turned red, unable to admit where she'd fallen asleep.

Adia snorted. "Is that what that smell is?" she asked. "I

thought you were trying out another beauty treatment. Honestly, Mallorie, instead of screaming at teachers you really should go take a bath. You smell horrible."

Adia ducked as Mallorie grabbed a heavy book off the table and hurled it at her head. A curtain flung itself forwards and quickly rolled itself up into something that resembled a bat, whacking the book out of Adia's way.

"Miss Amber," Gini said through gritted teeth. "I have to agree with Miss Kelbara. Go clean yourself up and calm yourself down. We can speak tomorrow."

"No," Mallorie said, stomping her foot. "No, no, NO. I came to this school to learn magic and I get treated worse than a servant. If I'm not going to learn any spells, then I'm going home. For ever."

"Is that a promise?" Adia asked, ignoring Gini's glare. She knew she wasn't helping, but Mallorie was so annoying. "The only time I have any peace is when you're knocked out. I'd love for that to be all the time, not just when I'm watching you drool into your salad."

Mallorie paused mid-tantrum. "What do you mean you have peace when I'm knocked out?"

Adia's stomach dropped as she realized what she'd just admitted.

Mallorie's eyes narrowed as she stared at Adia. "Are you saying you don't pass out?"

The girl was shrewder than Adia had given her credit for.

"You don't pass out because this isn't some poisonous gas. It's something...shamanic."

"I just misspoke," Adia said, though she could tell Mallorie wasn't buying it. "I meant I have peace because I'm passed out too."

"No, I don't think that's what you meant at all," Mallorie said slowly. "And you came racing here to the headmistress's office because she knows what's going on too." She stared at Gini. "All right, now that I know I'm not actually being poisoned to death, I'll keep everyone else calm. Because if you haven't noticed, you're about to have a riot on your hands. But they'll listen to me if I tell them not to worry."

"And what do you want in return?" Adia asked. "Because I know you're not doing this out of the generosity of your own heart."

Mallorie shrugged. "Would you knowingly get involved in something dangerous without asking for something in return?"

Adia winced. No. She wouldn't. But she wasn't going to tell Mallorie that her own fortune was payment for helping save Darian. Thankfully, Darian had just laughed when she told him she'd negotiated a fee before agreeing to help Gini exorcise him.

"So what do you want?" Adia asked.

"For now," Mallorie said, "a guarantee that if you can't put a stop to this, I'll be put on the first ship out of here."

"I guarantee that you will be the first student I remove from the Academy grounds," Gini said. Something told Adia that Mallorie would have been on that first ship anyway, just to spare them all a headache.

Mallorie nodded. "That'll do for now. I'm sure I'll need other favours soon enough. Now if you'll excuse me, I need to...see to my toilette."

Adia rolled her eyes and mumbled under her breath. "See to her toilette. Fancy way of saying you need to take a bath because you're covered in horse—"

"Adia," Gini said warningly as Mallorie flounced away. "Finally. A moment of peace. And why are you in my office?"

Mallorie's tantrum had sucked Adia of all her energy. She suddenly felt too ashamed to admit to Gini that she'd been the one to cause the blackout this time.

"I just saw Mallorie in a huff and thought you might need reinforcements."

"Mallorie's not the first spoiled princess I've encountered," Gini said with a wave of her hand. "Go on now. Try to get some sleep. You have a long boat ride ahead of you."

Adia nodded and slunk out of Gini's office, but she didn't feel like going to her room just yet. Everyone was still in the halls. Mallorie wasn't the only one desperate to go home. A few of the teachers were tearfully saying the same thing as everyone wandered around in their pyjamas, trying to figure out a way to get out of here.

"Adia, tell us what's going on!" Rusty shouted.

Adia sped up and turned a corner. She couldn't handle this right now. She made a beeline for a curtain that covered a hidden door and closed it shut just before Rusty reached her.

"She vanished!" he yelled. "She can turn herself invisible. I told you she's a witch."

"Ugh," Adia said in disgust as she stormed down the passageway as fast as she could.

She didn't have a particular destination in mind and just wandered around the Academy grounds for a while, grateful to have a moment to herself, even if it was a chilly night. But then she found herself standing outside the library enclave. Maybe she'd just sleep here tonight, she thought as she opened the gate. If she went back to her room, Rusty might break down the door trying to find out how she'd made herself "invisible". But she'd only taken a few steps when a chill went through her. She turned as a shadow moved from behind a tree and swallowed nervously when she saw who it was.

"Mr Chobly," she said. "I didn't mean to disturb you." So this was what instant regret felt like. She should have gone to her room just like Gini said, not wandered out into the night.

"Oh, you're not disturbing me," Chobly said. "In fact, I saw you heading in this direction and decided to take the opportunity to speak with you. I just learned the most fascinating thing from one of your friends."

Adia blinked. Her heart sank. Had she behaved like a complete fool again thinking she could trust Nami? No. He wouldn't. He knew she was going to help his mother. Nami would have no reason to betray her.

"Miss Mallorie Amber," Chobly said.

Adia gasped. "*Mallorie?* Mallorie's not my friend."

"Oh no?" Chobly said, his voice full of fake confusion. "She just rushed up to me out of such concern for you. And she told me the most astonishing thing."

Adia's stomach dropped. Of course. She'd spent so much time worrying about Nami betraying her again that she'd forgotten to take the most vicious person in this school seriously. Mallorie knew what Nami didn't. And she hadn't even been able to go a full hour without blabbing.

"You're immune to the sleeping sickness that's overrun Zaria," Chobly said, confirming Adia's suspicions.

Adia gave a laugh that sounded hollow even to her own ears.

"Mallorie loves to make up stories," Adia said, but it was pointless. He knew.

"I'm sure that's true," Chobly said. "But I don't think she's lying about this. Which makes me think one of two things. Either you really are as special as Emperor Darian seems to think, and your powers make you immune to illness, perhaps even impervious to pain—"

"That's ridiculous," Adia gasped.

"Or," Chobly said, ignoring her, "you're immune because you're the one who's causing this."

Adia couldn't even blame him for thinking that. If she were in his shoes, and if Chobly *really* didn't have anything to do with this, she'd be her number one suspect too.

"Of course I'm not causing this," Adia said. "I'm doing everything I can to try to *fix* it. That's why I'm always in the library trying to look for information about a cure."

To her surprise, Mr Chobly nodded.

"I didn't think you were," he agreed. "But I do believe you're immune. And as such, you need to be studied."

"Studied?" Adia said slowly.

Chobly cleared his throat.

"Perhaps that was the wrong word. What I should have said was, examined by physicians. In fact, I've wanted to have you examined for a long time. Think about it, Ms Kelbara. You say you want to help. That you're in the library combing books for answers. But what if the answer is inside you? What if your blood carries the antidote to this sleeping sickness plaguing the land?"

Now Adia was frightened. This man wasn't Olark's shaman. And he didn't want to use her shamanic ability for himself. He wanted to dissect her and see how she ticked. That frightened her more than all the reanimated corpses in all the world.

"Don't you want to help your friends? Your family? Your

kingdom?" Chobly asked. "Of course you do. And don't worry. I'll be there the entire time. You'll have nothing to worry about. It will be like any other examination you've ever had."

"No," Adia said. "You can't examine me without my permission."

"You're a child," Chobly snapped. "I don't need *your* permission. Your uncle has proven himself quite amenable to my cause."

"You mean he's easily bought," Adia snapped back.

Chobly took a step closer. "We both know he's going to give his permission so why not make things easier on all of us and agree to come with me willingly?"

"I'll never go with you," Adia said. The gate to the library suddenly opened itself so forcefully that a few bolts fell off. She dashed forward, but Chobly grabbed her before she could make her escape. Terrified, she didn't think as she called her power to her.

"What?" Chobly gasped as an agrias vine wrapped around his wrist, pulling him off her. His eyes went wide as he stared at Adia, whose hands were now glowing purple. She pointed a finger, and two more vines shot forward, wrapping them around Chobly's legs, causing him to fall. When she looked at him, she'd expected to see fear and confusion. What she saw instead made her blood run cold. Triumph. He started to laugh. "I knew it! You command the elements."

Adia turned and ran. She had nothing on her. No food, no

money, not even Bubbles, but she didn't care. She couldn't stay at the Academy for another second.

She ran through the yard, past the dorms and the kitchens, and right out the front gate, into the darkness.

CHAPTER 20

Adia shivered as she crawled out of the corner she'd slept in at the docks. The rain and wind had made it a miserable night, but it must have stopped at some point. Her clothes were damp and her nose was runny but the sun had finally appeared. She couldn't help the loud sneeze that came out of her mouth as she stood up. "Bless you," a dry voice said.

Adia jumped up and turned to see a furious-looking Darian and Thyme.

"We spent all night searching the Academy until we finally realized you weren't there," Darian said. "Then we spent the last few hours tracking you here."

Adia stepped back. She'd never seen Darian angry before. "You left without telling any of us. Without saying goodbye. What were you thinking? That you were going to find the High Queen's tomb all by yourself? You don't even know where to go!"

Everything he said was accurate, but Adia straightened her shoulders. She wasn't going to stand there and be chastised without defending herself. Not when she was trying to keep everyone from getting dragged into the trouble that followed wherever she went.

"I was trying to keep you all safe!" she exclaimed. "You don't understand how many people are after me now. Olark, the dead, Chobly, Uncle Eric probably. If I can just go somewhere no one can find me, this might all stop."

She told them what happened last night with Chobly and his plans to "study" her, and their irritation seemed to lessen.

"That does sound terrifying," Darian said. "But it's not safe for you to take off like that on your own. No one is fooling themselves. We know you're stronger than us. But just because you're the strongest person in the room doesn't mean you can do everything yourself. Gini can help protect you from Chobly. *I* can help protect you. You think the emperor is going to stand by and let his best friend get dissected like a lab rat?"

"I'm sorry," Adia cried. "I panicked. I just thought—"

"Thought what?" Thyme said. The anger had gone out of her eyes, but she looked sadder than Adia had ever seen. "That if you run away and disappear from our lives that's going to make Olark ever give up on trying to find Imo Mmiri? Trying to find *you*? Adia, I'm sorry, but it's never going to stop until you defeat that monster once and for all. And you can't abandon a quest. It's not what champions do."

"I'm not a champion of Nri like you, Thyme. And I don't go on quests."

Thyme rolled her eyes. "A champion of Zaria then. And you *do* go on quests. We're going to get on that ship and we're going to get a map from the bone thrower so we can find that tomb and lay the dead to rest. I know you. You might have wanted to run away from all of this, but I bet it would have taken you all of one day before you turned back around and went to find the bone thrower and get the locator map. Defeating Olark is your destiny now. Finding Imo Mmiri too. But you can't do it alone. So are you going to let us help?"

Adia closed her eyes. There was nothing she could say that would convince them to let her go by herself.

"So what do we do?" she asked.

Thyme pulled a bag off her shoulder. Adia hadn't realized Thyme had been carrying two. Thyme rolled her eyes and tossed the brown bag to Adia.

"Ran off into the dead of the night and didn't even think to take food or water with her," Thyme muttered to Darian as Adia sheepishly put the bag her friend had packed her across her shoulder.

"Gini covered for you with your aunt and uncle," Thyme said, "so they just think you left early and will meet them on the ship. And she told us how to find the bone thrower. We'll have to ditch your family and get off at the port for the Mbari Mines. From there we'll hire a small rowing boat to take us the rest of the way to the bone thrower's village. All right?"

Adia nodded. Thyme sighed and gave her a hug. "Come on. Let's go before we miss the boat."

By their second day on the boat, it became clear that Uncle Eric appeared to be suffering through a great dilemma. His mood changed every hour as he went from treating Adia like a treasured daughter to treating her like someone who needed to be locked up.

"Is your uncle all right in the head?" Thyme asked as Uncle Eric scurried away after handing Adia a plate of fish. Uncle Eric knew so little about her that he'd forgotten she didn't eat meat. Adia turned her nose up at the fish and handed it to Thyme as she stared at her uncle's retreating form. Her newfound ability to see auras was temperamental at best. Today she hadn't been able to see anything when she looked at people, no matter how much she squinted.

"He's trying to figure out the best way to get my money," Adia said in disgust. "But I think he's realizing it's way too late to start acting like we're a loving family, so I assume he's going to have me locked up instead."

"It'll be fun watching him try," Thyme snorted as she dug into her pocket and tossed Adia an apple.

"How's Darian?" Adia asked as she bit into it. It wouldn't do for everyone to know the emperor was on a transport ship, so poor Darian was forced to stay below deck for the entire trip to the Swamplands. At least she and Thyme could take a few minutes every now and then to get some fresh air when they were certain Uncle Eric wasn't around. She took in a deep breath of sea air.

"He's bored but fine," Thyme said. "So...are we going to talk about the *other* person who's on this ship?"

Adia rolled her eyes to the heavens. "Yes, how exactly did that happen?"

"He's been following me and Darian ever since we left the Academy," Thyme said. "He must have figured you were in trouble. Or he recognized Darian and wanted to know what I was doing with the emperor. He's done a terrible job of disguising himself."

Adia glanced at the corner where Nami was lurking. He quickly spun around and stared out at the sea, as if lost in thought. His Gold Hat apprentice uniform had been replaced with a brown shirt and trousers and he wore a floppy hat on his head.

"Let me go talk to him," Adia said, exasperated. "I don't know who he thinks he's fooling."

But then Aunt Ife walked past Nami. Adia sat up straight. "Actually," she muttered, "let me talk to *her* first."

She couldn't straight out accuse Uncle Eric of being a shaman. Her aunt would fall over laughing at the thought. But maybe Adia could get some information out of her.

"Auntie," she said, walking in step with Ife. "Nice weather today, isn't it?"

Aunt Ife spared her an annoyed look. "You've barely said two words to me or your uncle since we've been on this boat, and you refuse to join me for evening prayers. So I know you didn't come over here to talk to me about the weather. Out with it."

Adia had never thought she had anything in common with her family, but maybe she and Aunt Ife shared a similar bluntness of speech. She cleared her throat. "I was just wondering how the Swamplands is faring, that's all. What with the fires and the sleeping sickness."

"We're faring as terribly as everyone else," Aunt Ife admitted. "Your uncle more so than anyone. But he refuses to see a doctor."

Adia tried not to let her aunt see how curious she was about this.

"Oh?" Adia asked. "Is Uncle Eric getting sick?"

Aunt Ife pursed her lips. "He's just been disoriented. The first time we woke up he was calling out for your mother. He thought he'd seen her. That she was still alive."

"What?" Adia gasped. She knew from Nami and Maka that the impending convergence was causing people to have visions of dead loved ones. So why would Uncle Eric be having visions of her mother? Unless… She tried not to vomit at the thought.

"I didn't think my mother and Uncle Eric were close," Adia said.

"They weren't," Aunt Ife muttered. "But I'm sure Eric would have preferred if they were closer." Ife gave her an assessing stare. "You're starting to look just like her, you know. You're many things, Adia, but no one would ever accuse you of being plain looking. You're going to be as beautiful as your mother. Sounds like an emperor has already taken notice of it. I guess my beloved husband spends all his time staring into those wretched cracks in the earth hoping to see Zina's perfect face one more time."

Adia might not remember her mother, but she was sure that no one who had given birth to her would have such horrible taste. Her mother must have laughed in Eric's face when he came courting. Maybe that was another reason why Aunt Ife had been so jealous of her. Probably the main reason.

"Of course this is all because of the poisonous fumes," Aunt Ife said quickly. She looked embarrassed. As if she had revealed more than she'd wanted to.

Adia nodded. "Of course."

"I think I'll take my lunch below deck," Aunt Ife said. "I'm suddenly tired. Too much sun. At least we'll be home soon. EJ will certainly be thrilled to see you. He's been rather hurt that you haven't been writing to him, you know. I know you've got your new friends now but don't forget about your cousin."

Adia swallowed her anger. As if she would ditch EJ for new friends. And she most certainly *had* been writing him letters. Chobly had just intercepted all of them. But she couldn't say that, so she just gave her aunt an apologetic look and mumbled something about being busy with her classes. Her aunt seemed to accept her excuse and gave her a nod before walking off.

Adia watched her aunt go and her annoyance changed to pity. "Poor auntie," she said with a sigh. She turned to lean over the railing and stared out at the sea. How deep had Uncle Eric's obsession with her mother been? Deep enough that he would turn to the dark arts to try to bring her back? That he would align himself with a demon? Could this man really have hidden a shamanic ability from her and EJ and everyone in that house for so many years? Her confusion gave way to dismay at the sound of things dropping and rolling all around her. She froze. The water was calm. There was no reason for things to go falling unless…

"Oh no," Adia said. She spun around.

Everyone on deck now lay on the floor, unconscious, including the captain. The ship's wheel spun round and round with no one to steer it.

"I'll get Darian," Thyme said, running to the stairs. "Take the helm!"

"You might as well take your time," Adia called out as she leaped over the sleeping captain. "With everyone staying asleep for longer and longer, we might have to sail this ship all by ourselves except for a few corpses."

Thyme gaped at her. Adia gave her a wry smile and a shrug as she grabbed the wheel.

"I joke to hide my misery." But then she frowned as she stared down at the wooden spokes of the helm. "How do you steer this thing?"

"Just...stay away from land," Thyme said unhelpfully before disappearing below deck.

At least they weren't sailing through a storm, Adia thought. She just had to keep them on a straight path until the captain woke up. And she managed to do that for several hours. But then a loud thump from the side of the ship made her worry that she'd relaxed too soon. Had she crashed them into a rock? She ran to look over the side of the boat.

"Thyme! Darian! Get up here!" Four soaking-wet corpses stared up at her with fevered expressions, seaweed dripping off their bloated flesh.

"Adia," one said and began scaling the ship faster. Adia shuddered. These were clearly the bodies of people who'd drowned at sea.

"Your eyes?" one asked eagerly. As horrible as they were, Adia was filled with pity for them. The thing staring up at her, hopeful that she would say "Sure!" and let it take her eyes, had been a person once. And they deserved better than this. The best she could do was put them out of their misery as quickly as possible and send them back to the realm where they belonged.

She took a step back and called her power to her. She felt the seaweed stir and try to climb the side of the ship, but the corpses were already too high up. It couldn't reach. One was already at the top. All it needed to do was hoist itself onto the deck.

"I'm really sorry about this," she said with a grimace as she pushed the corpse back into the sea. She winced as the body hit the water.

"It's no use," Thyme said in disgust as she flung another one overboard. Darian had returned with her.

"They're already climbing back up," Darian said. "This isn't going to stop until everyone wakes up. And that could take hours. How are we supposed to sail if we have to fight the dead all day long?"

"We could burn them," Thyme said. "There's a furnace below deck. If someone gets me some oil and I can make flaming arrows, we can take them out while Adia mans the helm."

Adia didn't think she could stomach watching them burn the bodies. But maybe fire *could* help, just not the way Thyme was thinking.

"I'm going to try to contact Gini and tell her we're in trouble," she said as she dashed below deck. It was a long shot, but Gini was a fire master. They should have thought to practise whether Adia could send her messages in the flames.

Adia had to hop over unconscious bodies on her way to the furnace. To her dismay, two of those bodies were Uncle Eric and Aunt Ife. It looked like they'd been sitting at a small eating area and Aunt Ife had dropped her plate of food right on top of Uncle Eric's head when she fell asleep. Her uncle's face was covered in stew. He wasn't going to like that. At least Aunt Ife was clean and in one piece, snoring to the right of him.

Adia stepped over her unconscious relatives and went to the furnace, looking into the flames. It was hard to let herself drift and send her soul through the fire as several of the dead made it to the deck, leaving Thyme and Darian no choice but to fight them, but she did her best. It was a similar experience to going to the Underworld, but not as disorienting this time around. Adia knew what to expect now, so she didn't panic as energy shot up and down her spine before expanding to every part of her body.

She ignored the spirits reaching out to her and focused on finding Gini. She didn't know how long it took, as time was disorienting whenever she went into this space, but there – a glowing light that she recognized stood out among the distorted images of the spirit realm.

"Gini?" she asked.

"Not Gini," a familiar voice said. Adia's eyes flew open. In front of her was her mirror image – just minus the glasses and with three white lines running down each cheek.

"Viona!" Adia said. "What are you doing here?"

"Helping," her ancestor said with a grin. "It's good to see you. You've got a lot stronger. But the realm of the dead is in chaos. Our family is safe, though, don't worry. This foolishness isn't strong enough to touch someone from Imo Mmiri."

"Our family?" Adia asked. She wondered if Viona could speak to her mother. Were they in the same area in the realm of ancestors? And if Adia could speak to Viona, why hadn't her own mother tried to contact her? "Who do you live with on the other side?"

"There's no time for chit-chat," Viona said. "Get back to the deck. Your friends are in trouble." The dead were trampling over the unconscious living as Thyme and Darian tried to keep them away from Adia.

"Adia, what's going on?" Thyme shouted, ducking as a corpse tried to land a punch to her head. "Are you talking to Gini?"

"They can't see me," Viona said, stepping close to Adia with a frown. "I can't do much like this. Can I borrow your body for a minute?"

"Excuse me?" Adia shrieked.

"You're stronger now. You won't shatter into a million pieces if I take over for a few minutes like you would have before. These are people who drowned or were buried at sea. The water has to take them back. You can't communicate with water yet, but I can."

The idea of anyone, even someone she trusted as much as Viona, taking over her body again made Adia feel nauseous, but Viona was the one who'd shown up to help.

"Do it quickly," Adia said. She gasped when she felt Viona pushing into her mind. It didn't hurt, it was just...weird.

Relax and don't fight me, Viona said from inside her head. Adia tried to stay calm as her hands moved of their own accord. For a moment blue light shot out from her fingertips, and then her vision changed. Everything around her turned to a clear, rippling blue. It was as if she'd fallen into the sea. If not for Viona forcing her to breathe, Adia would have held her breath out of fear of inhaling water. Instead, she remained calm as Viona made her arms lift to the sky, more blue light spitting out of her hands, and she felt herself touch the spirit of something deep and primordial. Water.

"Whoa," Darian said, staring at her. The boat was now rocking back and forth. A few sleeping people rolled to the side.

"Make sure no one falls overboard," Thyme cried. "I'll keep Adia safe. I think she's in a trance again."

On all sides of the ship, the sea shot up with white foamy fingers. Adia couldn't believe this was Viona's power. If her ancestor had wanted to, she could probably flood the world. How had Viona mastered this so young? And how could Adia have ever thought she could do the same? She could only watch in amazement as Viona commanded the giant hands she was creating out of water to gently grab the corpses and carry them back into the sea.

That should do it, Viona said. *Your people should wake up soon.*

"How do you have so much power?" Adia gasped as Viona began to extract herself from her mind.

I'm from Imo Mmiri, Viona said. *You'll see. Once you've been there, once you drink the water, you'll never be the same.*

For the first time, Adia understood why everyone was after that land. Even after she had been dead for centuries, Viona's powers were still nearly as strong as an Alusi's.

Adia couldn't let Olark ever get his hands on that land.

"WHAT was that?" Thyme yelled. She was soaking wet. The entire boat was. Adia went back to the furnace and shut the door, creeping over Uncle Eric again and wincing as Aunt Ife rolled over in her sleep, causing Adia to trip over her.

"The water took them back," Adia said, returning to the deck. "Same as the earth takes back the corpses on land."

"But you can't control water," Thyme said. "Can you?"

"No, it wasn't me," Adia confirmed, rubbing her head. They should be safe now, but she was still tense. "Viona was in control."

"Viona?" Thyme said, whipping around. "Is she here?"

"She was," Adia said with a frown. "But she's already gone. Come on. We need to check on everyone."

Adia supposed she should start with her relatives. Then

check on Nami. But when she got to her aunt and uncle she frowned and turned to Thyme, putting her finger to her lips. She nodded her head towards the back of the ship and Thyme followed her.

"Adia, what is it?"

"I tripped over my aunt," she said.

"And that upsets you because…"

"Because I walked in the exact same direction before and she wasn't in my way. She was on the left side of my uncle before – and now she's on his right."

Which meant Uncle Eric had got up and moved while they were all busy dealing with the dead's attempts to take over the ship. He'd forgotten which side of Aunt Ife he should have been lying on, but Adia didn't forget anything. He'd been awake the entire time. Watching her.

Her stomach dropped as she began to see the horrible truth. She'd basically told Aunt Ife that she and Gini were close to finding a cure. And of course Aunt Ife would have told Uncle Eric too. Chobly had seemed such an obvious choice, but she'd been wrong. So wrong. Mr Chobly wasn't Olark's henchman. It was Uncle Eric. And he knew she was after the cure.

Which meant Olark did too.

CHAPTER 21

Adia had never been so terrified of her uncle in her life. She had no idea what he was capable of. She could only imagine the hell he would raise when he realized she had vanished off the ship.

Part of her wanted to go to the Swamplands and grab EJ and get him away from Uncle Eric. But Aunt Ife loved her son. Even if his father was working for Olark, his mother wouldn't let him be harmed again. Adia had to swallow her fears about EJ and stay focused on finding the bone thrower. It was the rest of Zaria she needed to be worried about right now. She needed to get to that cure.

She, Darian and Thyme had got off the ship one stop before the port to the Mbari Mines. It was earlier than they'd planned on leaving, but hiking the rest of way seemed like a better idea than staying trapped on a wooden boat with a sea of drowned bodies ready and willing to rise on Olark's behalf – and with Uncle Eric, now that she knew who he was.

"Can you see Darian and Nami?" Adia asked Thyme quietly. "Are they all right?"

Since Thyme had superior vision and could see for over a mile ahead, she'd stayed with Adia while Darian brought up the rear to protect them from any corpses, uncles and council members who might be tailing them. And further behind him lurked Nami.

Thyme nodded. "They're about half a mile behind us. I think Darian's holding himself back from confronting Nami. And Nami seems oblivious to the fact that we know he's following us. But I don't want to talk about them. I want to talk about you commanding the wind and seas."

"Lower your voice," Adia hissed. "We don't know who's listening to us. And I didn't command anything. I told you, it was Viona. I just…channelled her."

Adia didn't want to admit to Thyme how similar it had felt to possession. The only difference was that Viona asked first. Adia had given permission to let a spirit take over her body because she knew and trusted Viona but still…she was more unsettled that she cared to admit.

"Well, what I saw was you in a trance mumbling something under your breath as you made a body of water do exactly what you wanted," Thyme continued. "Even if it was Viona, it came through *you*. Channelling spirits is a power in its own right."

"It's the same thing I've always done," Adia protested.

"Only this time I wasn't channelling a plant spirit's power, I was channelling my ancestor's."

"And how do you feel now?" Thyme asked. "I'd think you'd be drained but I've never seen you move this quickly without me dragging you along."

Thyme was right. Adia was full of energy. Even her vision was sharper. Not better – she still would fall flat on her face if she didn't have her glasses – but as they passed by an old Neem tree, Adia saw a face in the trunk. Wise, hooded eyes above a pair of wrinkled cheeks. The tree's spirit was beautiful. Adia was more in tune than ever to the spirits all around her. Was this a lingering side effect of Viona's spirit merging with hers? An unexpected boost to her own powers? She frowned. If that was true, then she would also have to accept that she'd been changed by Olark's possession too.

"The river crossing should be just down that hill," Adia said, pointing below her, wiping her face. Thyme gave a whistle. They'd hiked for hours, and she was drenched in sweat. She'd never come this far past the Swamplands before. She could just make out the rocky cliff face of the Mbari Mines in the distance.

Darian caught up to them and peered down. "Gold Hats?"

Thyme nodded. "But why are Gold Hats guarding a river crossing?"

"I think I know one of them," Darian groaned. "He's under my mother's command. He'll recognize me for sure."

"You'll have to wait here then," Thyme said. "Unless I just take them out?"

"I can get past them."

The three of them turned around and glared at Nami, who held up his hands as he approached. When he locked eyes with Darian, he fell into a deep bow.

"Emperor Darian. I'm glad to see you looking so well. And I know what you must be thinking. How did I manage to track you all this time undetected? Well, you see—"

Darian sputtered. "Do you *really* think we didn't see you on our ship? I could have had you thrown overboard anytime I wanted."

Nami went red and Adia winced. Right now, Thyme and Darian were angrier at Nami than she was.

"I just wanted to help."

"Help us right off this cliff, you mean," Thyme said. "No one wants your help."

"I can get you past the Gold Hats," Nami said quickly. "They're standing guard because we've been ordered to stop travel to any area that's had an uptick in fires to make sure no one gets hurt. There are blockades going up everywhere. You'll be harder to find if you let me help you get down the river instead of Thyme leaving a trail of bodies. I assume you don't want to attract attention."

"Just wait here for a second, Nami," Adia said, pulling Thyme and Darian aside.

"You're not actually going to trust him?" Thyme said in horror. "Adia. You know who he is. He only thinks about himself. There's got to be an ulterior motive. Probably trying to get close to Darian and all his emperor power."

Adia couldn't believe she was about to defend Nami. "Look, I'm not saying I trust him, but since I've been back at the Academy he's done nothing but try to protect me. Even yelling at the council when he thought they were bothering me. A few months ago he would have shoved me straight into the dirt to get in good with someone he thought was powerful. But this time he didn't even hesitate to protect me. Even if it meant making a powerful enemy."

"That might be true," Thyme admitted, "but that doesn't mean he won't let you get hurt if it means saving himself."

Adia knew that was a possibility.

"Maybe you're right. But even if he hasn't really changed, he won't fool me again. I know there's always a chance he'll do something terrible to me to save himself, and I won't lower my guard around him. But I still say we let him help us get through the Gold Hats. Can we vote on it? If we don't all agree, I'll send him packing. And Darian really should stay here so no one spots him. It could be good to have another pair of hands to help us."

Darian frowned. "We don't need to vote. If you think we should let him help, we'll trust you. But if he acts up, you need to leave him behind, Adia."

"If he does anything suspicious, I'll lose him," Adia agreed.

They all agreed that Darian couldn't go with them. Not if Gold Hats were on patrol to get travellers off the road. But Adia didn't know what to do when the Gold Hat who peered at Nami's papers said, "You can only take one of them with you."

"But—"

"We shouldn't even be letting you go over there, so don't complain. You're just a trainee. We'll let you borrow a boat but it can only hold two people. So who's it going to be?"

"The two of us." Adia decided to speak quickly before Thyme started throwing Gold Hats into the river. "We'll be back in a few hours," she said to her friend quietly. "Just wait with Darian."

"I'm surprised you're not mad at me for following you," Nami said as they rowed down the river.

"I don't have time to be mad at you," Adia said. Which was the truth. But it was also the truth that she still didn't completely trust him.

"Are you sure this person will have whatever it is you're looking for?" Nami asked.

"I'm not sure about anything any more," Adia said with a heavy sigh.

"Maybe that's good for me."

Adia looked at him curiously.

Nami cleared his throat. "I mean, maybe it means you're not sure if you still hate me."

She stared at him thoughtfully. "I don't think I hate anyone," she said honestly. "Some people are just more disappointing than others."

"I wish I could do something to make everything go back to the way it used to be between us," Nami said.

Adia scrunched up her face. "I don't. The way it used to be between us was you liking me well enough, but mainly because of how you could use me for your own benefit. And me not realizing that's what was going on. Or worse, me realizing it but being so lonely I put up with it anyway. So why would *I* want to go back to being treated like that?"

Nami blinked quickly, as if he was fighting back tears, but nodded.

"That's fair," he said. "But maybe we could have a different, better friendship. Someday. If you ever felt like it, I mean."

Adia didn't answer. She still wasn't sure what role she wanted Nami to have in her life. But she couldn't deny any more that he *was* a part of it.

"This is it," he said when they came to shore.

"It should be just over the hill," Adia said as she scurried out of the boat. The road ahead of them was surprisingly crowded. Dozens of people walked behind carts and wagons that were packed to the brim. Where were all these people headed? "Keep your head down."

They walked up the short hill from the riverbank and fell in line with the group of travellers walking down the dusty road. Smoke rose behind them in the distance, making the world around them look perpetually dark and grey. Even though Adia had known the dead were setting fires throughout Zaria, being at the Academy had kept her removed from all the suffering it was causing. And from how close they really were to the world of the living and dead converging. Everyone around her looked exhausted and sad, and they seemed unconcerned by the sight of two children travelling alone. No one paid them any mind until Nami knocked into one of them.

"Watch it," a man carrying a crying baby said.

"Sorry," Nami said. "Hey, where are you all going?"

The man adjusted the screaming infant in his arms. "To see if the next town over has space for me and my girl. Others are going to find family to stay with, or to the river to see if they can get on a boat going as far away from here as possible. You'd be better off following us than going that way," he said. "The mines and this village have been abandoned. Half the houses were burned down yesterday. People grabbed what they could and fled. These lands are cursed."

"All of Zaria is cursed," someone muttered, and the crowd murmured in agreement. The voice got louder, emboldened. "Where we should be heading is to the capital to rip that crown off Darian's head!"

"Why stop there?" the man with the baby said. "I say we rip the crown from his head, then we rip his head from his body! He's sitting comfortably in his palace as we're driven out of our homes. You can't tell me this is natural. His new buddies are probably digging for gold while we sleep. What else could explain why the ground is burning and crumbling beneath our feet? If you ask me, someone is doing this to us deliberately, and Darian's signed off on it. He betrayed his own people for a crown."

Maybe staying silent about Darian's reign of terror actually being Olark's work hadn't been the right decision. As Zaria's future grew more and more bleak, people were looking for someone to blame. Of course, in their eyes the blame would lie with Darian. The innocent puppet Olark had used to make all of this happen. Adia pressed her lips into a tight, thin line to stop herself from saying anything as the crowd called for Darian's head.

CHAPTER 22

"I guess Darian's not as popular here as he is in the capital," Nami said.

"Oh, shut up," Adia muttered as she marched forward. "I can see the village. Come on."

They walked down the hill in silence. It wasn't hard to tell which one was the bone thrower's hut. Every other house was either sunk halfway into the ground or boarded up.

But one hut was surrounded by a field of fragrant wild flowers and date palms fed by a babbling brook. Everything about it was a little too inviting. It reminded her of something in a fable where a malevolent spirit would take the guise of a mortal in order to lure children to their doom with the promise of candied apples and golden combs if they came inside. It made her tense.

"This is so nice," Nami said, not sharing Adia's trepidation. He *would* be that child who got lured into a dark spirit's lair.

"Just don't eat any apples if she offers them to you."

"Huh?" Nami asked, but Adia ignored him and knocked on the door. After a few seconds, a small woman wearing a thin, grey shawl over her frail shoulders stared at them.

"Are you lost?" she asked.

"No," Adia said. "We were looking for you. I hear you're the person to come to if you need rare power objects."

The hut was jam-packed with trinkets and oddities and glass jars full of liquids. If Gini hadn't told her the bone thrower housed the largest collection of power objects in Zaria, Adia would have assumed she was a hoarder.

"And what rare power object do you want?" The bone thrower's voice was weary. "Something to help you pass your tests, perhaps? Or do you need to get a bully off your back?"

If only her problems were so simple.

"We need a bottle of ink," Adia said.

The bone thrower rolled her eyes. "And you think my home is a vendor's stall? The market is half a mile down the road. There'll be an old man who sells paper and ink towards the end of it. At least there will be if his stall wasn't already swallowed into the earth with the other half of this village. Don't let him charge you more than half a coin. You know how to haggle?"

"I do," Adia said. "But he doesn't have the ink I need. You do. It's made with the bones of an owl."

The bone thrower's eyes went wide. Then she gave them a tight smile and a knowing nod.

"Just one minute," she said. She walked into a back room.

"That was too easy, wasn't it?" Nami asked nervously. Adia ignored him even though she'd been thinking the exact same thing. The bone thrower came back into the room in a matter of seconds, but this time she was brandishing a heavy broadsword.

"You think I don't know a Soulless when I see one!" she yelled. "Get out of my house."

"What is wrong with you?" Nami shouted, his eyes wide as he fumbled for his weapon. "What's a Soulless?"

Adia stepped between them, holding up her arms.

"Nami, wait by the door," she said.

"But—" Nami was about to protest but a glare from Adia made him sigh and move back.

"I'm not a Soulless," Adia said. "My name is Adia and I'm a first-year student at the Academy of Shamans. See?" She flipped her collar open and showed her the pin of Ikenga's horns that all first years wore.

The mention of the school made the bone thrower tilt her head, but she didn't lower her sword.

"The Academy of Shamans?" she repeated. "So you found some mention in those dusty libraries of an ink that can create a map to lead you to treasure and thought to seek out your fortune?"

Adia blinked.

"Dusty libraries? Did you go to the Academy?" she asked.

The mention of being an Academy student must have made the bone thrower decide Adia was just a foolish child, not a Soulless under the command of some master. She lowered her sword.

"I did. Six years of my life I'll never get back," she muttered. "Although the Academy was nicer to me than it was to anyone else in my class. There was one boy who was so horrible the curtains wrapped him up one morning and dangled him outside the window in nothing but his underwear as he screamed. He's a government official now. Anthony Amber."

Adia cringed. "I think I know his daughter."

"My sympathies," the bone thrower said. "All right. I believe you are who you say. But you can't have that ink. It's not a magic toy for children to play around with."

"I know," Adia said. "And I'm not looking for treasure. I need to find something a lot more important than that. You can't tell me you haven't noticed what's going on here. The cracks in the earth, the fires, the new burned lands cropping up."

"The reanimated corpses running around burning those lands," the bone thrower added.

"The what?" Nami shrieked from his side of the room, but Adia ignored him. She approached the bone thrower cautiously. What she was about to ask, she didn't want Nami to hear. She didn't trust him enough yet.

"You see the corpses too?" Adia asked quietly.

The bone thrower's eyes narrowed. "I'm the only one who doesn't fall asleep. I think something in my house protects me."

Adia shook her head.

"It's not that. You've never taken Drops, have you?"

The bone thrower looked at her in shock. "No, I've never taken them. I couldn't believe how eager everyone in the village was to swallow the words and medicine of those missionaries, but I chased them out of here every time they showed up. Eventually they decided I was more trouble than I was worth, and they've left me alone ever since. So it's all linked to Drops, eh? But what does that have to do with the owl ink?"

Adia decided to go with her instincts and trust the bone thrower. Anyone who would stay cooped up in a house to guard a bunch of objects just because some great-great-grandmother she'd never met had said they were important seemed like someone who took things seriously.

"I need it to find a cure. For Drops," she said quietly. By now she figured Nami was piecing things together, but it still didn't mean she wanted him to hear her conversation.

The bone thrower shook her head.

"It doesn't work like that. It won't draw you a map leading to a person or to an object like gold. It can only lead you to a physical location like a town or a church or—"

"A burial ground?" Adia asked. "A person's final resting place?"

"Yes, that should work," the bone thrower said.

"Then I can give you what you need," Adia said. "I know the name, I just have no idea where in Zaria it's located. Will you help me?" She stepped back, speaking at a normal level now. "I can trade for it."

The bone thrower shook her head again. "This one's on the house. Wait outside. I'll need to prepare it, and you can't see how I do that. It's a secret only known to my family. What's the name of the location?"

"The High Queen's tomb," she said, then paused. Trying to track down that strange constellation from her vision of Imo Mmiri would take years. Even if she dedicated the rest of her life to wandering around the world chasing the stars, odds were she would never find it. But if she had an actual set of directions...

"Is there enough ink to make two maps?" Adia asked.

"Yes," the bone thrower said. "But don't waste your time. It won't show you Imo Mmiri."

Adia gasped. "How did you know I was going to ask that?"

The bone thrower narrowed her eyes. "An educated guess. It's what every Soulless who's slunk up to this house this past year has wanted. After the third one showed up trying to get the ink, I got curious and made a map. Imo Mmiri is just a myth. The way the ink works is that after you write the name of a place down, the ink spreads out and draws a map. But when I wrote *Imo Mmiri*, the page stayed blank. It couldn't create a map of a place that only exists in our imagination."

Adia's eyes narrowed. "Any chance you still have that paper?" she asked.

"The blank paper?" The bone thrower shrugged her thin shoulders. "It's probably around here somewhere. I'd never throw away a perfectly good piece of parchment."

"I'd like to take a look at it, if you don't mind," Adia said.

"Whatever," the bone thrower said, waving her to the door. "It won't do you any good, but I'll let you satisfy your curiosity."

"Thank you," Adia said. "We'll wait outside." She tilted her head at Nami, and he followed her out the door.

Now that she'd left the somewhat safe walls of the Academy, she was shocked at the state of Zaria. This village was completely demolished. All this destruction because of whatever mythical power Imo Mmiri could bestow upon its inhabitants? She believed Imo Mmiri still existed, but who was to say it wasn't a wasteland? Her vision in the Underworld had been of a cold, dark land with no life. Just black and endless water as far as the eye could see. After all these centuries maybe its power had dried up, leaving nothing behind but lifeless waters. Everyone who was after it might be hunting for something that was long gone.

Adia would have lingered in her depressed thoughts, but Nami wasn't a person who could handle silence for too long, no matter how hard he was trying to control his tongue. Not like Darian, who would have known to keep quiet so she could think.

"So what do we do if this map works?" Nami asked. "How are we going to get the cure to everyone?"

"Who's we?" Adia asked. "*I'll* go my way and you'll go yours. I can't believe that after everything you'd still jump on another boat to follow me."

"It's *because of everything* that I got on the boat!" Nami shouted.

"Are you yelling at *me* right now?" Adia asked in disbelief. Nami flushed.

"Sorry. I'm just... I don't know. I don't know what else I can do to show you how sorry I am."

"Look, if I said I forgive you, would you leave me alone?" Adia asked.

"No," Nami said, "because you obviously don't mean it."

Adia was starting to think she *did* mean it. She just wasn't ready to let Nami off the hook yet.

"You basically just admitted you'd only say that to get me to leave you alone. But you're right. You've been telling me to leave you alone since you got back to the Academy and I didn't listen, even followed you here. But you don't understand what this is doing to me. I wake up every day feeling horrible and—"

"And you want me to make you feel better?" Adia snorted. Every time she came close to forgiving him, he managed to annoy her. "Can you really not hear how selfish that sounds?"

Nami fell silent.

"Nami," Adia said, "I don't think we're ever going to be friends again, and we both know that's entirely your fault. You feel guilty because you did something horrible. The only way you're ever going to feel better about yourself is by being a better person in the future. I do think you're genuinely trying to be better and I'm glad of that. But you don't need me in your life to do it."

Nami's shoulders fell, his eyes damp. Adia felt a bit like crying too. But it was time for them both to face the truth. Forgiven or not, their friendship had died the night he'd had her thrown in the dungeon, and nothing was ever going to fix it.

The door opened and the bone thrower walked out, holding a long, wooden tube in one hand.

"It'll take a few days for the map to be created," she said, opening the tube and pulling out a rolled-up parchment. "The ink needs time to carve out the map. But it's working. Look."

Adia peered down at the parchment. At the bottom, written in a black box was *The High Queen's Tomb*. She watched in amazement as the ink began spreading out from the box, beginning to map out a terrain. She put the parchment back in the tube. In a few days, she would know exactly where to go to find the cure for Drops. She just hoped Olark hadn't somehow got there first and already destroyed it. The only thing that made her think he hadn't was that she couldn't see him trusting anyone with the information about where Sabo was buried. Not even his shaman. She still had a chance to save everyone. For the first time in a long time, Adia felt hope.

"And here's the other one," the bone thrower said, interrupting Adia's thoughts.

"Other what?" Nami asked. "I think you grabbed the wrong parchment. This one is blank except for the box at the bottom."

"I know," the bone thrower said with a snort. "But your friend didn't believe me. My ink only shows you real places, not imaginary ones."

Adia looked at the parchment and schooled her face into a blank expression even as her heart raced. Yes, there was a box at the bottom with *Imo Mmiri* written in it, but there was so much more. Nami and the bone thrower just couldn't see it. Usually when Adia committed something to memory it was completely unintentional. Words or an image just saved themselves into her brain, and most of the time she was surprised when she realized she had some random bit of information she needed buried in the recesses of her mind. But this was different. The map in front of her etched itself into every part of her soul so clearly that she felt as if she'd walked every trail already. This map was alive inside her mind.

"Everything all right?" Nami asked.

Adia blinked and looked away from the map.

"You're right," she said, hoping her voice sounded steady.

"I should have believed you, sorry. I guess I just needed to see it for myself. It's blank."

The bone thrower stared at her with an expression Adia couldn't decipher. But if she was going to say something, or call Adia out on her lie, she decided not to.

"You'd better get going," the bone thrower said. "You see that?" She pointed to the east, where grey smoke was rising. "Another crack just formed. It'll be here soon enough."

"Are you sure you're all right staying here by yourself?" Adia asked.

"The Alusi protect me," the bone thrower said. "But you know that, don't you? You have the look of someone who can speak to the stars."

"Thanks for the help," Adia said. She would have left it at that, but the bone thrower grabbed her arm and pulled her back.

"Consider me a member of your circle," the bone thrower whispered.

"What?" Adia gasped.

"When you reopen the circle of shamans. I'll come if you call me."

Maybe the shamans of Imo Mmiri or Viona could open and lead a circle of shamans, but Adia knew she definitely didn't have that kind of power yet. But she nodded at the bone thrower.

"Adia," Nami called out, pointing worriedly at the smoke

coming from the distance. "We need to go. Now."

Adia could barely contain her excitement as they ran. She'd seen the path that led to Imo Mmiri. It would take months to go that far north, but she finally knew where to go. But she couldn't do any of that until she was sure that no one – living, dead or demonic – knew where she was going. She wondered if it wouldn't be safer to not even tell Thyme and Darian, or even the Alusi. Right now, the information was contained only in her head. And only her eyes would be able to see the exact entrance.

The ground rumbled beneath them, shaking her from her thoughts. Adia screamed as she lost her footing and found herself falling. Her eyes filled with tears as her ankle twisted at an awkward angle. She'd always been terrified someone was going to fall to their deaths in one of these holes. Maybe it was going to be her. But Nami grabbed her just before she could slip into the chasm that was forming. She clutched his arm gratefully as he pulled her back up. But there was no time to rest or to pay attention to the pain in her ankle. The dead were coming.

"We have to get out of here!" he shouted, running away from the shaking earth and towards the river. Adia limped after him but quickly fell behind. After only a few steps her leg gave out and she fell to the ground. All she could do was watch helplessly as Nami rushed ahead. He was already at the boat.

"Get in!" he shouted as he untied the boat from the tree trunk. He turned around, finally realizing she wasn't behind him. "Adia!"

She'd expected him to just jump in the boat and sail away. She was shocked when he ran back without a moment's hesitation.

"My ankle," she said, tears running down her face.

He grabbed her under her arms and helped her up.

"Come on," he said, half carrying her. The crack was growing fast, the ground beneath them falling away.

"Just leave me," she said. "I'm slowing you down."

"Adia, shut up," Nami snapped. He was dragging her now, panting as he ran. But they made it to the boat. Nami dragged her in first, dumping her into the boat with a thud. Adia winced as her hands landed on the rough surface. Her empty hands.

"The map," she gasped in horror. "I must have dropped it."

Nami spun around. "I see it!" he said.

"Nami, don't," Adia shouted but he'd already taken off. Running straight in the direction of the cracked earth.

She closed her eyes, begging the ground to stop for just a moment, but her power was met with another. The plants didn't always listen to her, but this was a different thing altogether. Like her entire soul was being slammed into a wall. Her power was completely blocked. The other shaman. Uncle Eric. It had to be him. He might even be nearby. Because for the first time, she could feel the shocking level and precision of power Olark's shaman commanded. She pushed against it, but he pushed back harder and the crack continued to grow.

Adia's eyes went wide. This wasn't the power of someone who had only recently started dabbling in the dark arts, but the power of someone who had mastered their ability in a way she hadn't yet, and maybe never would. He was stronger than her. Much stronger. If they had to face each other head-on, right now, Uncle Eric would win.

"I got it," Nami said. "Push off into the water, I'll jump."

Adia got the boat clear of the water but kept it as still as she could so it didn't get too far away from Nami.

"Hurry!" she yelled. The entire road they'd just walked down was being swallowed, and Nami was about to be too.

Then, to her horror, when he was just a metre or so from the water, his eyes glazed over and he let out a yawn. Smoke began to rise from the crack, and the bony hand of a corpse climbed out. Nami blinked, as if trying to shake himself out of a stupor.

"No," Adia whispered. "Nami!"

The sound of her voice seemed to reach him because he slowly met her gaze. His face settled into a look of fierce determination. The crack behind him was growing, the ground splitting in two as everything that had once stood there vanished into the deep abyss that was seconds away from reaching Nami.

He raised his hand, even though it looked as if it was taking him the same amount of effort it would take to lift a ton of bricks. Balling his fist up, he hurled the map to the High Queen's tomb straight at Adia. It hit her smack in the middle of her chest and fell to the bottom of the boat, but she didn't even notice as the glazed look took over Nami's eyes one more.

"No!" Adia threw herself out of the boat and into the water. Gasping, she surfaced and spun around to start swimming back to the land to get to Nami, but it was too late.

He collapsed on the ground, fast asleep. And all Adia could do was bob up and down in the water as Nami was swallowed into the earth.

CHAPTER 23

Adia didn't know how long she drifted on the boat. She'd managed to climb back into it, but she'd given up on paddling as soon as she was safely away from the wreckage. All she could do was lie down and stare up at the sky as tears dripped down her face and became a part of the ocean. The pain of her twisted ankle and the bruise that was no doubt forming where the map had struck her was nothing compared to the pain in her heart.

She had just watched Nami die. They'd had the world's most complicated relationship, but in his final moments, Nami had chosen to be the boy she'd first met. The boy she'd called her first friend. He could have saved himself. He didn't have to go back for her. He didn't have to go back for the map, and he didn't have to use his last breath to make sure she had it.

Adia rolled onto her side and picked up the tube, fighting the urge to just throw it into the water. To let the cure stay buried in the High Queen's tomb with her bones. Let the world of the living become the realm of the dead. What was the point? This was always going to end the same way. With Olark winning.

Letting out a sob, she curled into a ball, hugging the map into her stomach. She was done paddling. She was done with everything. She closed her eyes and let herself drift asleep.

"Adia?" Someone shook her awake, but she kept her eyes tightly shut. Thyme. So the boat had betrayed her and taken her to shore. "Adia, are you hurt?"

She'd never felt angry at Thyme before, but right now she wanted to scream at her friend for waking her up. Sleep had given her a few hours of peace. She rolled over onto her side and sobbed. Eventually she heard someone running up.

"I don't know what's wrong with her!" Thyme said frantically.

"Adia?" Darian asked. "Where's Nami?"

"Of course her being in this state would be something to do with Nami," Thyme said. "What did he do, Adia? Did he hurt you again?"

Adia answered, but her voice was so small even she didn't hear it.

"What was that?" Darian asked.

"He's dead," Adia managed to choke out. "He died helping me."

Thyme and Darian fell silent. Adia didn't know if she fell back asleep or just blacked out, but the next time she came to she was being carried on someone's back. She lifted her head and saw Thyme marching ahead. Which meant Darian was carrying her. She lowered her head again. Let him carry her. Even if her ankle wasn't throbbing she wouldn't have had the strength to walk right now. Nami had died thinking she hated him. How could this be the way their story ended? With him falling into darkness so the dead could rise.

The dead could rise.

Her heart jumped as hope entered her body. This didn't have to be the end. He had only died a few hours ago. Zaria was overrun with the walking dead. She herself had reanimated one of them.

"I can bring him back," she mumbled, her tongue heavy.

"She's awake," Darian said, lowering her down.

"I'll bring him back," Adia said, laughing hysterically that she hadn't realized it right away. It was so simple.

"What do you mean?" Thyme asked nervously. "Adia, we came all this way to help the dead rest, not bring them back. I'm sorry about Nami. But you can't meddle with things like this. Look at the harm that's been caused already with the realms of the living and the dead converging on each other. You're meant to seal that crack, not add to it."

Adia ignored her. Maybe everyone else had to do nothing but weep as people they cared about died, but she had power. Of course she would use it to bring Nami back.

"Adia," Darian said quietly, "bringing back the dead comes

at the cost of draining the living. You'd have to hurt someone to do what I can see you're planning to do. What if you cost someone else their life at the sake of saving Nami's?"

She ignored him too. After everything she'd put up with this past year, the universe would have to forgive her for playing with life and death. The universe owed her.

"I think we should go back to the Academy," Thyme said. "Have Gini talk to her."

Adia pointed at Thyme. "I dragged you out of the Horrorbeyond. And you, Darian – I exorcised you after you spent a year possessed. But now, when I want to help someone else, you act like I'm evil?"

"Adia, you know that's not what we—"

"Just go," she said. "You got what you wanted from me and my power. I don't know why you're still hanging around."

Thyme snorted. "You're crazy if you think *that's* going to work. We love you and you love us. You can be as hurtful as you want but we're not leaving you."

Adia stared at them, realizing the truth in their words.

"That's true, isn't it?" she said. "I almost wish it wasn't." She closed her eyes and unleashed her power.

"Adia, don't do this," Darian yelled, but it was too late. Her power worked faster than it ever had before as she woke the forest. Roots stirred, knocking Thyme and Darian off their feet as vines shot forward, wrapping their branches around her friends more securely than any rope.

"You'll be set free when I'm far enough away that you can't follow me," Adia said. "I'm sorry, but I have to do this."

Adia ran without thinking about where she was going. Her only focus was on putting distance between herself and Darian and Thyme. *Especially* Thyme. Darian was athletic and strong, and Adia was a bookworm who used any excuse she could think of to get out of doing exercise. He'd have no trouble catching up to her in a few hours once he broke free from the vines. But Thyme, with her otherworld speed and eyesight, would catch up to her in a matter of minutes if Adia didn't make sure she was hiding her tracks.

She paused and knelt on the ground, asking the roots and plants to shift and hide her footprints. The ground wouldn't budge. She frowned and tried again. Nothing. This might be the first time the plants hadn't responded to her.

"Fine," she said. "Don't help me. I'll do this on my own."

She'd become too reliant on her power and on other people. Thyme and Darian seemed to think she required their permission before doing anything. And what right did they have to try to stop her? If either of them had been the ones killed, she would have brought them back too. Without hesitation.

She had just knelt again to begin covering her tracks the old-fashioned way, when the map tube fell out of her bag. For a moment, Adia felt nothing but fury as she stared at it. Going to get this map was the reason Nami had died. She wanted to tear it into pieces. But she couldn't do that. Not when he'd given his life to make sure she had it. She took it out of the tube and looked at it. It wasn't complete yet but it had to be almost finished because the ink was getting close to reaching the bottom of the page. Despite her wild running she was still on course.

Adia carefully rolled it back up. It wasn't the map that had got Nami killed. It was Olark. She would make it to the tomb and she would stop him. But first, she would bring back Nami. She quickly grabbed as many fallen branches as she could find and threw them in a pile to make a fire. Thyme could show up at any second. Adia had to get to Nami before Olark turned him into another one of his mindless minions. She didn't think she would be able to stand it if Nami showed up as a corpse, hissing—

"Adia Kelbara. We need to bring the High Queen your eyes." Not one, but three corpses holding torches stared at her with eager expressions.

So they were hunting her in groups now. Adia wanted to scream in frustration. The sun was setting and she was all alone in a forest when – judging by the size of the chasm that had swallowed Nami – there'd just been a massive occurrence of dead rising. She'd been careless. She didn't have time for this.

"We need—"

"I know what you need," she said, releasing her power.

She didn't have to exert much energy any more to get nearby agrias vines to grab the corpses and begin the process of decomposition. She could do it by instinct now. But exhaustion had made her sloppy, and she didn't notice another corpse sneaking up behind her. Adia gasped as it wrapped its arms around her neck, cutting off her air. Her legs flailed as it began to drag her off, and stars swam in front of her eyes. She hooked her foot under a root and forced the corpse to pause so it could try to pull her loose. When it did, she ripped herself free and grabbed a thick branch, swinging up and hitting it on the head. Yes, she could have used the plants around her to tie it up, but she wanted to hit something.

She screamed as she hit it over and over again, not caring if she alerted every corpse in the area to her presence. It covered its head with its hands and, for a second, Adia thought she saw something in its eyes. A flash of fear. A reminder that inside this corpse was a scared soul being controlled by a demon and the shaman who served him.

"What am I doing?" she gasped, dropping the branch. She didn't even call the vines around her into action. They leaped forward, wrapping themselves around the shaking corpse and helping it decompose.

"I'm so sorry."

Adia sat on the ground, too disgusted with herself to move.

She sniffled and wiped away the tears that were falling down her face.

"I'll fix all this," she said, crawling back to her pile of branches. "Just as soon as I get Nami back."

She fumbled around on her hands and knees until she'd gathered enough dried leaves to use as kindling, then set about building a fire. When it roared to life, she pulled the vial of Drops out of her bag and splashed some into the flames, settling herself in front of it.

"Bring me Nami," she whispered. Even sitting in front of a fire, a chill ran through her as she felt the door to the realm of the dead open. But almost as soon as the door opened, she was shocked when it slammed in her face. She opened her eyes and dropped the vial in shock, crying out in dismay as Darian put out the fire.

"How did you get here?" Adia gasped.

"I had a chat with the vine," Darian said, not even sparing her a glance as he stamped out the last of the embers. "It was a one-sided conversation, of course. Nothing spoke back; I'm not like you. But I guess someone was listening and agreed with me that I should find you before you do something you regret. They let us go."

"Then where's Thyme?" Adia asked.

"We split up," Darian said. "She begrudgingly admitted that I'm just as good a tracker as she is. And we needed to cover more ground since you've been using the forest to hide your tracks."

"But you found me anyway," Adia said. "How?"

Darian shrugged. "After a while I started to see your tracks again. Even the forest is trying to stop you from doing this. It's not helping you hide from me. Plus, you have a tell."

How could she possibly have a tell when she could bend the ground to her will? "No, I don't," she said.

"You do," Darian said, ignoring her protests. "But I'll never tell you what it is now that I know what a flight risk you are. I have to make sure I can always find you." He turned his gaze to the pile of logs. "So I guess you were about to start whatever it is you do to raise the dead. Even though you're going to send anyone within a mile radius to sleep so they can have their energy stolen?"

Adia held his gaze.

"Everyone wakes up eventually, don't they?" she asked. She wasn't going to back down. After everything she'd put up with, she deserved to bend the rules just this once.

"At first they woke up after a few minutes, then it became hours. Soon it'll probably be days and after that... We've been getting closer and closer to this turning into a permanent sleep as Olark gets stronger. Not to mention all the injuries happening when people lose consciousness at the wrong place at the wrong time. You really want to risk hurting someone? Risk getting someone killed?"

Adia refused to let him make her doubt her plan.

"I *already* got someone killed," she said. "You can't stop me,

Darian. I'm getting him back. If someone falls asleep and falls down a flight of stairs as a result, I'm sorry. But if they'd been strong enough to refuse to take Drops they wouldn't be in this situation, would they? The bone thrower is fine. I'm fine. You and Thyme are fine. Because we didn't blindly drink a poison just because someone said it would give us power."

"All right then, Adia," Darian said as he reached into his pocket. "Do what you need to do. But you're going to have to look me in the eye when you do it and watch me lose control of my body again." He held out his hand. Adia's mouth fell open. She turned to look at the remains of the fire where she'd dropped the vial of Drops, and it was gone. He'd snatched it when she wasn't looking.

"Darian, stop!" she screamed. Adia lunged and knocked him to the ground, but it was too late. He'd taken Drops.

"How could you do this?" she said. She tried to shove her finger down his throat to make him throw it up, but he just swatted her hand away as he rolled to his side.

"It's disgusting," he muttered to himself. "How do people manage to take that every day?"

"What were you thinking?" she whispered. "We have no idea what else Drops will do to a person in the long run. You had an immunity, never taking it."

"And are you still going to build another fire and pull the dead to you, knowing it'll steal my life force? That I might never wake up?"

"Of course not," Adia said with a gasp. "You know I won't."

"Then I have no regrets," he said. "I spent a year of my life living in complete darkness. I'm not going to sit back and let you walk right into it."

Adia buried her head in her hands. She felt like Darian had just dragged her up out of dark, murky water and she could breathe and see light again. He'd stopped her from doing something that would have changed her for ever. But at what cost?

"I'm so sorry," she said, her voice thick with tears.

"You don't have to be sorry," Darian said. "You watched Nami die and instead of being allowed to lie down and cry you're supposed to go save a kingdom. You're allowed to grieve for as long as you need but you're not allowed to become a demon."

Someone came crashing through the trees.

"You found her," Thyme said in relief. "Adia, if you ever do that to me again—"

Adia jumped up and gave Thyme a hug.

"I'm so sorry," she said. Darian could say whatever he wanted but she'd be apologizing to the two of them for a long while. What she'd done was inexcusable.

"Did you do it?" Thyme asked, pulling back. "Did you reanimate Nami?"

Adia shook her head.

"Good. The other time was an accident, but you can't use

that type of power again, Adia. It'll just become easier and easier for you to justify doing it. Don't even tempt yourself."

Adia knew what they were saying was true. This must have been how the shaman helping Olark and the High Queen had turned to the dark. Something that made them feel justified in using the power they'd been blessed with for selfish reasons, no matter the consequences. Sure that they would never hurt anyone. They must not have had a Darian and Thyme to stop them.

"I don't know what to do," Adia said.

"We get you to that tomb and finish this," Thyme said.

At that, Adia turned to Darian. In her panic about him poisoning himself with Drops she'd forgotten where they were supposed to be headed before she took them all off course.

"You're going to be all right," she said. "There's nothing that will stop me from getting the cure now."

CHAPTER 24

They were moving slower than Adia would have liked. They'd lost half a day already because Darian had lost consciousness in the afternoon yesterday. And since Thyme refused to entertain the idea of staying behind and watching over Darian while Adia made the rest of the journey by herself, they'd had no choice but to stop early for the day and make camp. But now it was the next evening, and there was still no rousing him. Thyme kept reminding Adia that he'd wake up soon enough, but she was inconsolable. Darian was in this situation because of her.

"He's been asleep for so long, Thyme," Adia said. "You can't say for certain any more that anyone will wake up. The world is spending the whole day asleep now. Olark is getting close."

Thyme rubbed her forehead.

"Check the map. How far are we from the tomb?"

Adia pulled the parchment out of her bag. The ink was still working its way across the paper, but it was almost complete.

"I think we can be there in a few days. The only thing in this direction is the Sunless Mountains. It must be around there. Hopefully Darian will be well enough to travel soon."

"If not, I can carry him," Thyme said. "So what's the plan once we find the cure? How are we supposed to get it to everyone in Zaria? Have you thought about the fact that some people won't want to take it? By now everyone should realize they're losing hours of time every day, but they probably think it's just a side effect before they get their magical powers from Liquid Gold."

Adia knew Thyme was trying to distract her. Losing Nami and Darian becoming yet another victim of Drops was more than she could handle. She knew she was barely hanging on right now and she guessed Thyme knew it too.

She was about to say she'd pour the cure down everyone's throats one by one if she had to, but then she remembered her initiation. Just because she had a cure didn't mean she could force people to take it.

"We'll have the emperor on our side. Darian's influence will get a decent amount of the population to take it. Gini and Mbari too. It shouldn't be hard to convince parents that letting their kids sleep through their studies isn't a great idea and that they need to detox from Drops. People have to see by now how dangerous this new formula is."

"So you're appealing to people's sense of reason?" Thyme asked. "You have more faith in the world than I do."

"The world is falling apart," Adia said. "They might not know the whole story, but it shouldn't be hard to make up some lie about it being related to the production of Liquid Gold. It might take a bit of time to get the cure to everyone, but we'll fix this."

Darian groaned and shifted his head.

"Thank the stars," Adia cried. She almost wept with relief when Darian at last opened his eyes.

"I guess that wasn't a normal sleep," he said with a sigh as he sat up. "How long?"

"Since yesterday afternoon," Adia answered. "Here. Drink some water."

He took a long swig from the flask she handed him.

"I'll slow you down if you have to stop to watch over me every time I pass out," he said, handing the water back to her.

"It was getting dark anyway," Thyme said. "We've made camp here. How do you feel?"

"Exhausted," he admitted. "That's definitely not a restful sleep."

"Do you remember anything? Any dreams?" Adia asked.

Darian nodded. "I remember everything. It felt exactly like being possessed. My mind and soul were trapped and couldn't break free. Except this time I wasn't trapped in my body. I was trapped in a tomb. Honestly, I don't even know if I was me. I think it might have been Sabo's misery I was experiencing. Or maybe it *was* mine. She and I went through the same thing.

Bound and forced into doing Olark's bidding. I felt... connected to her."

Adia gave him a worried look. Lebechi had barely remembered anything about her dreams when she was unconscious. She hadn't even remembered she'd had any until Adia asked about it. But Darian had woken up clear-eyed and feeling connected to Sabo. She didn't know if this was happening to everyone in Zaria now, or if it was all that Darian had been put through that made it easier for him to feel these things.

She relaxed the hold on her abilities and let herself see Darian's energy. It was the same as before, no alterations.

Sabo was right. It *had* become harder and harder to hold on to things Adia had seen in the Underworld. But something was nagging at her. What had Sabo looked like in her true form? Beyond her obsidian skin and feathers and the giant crown on her head. What had her energy looked like?

"We should try to get some sleep," Adia said. "Even if you've just been asleep for all day, Darian, like you said, it wasn't a restful sleep. And we'll need to cover a lot of ground tomorrow. I'll take the first watch."

Thyme and Darian nodded. She wasn't a fighter like them, but they knew Adia was the strongest person in their trio when it came to handling reanimated corpses.

"Wake me in two hours," Thyme said.

Thyme fell asleep within a matter of minutes. It took a bit

longer before Adia was sure Darian was too. But when she was satisfied that they wouldn't see what she was up to, she moved closer to the campfire. After the scene she'd caused trying to reanimate Nami, it didn't seem likely they'd agree to her using the fire to speak to spirits right now. But she still wanted to see if she could find Sabo since her last attempt to meet the High Queen again had been such a failure.

Unfortunately, she couldn't see anything through her tears. The sight of Nami passing out and falling into a chasm was going to be a part of her memories for the rest of her life. She didn't know how she was supposed to live with it. His non-stop talking had always annoyed her. She didn't realize that it would be even worse to never hear his voice again.

"The letter!" she gasped, quickly crawling to her bag. Whatever Nami had written in that letter he'd given her back at the Academy were the last words she'd ever hear from him. Thank the stars she hadn't thrown it away.

She flung everything out of her bag in a messy pile until she pulled the crumpled envelope out of her bag. She held it for a while, almost not wanting to open it. Because once she'd read it, that was that. She'd never hear Nami's voice again. She couldn't help the shuddering sob that escaped her throat as she slowly unfolded the paper until she was looking down at Nami's surprisingly beautiful handwriting.

"You were always neat," she murmured. It must have been his Gold Hat training.

Dear Adia,

I don't know if you'll ever forgive me, and I know you don't have to. But I want you to know I don't think I'll ever forgive me either. It took me a while to admit it, but I did become your friend because I thought you'd be able to help me get closer to the students at the Academy and that maybe one day they'd be back at their fancy houses and remember me and request me as a guard or military adviser. I was hoping you'd be another person who could help me get back what my family lost. All I was thinking about was myself.

It wasn't until the day you saved Darian and looked at me with so much hurt and disgust that I realized I wasn't just a good son, trying to get my family out of debt by any means necessary. I was a villain. The villain of your story. And I knew that I never wanted to be that again.

So I just want to say one more time that I'm so sorry for what I did. I know I killed our friendship and that you have every right to wash your hands of me. But if you ever need help and there's no one you can turn to, please come and find me. I owe you one. Because I think you might have saved my soul.

Your first friend,
Nami Watson

Adia wiped her face, but the tears wouldn't stop. When

she finally gained control of herself, she closed her eyes and took a deep breath.

"What...are you...crying?"

"Nami?" Adia jumped up. The voice coming through the fire was just a whisper and she could only make out some of the words, but it had to be Nami. She'd wanted to see him so badly.

She closed her eyes, imagining a path in the fire, letting herself connect to him. Her shoulders slumped in disappointment. It wasn't Nami's spirit she touched. It was Sabo. Adia shook herself. Sabo was who she'd been trying to contact in the first place. The High Queen's voice came through clearer now. As did her annoyance.

"I said, what are you doing, sitting here crying? How could you be so foolish as to pull me through the fire?"

"Sabo! You're here! I needed to speak to you."

"You silly girl," Sabo snapped. "Don't you know why it was so easy for you to call me now? The barrier between the realms of the living and dead is almost gone. The convergence is almost upon us, and you do this? I'm *bound* to Olark. The only way I could get around it in the Underworld was fooling you into eavesdropping on us. But calling me to you? Don't you know I'll have no choice but to tell him I spoke to you? Or do I need to remind you about the terms of our contract?"

No. Adia remembered those terms. She hadn't paid as much attention to it as the first curse. This one only affected

Sabo. Or so she'd thought. But if what she was beginning to suspect was right, there could be something in Olark's words that she could use. He was sloppy when he weaved Words of Power. It was how she'd beaten him the last time. Finding a loophole in his weaving. She replayed the contract in her head.

Hear my words throughout the world
And read them in the skies.
Until this crown falls from your head
Your soul is bound to mine.
My every wish is your command
From now until you die.
And even in the realm of death
Our souls will be entwined.

The crown that physically couldn't come off Sabo's head.

"Are you even listening?" Sabo's irritated voice shook Adia out of her thoughts. "Olark will know what you just did. He'll know that you're speaking to me. And he found out you've left your school and are probably trying to find the cure. Whoever his shaman is, they know you left the safety of your school and will no doubt send an army of the dead after you. You're easy pickings without Ginikanwa's protection."

"I know who his shaman is," Adia said in disgust. "I don't know how he came to have shamanic powers, but it's my uncle. I know it. And he knew I left the Academy because he's the one who took me out of school. But I got away from him."

"For now," Sabo said. "There's no way he isn't already coming after you. And not just him. Olark is almost strong enough to return in spirit form to Zaria. If he does, he'll immediately find another body to possess."

"You're right," Adia said. "But I still needed to talk to you. Olark didn't kill you. You said you should have died with your people, but he wanted to keep you alive. And you told me that you liked going to the Underworld because it was easier for you to remember one of your past lives. I thought you meant your life on the Dog Star – but that wasn't it, was it? Because why would you want to remember something so horrible?"

For a moment there was silence, and Adia was worried she'd lost the connection but then Sabo spoke.

"You know that Ginikanwa banished Olark after he turned my world into the bloodstained star? That she's the one who inflicted him on your people?"

"I know," Adia said. "She meant to cast him from the sky and rid the world of him, but she accidentally sent him to Zaria."

"It wasn't an accident," Sabo said. "It also wasn't her fault." The entire time they'd been speaking, Sabo had just been a whisper coming from the flames, but now a shadow stepped forward. Giant, with onyx feathers shooting out of the back and a crown casting jagged shapes on the ground.

"Olark knew Ginikanwa and the other Alusi were coming for him. That she was about to cast him into an abyss he would never be able to claw his way out of. But I was bound to him by then. So he cast me down to a world that the Alusi Imo had gifted with her power. I was his tether, you see."

Adia leaned back. She was beginning to understand.

"Your bargain," Adia said slowly. "Your curse. It wasn't just to tie your power to him. Gini *should* have banished him. But he'd put a safety net in place." Someone whose soul was so linked to his that he could latch onto it and find them, no matter where they were in the universe. In another world, in the realm of death. Wherever Sabo went, Olark could grab onto her soul like a rope and use it to drag himself to safety.

"I was already on Zaria. Because that's where he wanted me to be. And when he fell through the skies, my soul pulled him here.

"So I hid. And for a very long time I stayed hidden. Which was hard, seeing as how I'm cursed to live with this crown on my head. And of course, to your people, I looked like a monster. In the end I gave up. I lay down on a hill, waiting to die. But a group of women who lived high up in those hills happened upon me. They took me in and nursed me back to health and let me stay with them. No matter what I said, they swore that I was a fallen goddess they were meant to save."

"The Hill nuns," Adia said. Revered but deeply isolated women who the world knew little about.

"I lived with them in peace for years. But one day a man came. They allowed certain outsiders with special skills into their convent from time to time. He was a great builder of musical instruments, and they commissioned him to replace some of their broken harps. He happened upon me by accident. I thought he would kill me. Mistake me for some beast and murder me. But he was fascinated. We became friends. Exchanged letters after he was gone. And eventually, he convinced me to leave the Hills and go to him. Then, to the great shock of my life, we had a child together. By some blessing of the Alusi, the child looked entirely mortal. But giving birth to him... His face was the last thing I saw before I left Zaria. It was my final life. I thought maybe it was my atonement. That I'd passed on the lineage of the Dog Star, even if no one would ever know. That my son was the last of our people."

Adia closed her eyes. Stardust was all over Darian's aura. They'd assumed it was because Olark had possessed him. Some lingering side effect from the demon that had lived in his body. But that wasn't it. That wasn't what had felt so familiar to Adia when she'd seen him clearly. Seen the colours of his soul.

"Your husband on Zaria," Adia asked. "What was his name?"

"Daniel Edochie."

And there it was. The final piece of the puzzle.

It hadn't been a random choice for Olark to possess Darian. And Darian hadn't survived the possession for as long as he did solely because of his internal strength. Like Adia, Darian was descended from an extraordinary bloodline. A *royal* bloodline. And it wasn't just Sabo's energy that reminded her of Darian.

The voices she'd been hearing all this time. It was Darian's ancestors from long ago who'd been trying to warn her. Those voices were the people who'd once lived on the bloodstained star.

Gini had told her once that the host usually killed the body it was possessing in a matter of weeks. Maybe a month. But Darian had survived Olark's possession for a full year. He'd survived something no mortal should have been able to survive.

Because Darian Edochie was descended from the stars.

The beginning of an idea was starting to form. She had been able to channel her own extraordinarily powerful ancestor before. Viona had let her borrow her power on that ship. And just like Adia, Darian had an extraordinarily powerful ancestor too.

Thyme and Darian had been right. She couldn't do everything on her own. In fact, *she* might not be the person who was meant to stop this. All this time she'd thought freeing Sabo from Olark's curse was impossible. That the only solution was finding a cure for Drops. But now, knowing what she did about Sabo and Darian's connection, she might be able to free the High Queen's soul after all and leave Olark with no way to ever use Sabo's knowledge and skills again.

She just didn't know if Sabo and Darian would go along with the plan that was beginning to form in her mind.

"Can Olark hear what we're saying?" Adia asked.

"No," Sabo said. "Though I'll have no choice but to tell him the truth when he sees me next. I couldn't lie to him if I tried because of our contract."

"You're not going to have to lie," Adia said. "In fact, you're going to be completely honest. This is exactly what I need you to say."

CHAPTER 25

Darian and Thyme hadn't asked any questions when Adia woke them up and told them they had to leave. She was amazed her friends still trusted her after how badly she'd behaved. Or maybe they were giving her grace because of Nami. The thought of him made her eyes fill with tears, blurring her vision. She would have tripped over some upturned roots if Thyme hadn't caught her.

"Let's rest for a minute," Thyme said. "We've been going uphill for hours. If I feel exhausted the two of you must be completely past your limits."

"Not for too long," Adia said. She was physically the weakest of the three of them, and it was taking every bit of strength she had to force herself to keep going when all she really wanted to do was cry about Nami, so she knew that this rest was more for her benefit than anyone else's. But she couldn't shake the gnawing feeling that Uncle Eric was getting close. "We shouldn't linger. Something feels off."

"Just a ten-minute rest then," Darian said. "And we should check the map again. It should be finished by now."

Adia sat on the ground, wrapping her arms around her knees and lowering her head to hide her tears as Darian dug the map out of her bag.

"What happened last night?" Thyme asked gently, putting an arm around Adia. "Did you have a vision or hear a spirit?"

She knew what Thyme was asking.

"Yes, but it wasn't Nami."

She wiped her face and took a deep breath trying to compose herself enough to tell them about her night-time conversation with Sabo. When she finished, Darian stared at her in disbelief.

"Edochie?" he gasped. "Are you saying I'm related to the High Queen? That I really *am* a royal, not just a boy pretending to be an emperor?"

Adia nodded. "You really were Olark's perfect target to possess," she said. "It wasn't a coincidence. He knew who the Edochie line was. High Queen Sabo is your great-grandmother about a dozen times over. Your bloodline is just as rare as mine. Or Thyme's."

"The three of us all being descended from lands with incredible power," Thyme said with a shake of her head. "And then ending up together? That doesn't seem like a coincidence either. More like someone is pulling strings like a puppet master, making sure all the right weapons find their way to each other before some great war."

"At least we know we're on the right side," Adia said, not wanting to think about the weapons being pulled towards Olark.

"Everyone fighting a war thinks they're on the right side," Darian said. "No one is willing to die for something they don't think is right."

Adia tilted her head and studied Darian for a moment. He looked at her curiously.

"What is it?" he asked.

"Nothing," she said. "It's just that you've always sounded like a wise king and turns out that's exactly what you are."

"Only by a technicality," he said, rolling his eyes. "And not even a king of Zaria. King of a star that was destroyed centuries ago. I don't think that counts."

"It counts well enough," Adia said. "What's the map doing? We shouldn't rest for too long."

Darian handed it to her as Thyme leaned in to look at it too. "I think it's finished."

Yes. The ink was no longer spreading forward and there was now an *X* at the top of the map. Right at the base of the Sunless Mountains.

"We're close," Thyme said. She walked over to the edge of the canyon they'd climbed to bypass spending days walking through the Mbari Mines. I think we can make it in a few—" A thud interrupted her as Darian collapsed to the ground. "Oh no. Not again."

Adia quickly walked over to where Darian was now lying and stared at him in dismay. Her plan would never work if Darian couldn't stay awake long enough for her to do what she needed to do. What she hoped Sabo would help her do. "It's like after his exorcism when he was still under the curse and would lose it whenever he heard Olark's name," Adia sighed. "At least back then all we had to do was watch what we said. Now I guess we have to wait and watch for the dead to show up. Can you help me move him to the tree so he's not as exposed? Thyme?"

Adia looked up to see why Thyme hadn't answered. It took her a second to register the expression on Thyme's face because she had never seen it before.

Terror.

"Thyme?" Adia and. "What is it?"

"We don't have to wait for the dead to show up," Thyme said slowly. She pointed at something in the distance. Adia pushed up her glasses and joined her at the edge of the canyon's rim. Below them was the base of the Sunless Mountains. Their final destination. But they weren't alone.

Hundreds of skeletons stood motionless in a line that stretched as far as the eye could see. Like soldiers standing to attention, waiting to be commanded.

Adia shook her head in disbelief. She didn't know what she had expected when she reached the High Queen's tomb. A unkempt mountain graveyard overrun with weeds, perhaps, or a crumbling sepulchre. She should have known the second Sabo told her Olark knew where she was headed that he'd send an army of the dead to wait for her.

"There are too many," Thyme whispered, pulling her back. "Sometimes the best thing to do is retreat. And this is one of those scenarios. I'm sorry, Adia, but we'll never get past them."

But Adia only narrowed her eyes. She didn't have to get past all of them. She just had to get past one.

"The other shaman is close," she said quietly. "Very close. I can feel them."

It was that same foul energy as when Nami had died. Rage ran through her. This person wasn't just some misguided soul who'd been mind washed by Olark. They were a murderer. They'd killed Nami. Maybe it was her rage that made her feel so in tune with their presence because she could feel them watching her.

There. On the other side of the canyon. A lone figure sat atop a black horse, as still as the skeletons they commanded. Their long black robe blew in the breeze behind them. A flood of heat rushed through Adia.

"I see you!" she shouted, taking off at a run.

"Adia!" Thyme cried. "You can't catch someone on horseback!"

"Stay with Darian!" she called back. "It's my uncle."

It had to be. Uncle Eric must have got off the ship as soon as he'd realized they were missing and chased after them. The dark rider turned their horse and galloped away, heading back down the canyon. It didn't take long before they were too far away for Adia to still see them, but she didn't slow down. Not until an agrias vine shot forwards and tripped her.

She landed face forwards, barely managing not to crack her glasses in the process. She pushed herself up and spat out a mouthful of dust. She knew enough about spirits now to know that this vine hadn't tripped her by accident.

"What is it?" she asked quickly. Then she saw it. A bright red flower with a spotted stem. A flower she had seen before in herbology class. Wonderflower as York called it. *Chincherinchee*, as the plant told Adia it preferred to be called. It could cure plant rot when prepared properly. And when it was prepared improperly...

Adia gently plucked the flower. It pulsed between her fingers. She stood up and started running again. It had taken them all morning to climb across this canyon. But the rider had set off as if Olark was at their heels. They had to have done something to grant them otherworldly speed because they were already at the bottom.

There was no time to make tonics or potions, but the power of this plant lay with its spirit first and foremost. Adia knew Uncle Eric was stronger than her, and that he also knew how to work with agrias. Which meant he had command over the plants, same as her. But she could only hope that the plant spirits were so angry at her uncle for the twisted poisons he was creating from them that they would be on her side right now. "Blind him," she whispered, holding out the flower and hoping its spirit would hear her.

The petals lifted themselves off the stem one by one and hovered in the air in front of Adia before floating down. As they did, Adia could see it – a spirit made of red lights. It shot forward like an arrow and reached the horse and rider. The horse reared up, almost throwing its rider off as the red lights turned into a thick red smoke.

Then Adia called every agrias vine in the area. "And bind him."

She couldn't make out the vines, she was too far away, but she watched as the rider jerked back and fell off the horse. The horse screamed and ran. Good. She didn't want to hurt an innocent animal. But as for the hateful shaman she had just unseated? She felt nothing but cold fury when they landed hard on the ground and fell still. She didn't know if the fall had merely stunned them or killed them, but they didn't appear to be getting up anytime soon.

"Adia!" Darian called. Thyme's voice joined his. Good. If Darian was awake again, then the dead weren't. She stared down at the person she knew had to be her uncle. She made a sound of disgust and turned away, running back up the steep canyon to get to her friends. Olark was on his way to the tomb. This might be their last chance to get to it first. The other shaman would have to wait.

She ran back to her friends. Thyme pointed beneath them. "What did you do? The skeletons all collapsed."

"I knocked out the shaman," Adia said. "But I don't know for how long. We have to hurry. Thyme, build a fire. Darian, are you ready to do this?"

Darian grimaced. "As ready as I'll ever be. Are you sure this is safe?"

"No," she said honestly. She knew what she was asking him to do. And how potentially traumatizing it might be to make him go through this again. She wanted to give him another chance to back out of her plan. "If you don't want to do it, we can think of another way."

Darian didn't respond. He just pulled the emperor's crown from the large pockets of his robe and placed it on his head and gave her a look of complete trust. There was no hesitation in his eyes.

"Fire's ready," Thyme said. Adia nodded. What had Viona said before she'd taken over her body?

"Relax," she said, walking over to Darian. "And don't fight me."

A few minutes later they reached the bottom of the canyon and the base of the mountains. The skeletons were strewn all around them.

"Let's go," Adia said.

"This isn't right," Thyme groaned as they climbed over the bones.

"Just look for the entrance." Adia carefully held a torch over her head as she pushed a skeleton out of her way. She needed the fire to maintain her connection to the spirit world. Sweat beaded on her forehead. It was taking a lot of energy to do what she was currently doing to Darian, but it was working.

"How are you feeling?" Adia asked, helping Darian as he struggled to walk. It was unnerving seeing someone who was always so solid look so unsteady. But after what she'd just put him through a few minutes ago, it was to be expected.

"I'm fine," he said sharply, shaking her off him. "The entrance is just up ahead. There's a door cut into the rocks that will lead to a staircase. The tomb is down there."

They followed Darian inside. The tunnel carved into the mountains reminded Adia of the path Sabo had led her through in the Underworld. Cold and dark and eerie. But at least this time she wasn't alone.

"Adia," Thyme said in a low voice as Darian walked in front of them. "Are you sure about this? You're putting a lot of faith in Sabo holding up her end of this plan."

"No," Adia said. "I'm not sure. But it's our best chance. If this works, we'll cut off Olark's access to our world for ever. The cure would have just been a temporary fix. As long as Olark can get to Sabo he'll use her again and again to create new and terrible formulas to help him get what he wants."

"All the more reason not to trust her," Thyme said. "How do you know she won't double-cross us in the end? The High

Queen isn't some innocent creature. She's the reason Drops existed in the first place. The reason her people got massacred."

Adia didn't respond. She knew she was taking a risk. But she had to trust that Sabo wanted to be free of Olark just as much as she did. Even though she was feeling more nervous with every passing minute as they walked without end.

"This way," Darian finally said. "The air is getting thinner. We're close."

"You just stay out of sight and find the cure while I deal with Olark and freeing Sabo," Adia said to Thyme, watching Darian cautiously as he turned a corner. "And keep an eye on Darian."

"Wait," Darian called up from ahead. "Be careful with this turn."

Thyme moved in front of Adia. Jutting bits of mineral, ready to spear you right through if you turned too quickly or moved the wrong way, lined the floor and walls of the passageway. Thyme leaned forward and carefully sniffed one of them.

"I haven't seen this in ages," she said as she lifted her head. "Don't let the tips touch you."

"Why?" Adia asked, noticing a sticky mucus-like substance at the end of the stalagmites. "What is it?"

"Poison from the claw frog. It won't kill you, but it will incapacitate you. We used it in Nri if we wanted to catch someone, but still needed them alive for questioning."

They had to move slowly to avoid the hundreds of poison-ridden stalagmites. Adia winced as she brushed past one and it touched the hem of her skirt. She'd make sure to burn all her clothes when this was over. Darian turned a corner and disappeared out of sight again.

"Is it just me," Thyme said, "or is our friend trying to lose us?"

Adia swallowed. She'd made so many mistakes lately. She hoped this wasn't about to be another one. To come all this way only to end up buried alive under the Sunless Mountains. But then she heard Darian call out to them.

"It's here!" Darian shouted.

Adia and Thyme gave each other a cautious look, then hurried to catch up to him.

"This is the tomb."

A drop of water fell onto Adia's glasses, making her look up at the cave ceiling. The entire chamber was full of more poisoned stalactites. It was like a death trap. And in the centre of it all lay a long, golden coffin.

"I'm ready," Adia whispered to Thyme. "Light the fires and stay hidden."

Thyme vanished almost immediately as Adia slowly moved closer to Darian, who was peering into the coffin.

"Darian? Are you still with me?"

Darian didn't answer. He ran his hand across the coffin as he walked the length of it. Adia walked on the other side of him, her eyes never leaving his face, which grew more and more illuminated as, one by one, the torches in the cave caught fire. Thyme was doing her job. Now Adia had to do hers.

Come to me. Adia willingly gave every spirit who wanted to come through the fire the ability to do so. If Olark's spirit was strong enough to return to the land of the living now, she'd give him a direct and clear path to follow.

She forced herself not to shudder as she felt the spirit world turn its eyes on her. Eager spirits began to flood her senses. Even with her shields up she knew she would only last a few minutes before they completely overwhelmed her. She swallowed her nausea when the spirit she was trying to bring through felt her soul. She took a step back as Olark's energy began rushing forward. He was so desperate to reach her he didn't seem to think or care about whether this was a trap. Because why else would Adia Kelbara be willing to call him to her?

"I can feel him," Darian finally said, his voice soft and cold. He touched his crown and gave Adia a grim smile. "Can you feel it? How happy he is to see you again? I can."

Adia didn't answer as the air around them went cold. A gust of wind blew through the cave, blowing out one of the torches. He was here. Not in solid form. Not like before. But Olark was here. And just because she'd called him to her as a spirit didn't make him any less dangerous. She let her eyes go soft and searched the cavern for his energy, and had to swallow back her nausea when she saw it. Mallorie Amber's aura might have been a murky mess, but she had nothing on Olark. His energy wasn't just a massive, dense fog of darkness. It had wormlike entities circling all around. The darkness inched closer to them until it was also at the coffin.

"Are you really here?" Adia asked. That he wasn't fully corporeal meant the convergence hadn't happened yet. But for him to be visible at all could only mean one thing. Olark's shaman had regained consciousness. And a large population of Zaria must currently be unconscious. She glanced at Darian. Before she'd done what she did through the fire, he would have been one of those passed-out people. But now, Darian was completely alert as he stared down the shadow.

Could Olark even see her? Unlike the last time they'd met, he seemed completely uninterested in her. He didn't look at her as he ran a smoky hand along the coffin.

"Part of me is," he finally said. "Why? Did you miss me, Viona?"

CHAPTER 26

"My apologies," Olark said, turning his gaze to her. "*Adia.* I won't make that mistake again. Your name is burned into my soul now. Do you know how much pain you caused me? When you flung me out of your body there was almost nothing left of me. The only reason I survived was that old contract I made with Sabo. As I was being ripped from existence, my soul drifted past the realm of the dead. I knew I wasn't welcome there, of course. But then I saw a light – Sabo's light. A soul that was bound to mine even in death. And I reached out my hands and she took me in her embrace, welcoming me into the realm of the dead."

"I'm pretty sure she was trying to strangle you," Adia said bluntly.

"But now," Olark said, dismissing anything he didn't want to hear, as usual, "my beloved Sabo has gone beyond my gaze. Somewhere I can't reach her. I assume you have something to do with that. Though I must confess, I can't understand how.

How could you have broken through a soul binding like that? Where have you hidden her?"

"Again you're overestimating your ability with Words of Power," Adia said. "I don't know why you won't just give up. You're not good at this."

"I won't give up because I can't," Olark said, his voice eerily calm. "This is my destiny. I've known it since I was a child. I was meant to be a god. All this? It's my trial. *You* are my trial by fire. To give up would be to admit that I'm unworthy of the destiny the universe has laid out before me. So I hope you're prepared. Because you *will* lead me to Imo Mmiri, Adia. It's already been written."

"And what about me?" Darian said. "Why did you drag me into all this?"

Olark's spirit turned to Darian as if he'd just noticed his existence.

"Drag you into it? You wretched, ungrateful boy. I gave you your birthright. You were always meant to rule. But you would have wasted your talents. Your royal bloodline. The last heir of the bloodstained star but you would been satisfied to grow up to be a farmer if I hadn't put that crown on your head. And this is how you repay me?"

"Oh please," Darian said. "I would have become emperor one way or the other. Even now I spend my days cleaning up all the messes you made. It may take a few more months, but soon enough, Drops will never be allowed in Zaria, no matter how hard you try. You have no power in Zaria. I'm still the emperor now, not you."

"Is that so?" Olark asked drily. "Even in this weakened state I have more power in my little finger than you do in your entire weak, mortal body. Don't mistake your lineage for true power. You're nothing like me. Like Adia. And the power we could have, Adia, if you joined forces with me. Shall I show you the strength of my shaman? Perhaps this will be what finally makes you come to the winning side. Think what you could learn with us. The power you could wield."

Olark's shadow grew larger, looming over the two of them.

The walls around them began to shake.

"You could bring down mountains!" Olark shouted, his voice echoing as the ceiling began to cave in. Darian pushed Adia out of the way just before a giant rock fell on her head.

"Do something," Darian snapped.

The sharp words spurred Adia into action. She reached into the spirit realm, pushing past everyone in her way as she tried to find the other person who was journeying, and forcing the realm of spirit to bend to their will. She had no idea what kind of shamanic ability could bring down a mountain, but Olark's shaman was going to do just that if she didn't stop them.

There. Adia felt it – the soul of a mortal, just like her, who was both in this world and a dozen others all at the same time. Their energy was terrible in every sense of the word. And in all that terribleness, there was something familiar. A feeling of home. Of the Swamplands.

Memories of Uncle Eric and Aunt Ife glaring at her for her strange behaviour. When all the while, her uncle had been watching and waiting for her powers to manifest so he could alert Olark that the descendant of Imo Mmiri had woken to her power and could now find the lost land. She slammed herself into it and felt the dark shaman's surprise as she used her will to fling him back into his physical body, wherever it was. She wasn't strong enough to hold them off for more than a few seconds and she marvelled at the fact that they'd kept her locked out of her own body for close to a week in the Underworld. The amount of mental strength that must have taken was now clear to Adia because she felt weak just from forcing the other shaman out of the realm of spirit.

Which was why she didn't have enough strength to fight them off when they attacked her again. She screamed as something she couldn't see wrapped around her torso and dragged her back, slamming her into the wall. Darian ran towards her, but the same energy shot forwards and threw him to the side.

"Release her," Olark said. Adia fell to the ground with a thump. Tears came to her eyes as she scraped her knees on the cold, rocky floor. "You see, Adia, this is what it looks like when a shaman has trained their entire life. Complete mastery of the elements. Spirits who have no choice but to obey their command. The ability to communicate with the dead. Even me."

"Communicate?" Adia sputtered. She knew what she was about to say would infuriate Olark, but Uncle Eric had killed Nami and he was trying to kill her. And no, she wasn't strong enough to fight him in the spirit realm, but stars above, she knew she was smarter than her doltish relative, who'd been foolish enough to align himself with Olark. "Don't you know how I figured out the cure was in Sabo's tomb? I was in the Hollowgate that night. Your shaman knew and they kept that information to themselves. Maybe you're not quite the dynamic duo that you think. After all, why should they help you find Imo Mmiri instead of just taking that power for themselves?"

The walls around them stopped shaking as the mountain settled back down. Olark's shadow went still. Adia could practically feel his cold fury. She knew she had just shoved a wedge between the demon and her uncle. But she didn't care what the ramifications would be for Eric. He deserved whatever punishment Olark doled out for betraying him.

"You may have your servants, but I have something better. I have friends who want to stop you for no other reason than you're a danger to the world and everything good. And that's why you'll never win. There will always be someone ready and willing to die to stop your hatefulness. Viona, Thyme, Gini, Darian, me." Adia blinked back tears. "And Nami Watson.

You'll never beat us. And you and your shaman and dead queen who works in the shadows will never beat me and Darian. We're a living emperor and shaman. This is our world now and you're no longer welcome in it."

Olark's attention turned back to Darian.

"*A living emperor?*" he scoffed. "You think that gold object on his head protects you? *I* was the one who put that crown there. Perhaps it's time I took it off."

He stretched a shadowy hand forwards and touched Darian's crown. It began to vibrate as pieces of it flaked off, surrounding Darian's head like an aura of gold stardust. Adia held her breath, willing Olark to do exactly what she wanted him to do.

Olark froze. "What's this? You're not the boy. You're... Sabo?"

Darian fell to his knees, clutching his chest. Then his body flung itself back of its own accord, his eyes wide and frightened. Adia hated to see him go through this again. It was the same as last time when Gini had exorcised Olark from his body. Except this time, the spirit who was currently possessing him was trying to exorcise herself. Sabo was trying to hold up her part of the plan, but she was struggling to break free.

"Sabo, take my hand!" Adia yelled.

It was clear that Sabo didn't have much strength left, but Adia's voice reached her. She held out her hand and grabbed on. Adia called on every ancestor she had to help her. Viona, Ovie, her mother. She threw in the Alusi too, hoping Gini would feel her frantic plea for help as she connected with Sabo's spirit and used every drop of her power to yank the queen out of Darian's body.

They had stood in front of the entrance to the tomb and built a fire, then Adia had called Sabo to her. They'd had to act fast before Olark realized what was happening. As soon as Sabo's spirit had come to them, she'd possessed Darian the same way Viona had possessed Adia on that boat. No, not possessed – Sabo and Viona hadn't done anything violent. What they'd done was briefly allow their descendants to channel their power.

From the moment they'd entered that tomb it hadn't been Darian with them, but Sabo in Darian's body.

And now Sabo's spirit stood in front of her. Tall as ever, with an imposing plume of feathers that were now stretched out in a remarkable wingspan, casting a shadow of an avenging angel on the wall across from Olark's shadow. And this time, there was no longer a crown on her head.

"'Until this crown falls from your head,'" Sabo recited, touching her hair in amazement as Adia ran to Darian.

"Sabo," Olark gasped. He was already vanishing. "But...I couldn't feel you. Your soul vanished."

"Young Darian was kind enough to let me borrow his body for a few minutes," Sabo said. "You failed to mention *whose* crown bound you to them, and you've crowned two of us now. It seemed like poetic justice that Darian be the one to banish you this time around. And that's what you are. Banished. Our contract has been voided, according to your own words. And something tells me the realm of the dead isn't going to be a safe space for you to linger without me to tether you there."

Shadows crept out of the walls, moving towards Olark's spirit. Adia shuddered as they descended on him. He'd been tormenting the dead for weeks. It looked as if the dead were about to return the favour. His shadow was overwhelmed by the others until Adia couldn't feel his presence any more.

Sabo rushed up to them. She was also beginning to fade from view.

"Is the boy unharmed?"

"I'm fine," Darian said, wheezing as he got used to having control of his own breathing again, but Adia didn't believe him. Even if he'd agreed to it, and even if Sabo had only possessed him for a few minutes, she knew that, like her, not being in control of his own body was his worst nightmare.

"Thank you for trusting me," she said.

Darian squeezed her hand. "Always. Now help me up. We'd better get out of here."

"Not without the cure," Adia said. "Sabo, where is it?"

Sabo grinned. "Tap into the fire and open your eyes. Do you see it?"

Adia frowned. She quickly linked her energy with every torch in the chamber and looked around. Something shimmered in a corner. She rushed over and picked it up.

"Olark placed a shield over it," Sabo said. "Not unlike the one your ancestor placed over Imo Mmiri. Only a true shaman would have been able to find it."

Adia frowned. Such a small vial. Her shoulders sagged. "Maybe this is enough to cure one person, but it's not enough for all of Zaria."

"It's enough, I promise," Sabo said. "Just one drop placed into a well would be enough to cure an entire village. It's not made of simple plants. It's an alchemical combination of stars and plants and minerals. But now that I'm free of Olark's binding, I can also give you the formula. May this be my final act of atonement."

Sabo closed her eyes as smoke filled the room, quickly turning into the forms of letters and numbers.

"What is she doing?" Darian asked. "What do you see?" But Adia held out a hand. She needed quiet. The formula was long and involved and full of mathematical symbols. She said it to herself under her breath as she burned it into her memory.

"Did you get it?" Sabo asked.

"Got it," Adia confirmed. "Thank you for everything."

Sabo nodded. "Thank you. I hope I never see you again."

Adia nodded. "I'll take that as a compliment."

"You'd better get out of here," Sabo said as a large rock fell from the ceiling and Adia barely jumped out of the way. "This tomb was hidden with bindings that no longer hold. It's all going to come crashing down in a matter of minutes."

"Where will you go?" Adia asked.

She could feel Sabo's happiness. "Wherever I want. I'm free now."

Thyme came out of hiding just as Sabo's presence faded. Adia didn't know if the High Queen would ever know true peace when the guilt she rightfully carried over the blood-stained star was so heavy. But Sabo had never stopped trying to right her wrongs, even in death. Adia hoped that wherever she was going, she did find some peace there.

Adia had never seen Thyme look more relieved in her life. She'd been positioned in a corner with her bow and arrow, ready to incapacitate Darian's body if Sabo didn't agree to leave it willingly.

"Darian," Thyme said, surprising Darian when she gave him a hug. "I'm so glad I didn't have to kill you."

"Kill him?" Adia gasped. "I thought you'd just shoot him in the leg or something if Sabo tried anything."

"I—" Thyme said, scrunching her face up in confusion as she grabbed a torch off the wall. "Yeah, sure. That's what I was going to do."

"Sure you were," Darian said, glaring at her. "Let's get out of here. Sabo's right. We'll be buried alive if we don't move."

They ran back through the passageway. A large rock

narrowly missed Adia's head as everything collapsed around them. Wouldn't this be a cosmic joke – to save Sabo's soul only to be buried alive in her tomb. Adia glanced behind her. The path they'd taken was already buried in rocks.

"We're not going to make it!" Thyme shouted.

Adia looked at her frantically. The flame from Thyme's torch illuminated her eyes, and Adia saw how scared she was. But Adia focused on the fire and all the spirits who were always around her. Plant spirits, human ancestors, beings from other realms like Sabo who could journey just like her.

"We'll make it," Adia said firmly.

The days of thinking that she could stop Olark all by herself were long gone. The dead would be allowed to rest now because of her. They owed her a favour. Adia took a deep breath.

If anyone can hear me, please help. I'm not strong enough to stop a mountain from falling down. Shamans, ancestors, spirits. Anyone. Lend me your power.

Her entire body vibrated as she felt the energy of hundreds of spirits come to her. It wasn't just her hands that glowed now. Her entire body was engulfed in light, and she swore for a second that her feet levitated off the ground. She gasped as a blast of energy shot out of her. And the mountain went still.

"Go!" she shouted. She didn't know how long she could channel such a huge amount of energy.

They raced up the stairs and collapsed in relief when they

reached the surface. Adia felt the spirits leave her with a whoosh. As soon as they did, the rocks began to fall again and within seconds, the entrance to the High Queen's tomb was buried by rubble. No one should ever be able to find it again.

"Come on," she said, wanting to put all this behind her. "Let's go home."

CHAPTER 27

The journey back to the Academy had been a solemn affair. Olark was out of their lives for the time being, but they all knew it wouldn't be for long. They stood outside the Academy gates. None of them seemed eager to walk through them.

"How long can you stay?" Adia asked Darian.

"Not long," he said, "but I'll hang around for a couple of days. Gini can help me come up with a story to tell my advisers about what's been going on."

"You'll go back to the capital then?" Thyme asked.

"Yes," he said. "But first I'll visit Nami's mother. And the palace will take care of her and her medical bills."

During their journey home Adia had told Darian and Thyme why Nami had done all the terrible things he had. That he'd been trying to keep his mother safe. And that even when Chobly offered him a deal that could have taken care of all his problems, he hadn't taken it because he wouldn't harm Adia again.

"I have the money," Adia said, but Darian shook his head.

"No. Nami died a hero. And maybe the world will never know what he did, and that we never would have made it to the tomb without him, but all of Zaria owes him a debt. It's the least I can do to make sure his mother is taken care of."

Adia nodded. "And make sure you tell her that. That he died a hero. That he saved your life. All our lives." She would do the same when she told the Gold Hats about his death. "And you have my letter for EJ?"

"Right here," Darian said, tapping his shirt pocket. "I'll make sure it's delivered to him, and him alone."

Adia had written a short note to EJ saying as much as she could. She didn't know if Uncle Eric had been working with Olark all along, or if EJ's kidnapping all those months ago had been the event that made her uncle put two and two together and figure out that Olark was back in the world. Some small part of her hoped that it was the latter. That her uncle hadn't really been ready to sacrifice his own son in his misguided attempt at power. But whenever Uncle Eric had sold his soul to a demon, EJ needed to know that his father had somehow managed to acquire a shocking amount of shamanic power. And hopefully find a way to report back to Adia on whatever her hateful uncle was up to.

Adia nodded. "I'll go let Gini know we've made it back."

"And I'll go check on Maka, Lebechi and Bubbles," Thyme said. "Darian, come with me. I'll help you sneak in."

Adia walked the path to Gini's office alone, but everywhere she turned, people noticed her.

"The gas leak ended pretty soon after you left."

Great. Rusty. Adia couldn't help letting out a groan.

He fell in step with her. "We were all about to head back home when the council said it was safe to stay."

The council. Chobly. She knew now that he wasn't a shaman, but that didn't mean he wasn't dangerous. Between Chobly, Uncle Eric and Olark, she was going to have her hands full. Danger was waiting for her at every turn.

Adia managed to give Rusty a nod. "That's good to hear."

Rusty stared at her intently. "You look like you haven't slept in a week."

"Rusty, I'm sorry, but I'm really not in the mood for this," she said.

"No, I know," he said quickly. "I just – *we* just wanted to say thanks. If you had anything to do with it, I mean."

That's when Adia realized everyone was staring at her. Not with disgust or fear, but with gratitude. They might not know what she'd done, but her classmates weren't as clueless as she'd originally thought.

"Glad you're back, Kelbara," Mallorie's friend Wren called out, giving her a smile.

"Welcome home, Adia," someone shouted.

Adia didn't know how to handle everyone's new, friendly attitude towards her and kept her head low until she finally reached Gini's office. Gini took one look at her and poured her a glass of water.

"Sit down, drink this and tell me everything."

Gini bowed her head when Adia got to the day they'd lost Nami and, to Adia's surprise, wiped away a tear.

"His loss wasn't in vain. There've been no more incidents of people losing consciousness. It's over."

"Over?" Adia got up and walked to the window, staring down as students rushed around the yard.

There was nothing to be done about the new chasms that now ran through Zaria. The kingdom's topography had been changed for ever. As the reports came in, they'd learned that some of the chasms had been so bad entire villages were now split in two because the only way to get to the other side was to walk for days around the gaps that now separated families and neighbours.

The "gas leak emergency", as officials were calling it, had been declared over. But just because everyone was once again in control of their bodies didn't mean anyone was safe. Olark had shown his strength and determination to get to Adia. And Zaria was a disaster because of it.

Not to mention that just because Olark no longer had access to Sabo's ever-changing formulas any more, it didn't mean he couldn't figure out another way to use the energy of those who'd taken Drops. Which was why it was time to distribute the cure. And hopefully make more of it, if she could replicate Sabo's formula.

"I have to get to work," she said, her voice exhausted.

"Adia," Gini called out, forcing her to pause at the door. "We won this time. And we'll keep winning. Even if we're now fighting against a demon and another shaman."

"The thing is, Gini, I don't want to have to keep fighting for the rest of my life. And this isn't a win to me," she said. "If we'd won, Nami would still be alive."

Adia stared at the row of vials in front of her. She'd been working on replicating Sabo's formula for the last two days straight. "Maybe I should make a few more just to be sure it's right?"

She and Darian were sitting in York's classroom.

"Adia, you've been working on this for days. I trust you." Darian picked up one of the vials. "It's time to test it out."

Adia wished he would have taken a dose from the vial they'd got from Sabo's tomb, but he'd insisted that he be the one to test out the formula Adia was trying to replicate. She sighed but nodded. "Sit over there and let me look at you."

Darian's energy was as calm as it always was, but there it was. The knot around his heart where the Drops had taken hold.

"All right. Take the cure."

She held her breath as Darian swallowed the tonic she'd

created. At first nothing happened. But then she squinted as the knot around his heart began to quiver and loosen. She gave him a triumphant smile when it vanished.

"How do you feel?" she asked eagerly.

Darian blinked slowly and smiled back.

"Lighter," he admitted. "I've felt a fogginess ever since I took them, but it's gone now. This is incredible."

"Yes, but how am I going to convince people to take it?" Thyme had been right with what she'd said before. Just because there's a cure doesn't mean anyone's going to want it.

"I don't think it's your job to convince anyone to do anything," Darian said. "You've given Zaria an option. I'll do what I can as emperor to encourage them to take it. We'll start mass-producing it right away."

"So you're leaving?" Adia asked. Nami was gone, and now Darian was going to leave her too.

"Just for a little while," he said quickly. "This charade of me being an emperor is going to come to an end soon enough, but I want to do what I can to help you while I still have power. I—"

He stopped speaking and turned to the door. Mimi gaped at him in shock.

"Emperor – Emperor *Darian?*"

Adia bit back a groan. Thyme was supposed to be guarding the door to make sure none of their classmates interrupted her.

"Mimi," Adia said, rushing up. "Look…Darian isn't supposed to be here."

Mimi's mouth opened and closed like a fish gasping for water on dry land, but thankfully she managed to compose herself. She cleared her throat. "Of course, of course. I won't say a word. But…what is all this? What are you doing?"

"It's a cure for the poison you call Liquid Gold," Darian said. "I asked Adia to work on it and she's figured it out."

"Poison?" Mimi squeaked. "I mean…I knew it wasn't really going to give us powers, but *poison*?"

Adia waited for Mimi to freak out but the girl just made a sound of disgust. "What is going on in Zaria right now?" Mimi muttered. "All right then. How much?"

"How much what?" Adia asked.

"How much does it cost? You're selling it, right?"

Adia quickly grabbed an empty vial and poured some in. "Free of charge," she said, handing it to Mimi. Mimi chugged the tonic down without hesitating. After a few seconds she tilted her head.

"This is so strange…I feel better? I didn't even realize I didn't feel good before."

"Spread the word," Darian said.

Mimi nodded. "I will. I don't understand what's going on but I trust Adia. We all do. I mean, not Mallorie Amber, but the rest of us aren't clueless. Whenever something is wrong, Adia helps fix it."

Adia felt herself heat up and she looked away in embarrassment.

"I'll leave you two to it then," Mimi said.

"See," Darian said. "You don't have to convince anyone. People trust you more than you realize. I'm going to let Gini know we have the cure. You should take a break for now."

Adia sat alone in silence for a few minutes before standing up. She winced at how stiff she was. When was the last time she'd breathed fresh air? She walked outside until she reached the forest. The bad memories were still there. Olark possessing her, the reanimated dead trying to steal her eyes, even the chasms still lingered. There was nothing she could do to fix those. She blinked back tears and reached into her pocket to pull out Nami's letter.

...So I just want to say one more time that I'm so sorry for what I did. I know I killed our friendship and that you have every right to wash your hands of me. But if you ever need help and there's no one you can turn to, please come and find me. I owe you one. Because I think you might have saved my soul.

Your first friend,
Nami Watson

Adia had done her part in reproducing Sabo's cure. She would have to leave it to Darian, Thyme and Gini to handle distributing it. She had something more pressing she needed to deal with. Like figuring out how to get to the realm of the dead. She wasn't going to use Drops. Watching Darian lose control of his body over and over again had taught her that the price was too high to reach the realm of the dead that way. But there was one place she could go to get all the power she needed.

"Don't worry, Nami," she said. "I'm going to find you."

And she was going to find Imo Mmiri.

EPILOGUE

Back in the Swamplands, a shaman stared at an agrias vine. The new formula should have been written on it. That was how the Bright Father delivered his instructions on how to circumvent the vines' tricky tendency to not let the same formula work more than once. They crushed the vine in their hand in fury. Sabo had well and truly been set free. All of her knowledge gone with her. And without it, they had no way of making Drops ever again.

The girl. This was her doing. She'd done something to make the Bright Father lose faith in their alliance. It was the only explanation for the sudden silence.

Someone knocked on the door and the shaman glared as they flung it open. A boy stared up at them.

"Are you all right?" the boy asked. "Your eyes are still so bloodshot."

Yes. Being choked by a smog of wonderflower poison would do that to a person. Their vision was *still* blurry.

"Never you mind about my eyes," the shaman snapped. "What do you want?"

The boy rolled his eyes. He was bold now. Nothing like the sickly, snivelling mess he'd been a year ago.

"Just letting you know that there was a letter. The Academy is remaining open now that the toxic gas is gone. Adia's not coming to the Swamplands any time soon."

The shaman gave the boy a cold look.

"Fine with me," they said. "But she'll give me what I want eventually."

The boy gave them a small smile. "No, she won't. The two of you will never see a cent of Adia's money." With that he walked away.

"Money," the shaman scoffed as EJ walked away. "As if that's what I want from my beloved niece. But you're wrong, EJ. I'll get *everything* from that little bug."

She slammed the door shut and hurled the vine into the fire.

"A bug that the master and I will crush," Aunt Ife said, her voice full of hatred.

"Just like I crushed her mother."

LOOK OUT FOR MORE ADVENTURES TO COME IN ADIA'S WORLD

ACKNOWLEDGEMENTS

As always, I have to start by thanking my champion and agent, Pete Knapp. From the very beginning, you've believed in me and this story, and I couldn't ask for a better advocate in my corner. Endless gratitude to Stuti Telidevara, Danielle Barthel and everyone at the legendary agency that is Park, Fine & Brower. Your support and guidance mean the world.

No book is written in isolation, and this series wouldn't exist without the incredible talents of my editors, Kristin Rens and Rebecca Hill, along with the hard-working teams at HarperCollins and Usborne. A heartfelt thank you to my UK agent, Claire Wilson, for her support across the pond. I also owe a huge thank you to my friend and mentor, Sylvia Liu, for her invaluable feedback and unwavering support.

And most of all, thank you to the readers – for coming on this journey with me and Adia. I'm so excited to share this adventure with you!

ISI HENDRIX

is a Nigerian American children's book author who has been lucky enough to live and work all over the world, from the Himalayas to the Amazon rainforest, during her past life as an anthropologist. Now she's based in her hometown of Brooklyn, NY, where she lives with a rotating roster of foster kittens and a stubborn refusal to accept that she is highly allergic to cats.